GUN-BOSS REYNOLDS

Center Point
Large Print

Also by Chuck Martin and available from
Center Point Large Print:

Sixgun Town
Hell-Bender from Texas

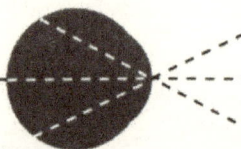

**This Large Print Book carries the
Seal of Approval of N.A.V.H.**

GUN-BOSS REYNOLDS

CHUCK MARTIN

CENTER POINT LARGE PRINT
THORNDIKE, MAINE

CHAPTER I

Roaming Reynolds raised his head to listen, as the shrill scream of a stallion keened across the high desert mesa of the Arizona Strip. Outlaw country where the badlands citizenry found both refuge and profit, and where the law was carried in holster leather thonged low for a speedy draw.

The stallion screamed again with a note of whistling terror easily recognized by any man who could understand horse-talk. The tall cowboy narrowed his blue eyes and gigged his roan toward a patch of greasewood and mesquite tangle. Only the subdued song of seasoned saddle-leather murmuring softly as he pushed through the brush.

He drew his Winchester from the scabbard as he slid from the high saddle, and his eyes flamed hotly when he cuddled it to one broad shoulder and squinted down the long barrel. A big chestnut stallion was hog-tied with all four feet bunched while two men cinched a heavy saddle on the broad back. A Spanish curb-bit gleamed brightly between the great snapping teeth, but it was the check rope that made Roaming Reynolds buy chips in a game where he had drawn no cards.

One of the buckaroos was a square-shouldered fellow with two guns belted high on his hips. The

5

other was a tall lathy man with crafty little eyes set too close together. Three horses grazed just outside the little clearing, and the tall cowboy held his bead until the big man straddled the scarred saddle and gripped the split bridle reins. A rope ran from the head-stall to saddle-horn to prevent the stallion from bogging his head between his knees during the ride.

"Turn him loose," the big man growled hoarsely. "I'll ride him into the ground, or bust his heart!"

His slat-like pard jerked the piggin' strings and jumped away when the big Morgan stud levered to his feet. Nearly seventeen hands high with the deep barrel of the mountain-bred horse; red-gold shining through the thin skin that rippled like smooth silk in the bright sunlight.

The big stallion trembled and fought for his head when the sharp rowels pedalled back and forth from shoulders to rump. Roaming Reynolds smiled grimly and pressed the trigger of his Winchester. The rifle spat flatly in the high air, and the check-rope parted in the middle as though a sharp knife had severed it.

Hell broke loose in the greasewood when the big stud swallowed his great head between his knees and leaped high with back arching like a cat on the fight. He came down on all fours to make the ground tremble, and his right knee buckled suddenly to produce the deadly cantle-spank. The hurry-board slapped forward like a projectile, and the big rider shot over the stallion's smooth neck like a sack of barley.

Arms and legs spread wide like a huge bird in sudden flight, and then the luckless buckaroo thudded heavily to earth. He looped into a roll instinctively and brought up behind a thick clump of mesquite with spurs biting deep in the loam. The stallion broke into a bucking run and sky-hooted across the rolling mesa with the whites showing in his rolling eyes to tell of his terror.

Roaming Reynolds cradled the smoking Winchester against his lean hip and covered the two buckaroos. The thin fellow raised his hands with a scowl twisting his face while his partner crawled out of the brush slapping at the twin holsters high on his hips. The tall cowboy smiled frostily and jerked his head to the side.

"You spilled yore hardware when you joined the bird gang," and his deep voice was crisp. "I don't know you two hombres, but you better step across yore hulls and fog it away from here before I change my mind. Pick up yore tools and holster 'em deep before you get ideas and turn around!"

The barn-shouldered fellow glared until his partner warned him in a thin nasal voice. "Better do what he says, matey. Right now he holds high-hand with his thumb earing the hammer back. He don't know what he's bucking, but the blighter will bloody soon find out!"

"I'm Hip High Hardy, feller," the big gunman snarled. "If I don't get you for cutting in on this play, Eagle Dupree will draw cards. C'mon, Canuck!"

He turned his broad back and picked up his sixguns. Jammed them deep in hand-moulded leather before he turned around to scowl at the tall cowboy behind the rifle. Then the two men stomped over to their horses and mounted up while Roaming Reynolds swung his saddle gun to hold the drop. Not until they had spurred away did he pay any attention to the third horse.

"Funny," he muttered softly, and lowered his rifle. "I wonder where that third rider disappeared?"

He whirled quickly when a muffled groan came to his ears from back in the thicket. Rifle at the ready, he made his way cautiously through the tangle toward the sound. Then he was on his leather-covered knees with left hand reaching for the skinning knife at the back of his broad belt.

"He couldn't be with that outfit," he muttered. "Now I know how come that third hoss yonder."

A big bearded man of forty-odd years was lying on the ground bound and gagged. The cowboy jerked the bandanna away and severed the piggin' strings from ankles and wrists. Black broadcloth suit and flat-crowned black hat marked the prisoner for a Mormon, and the cowboy helped him lever to his feet and stepped back to sheath his knife while he waited for the explanation.

"Blast them," the big man said angrily, but his voice was slow and cool. Like the chill of a deep-flowing mountain stream. "You have done me a great favour this day, young man!"

"I didn't even see you," the tall cowboy admitted. "I heard the stallion scream, and when I rode up for a look, them two buckaroos was fixing to ride him with a Spanish curb and a check-rope. All I did was shoot the rope in two to give the hoss a fighting chance, and the big hombre fanned the air when the stud come apart."

The big man studied the young face carefully. "You mind telling me your name?" he asked in his deep soft voice.

"I'm Roaming Reynolds," the cowboy answered promptly. "I'm new up here in these parts."

The Mormon smiled and held out his big hand. "Folks up here in the Strip call me Mormon Tucker," he said in his deep booming voice. "I run the M T horse ranch over on the Virgin River. What might you be doing up here in outlaw country, if you don't mind me asking?"

The cowboy kneaded his fingers gently after that powerful grip had turned loose. "Looking for a riding job," he answered without hesitation. "Buckaroo by preference if you happen to have any work in the breaking tank."

Keen dark eyes studied him from behind the black beard that covered the Mormon's face. Mormon Tucker was deliberate in all his movements and speech, but his big frame carried the suggestion of enormous strength held in reserve. Straight nose and square jaw, with full lips that parted to show even white teeth while he looked the cowboy over carefully. Like a man who knows his business, checking the points of a horse before making a buy.

Roaming Reynolds returned the glance without winking. His six-foot frame carried a hundred and sixty-five pounds of seasoned fighting bone and muscle, and his tanned face held the look of a man who knows his way around. Mormon Tucker nodded approvingly with a hard little smile curling the corners of his mouth.

"Sixty a month and grub for riding," he said slowly, and his wide eyes were steady. "A hundred a month and cartridges if you want to sell your guns in the cause of Right!"

A brief smile passed across the cowboy's tanned face. "Call it a hundred," he drawled softly, and his right hand rubbed the handle of the gun thonged low on his leather chaps. "You mentioned outlaws."

Mormon Tucker was studying the riding gear on the cowboy's horse. Came back to scan his rigging while his dark eyes smiled humorously.

"I see why they call you Roaming," and he

nodded his head. "You've been working Texas, Arizona, and Montana from the look of your gear. Looks like you don't stay put long in any one place."

The cowboy shrugged. "Itching heel," he explained soberly. "There's always something new on the other side of the hill. But looky, boss. Who was them two fellers that jumped you a while back?"

The Mormon scowled. "Outlaws," he boomed slowly. "They drove off the Morgan stallion from my west pasture up near the cliffs. Tied me up when I took after them and blundered into the trap they laid for me here in the brush. The thin man was Canuck Avery, a Canadian-Englishman who does most of his killing with a hide-out gun."

The cowboy nodded while his brown fingers rolled a smoke. "The big jigger who tried to make a ride?" he prompted softly.

"That was Hip High Hardy, so called because he belts his guns hip-high and uses a flip draw with the butts turned out."

"Flip draw?" and the cowboy stared at the Mormon's face. "I figgered him to use the cross-draw from the way he packed his irons."

"He's fast," the Mormon answered thoughtfully. "But not half so fast as Eagle Dupree who rods that outlaw spread. They have a hide-out over in Rainbow Canyon where a smart horse

11

couldn't find his way home in broad daylight."

"Best looking country I was ever in," Reynolds drawled. "Them Vermilion Cliffs yonder just keep on changing colour with the sun, and lush grass knee-high to a tall hoss in all them draws. Sounds like a hoss-backer coming our way."

Mormon Tucker looked up with a frown of annoyance on his bearded face when he located the sound of drumming hooves. A rider was racing across the mesa toward the two horses, and Roaming Reynolds drew a deep breath when a girl slid her horse and hit the ground running. Mormon Tucker put out a big hand to steady her, and he tried to kick the cut ropes behind him into the brush.

"They got you," the girl said quietly, and stared at the tell-tale piggin' strings. "You were foolish to start after those men alone, Father. They might have killed you!"

Mormon Tucker removed his black hat and bowed. "Mister Reynolds, allow me to present my daughter, Betty. Reynolds came along in time to save me from trouble, daughter. I've hired him and his guns to help me fight these outlaws here in the Strip."

The girl turned slowly to study the cowboy, and he saw that she was not more than twenty, with black hair and eyes. Straight nose and full lips, with the sober, serious expression that marked her father. Deep-chested and strong, with a natural heritage of health that radiated from her like a strong current.

"Thank you, Mister Reynolds," she said in a rich, throaty voice, and held out her right hand. "But I'm sorry about the guns."

Roaming Reynolds took her hand and gripped hard, man-style. "This Strip is outlaw heaven, Miss Betty," he reminded her bluntly. "From what I can make out, the M T spread is just raising hosses for these long-riding owl-hoot buckaroos."

"Our men have never carried firearms," the girl almost whispered, and shuddered when she glanced at the heavy forty-five Colt on his right leg.

Mormon Tucker settled back on his heels and frowned with disapproval. "After this you will stay close to the ranch, Betty," and the expression on his bearded face showed that he expected to be obeyed without argument. "Remember what I have said, daughter."

The girl bowed without speaking. Roaming Reynolds stared at her bench-made boots and allowed his eyes to travel from the worn chaps, over faded Levi's and up to her swelling figure. Rough wool shirt and calf-skin vest that failed to conceal her alluring beauty. Then he shook his head impersonally.

"You better stay home," he said bluntly. "An outlaw would forget all about horses if he laid his eyes on you."

13

The girl flushed to the roots of her black hair and changed the subject quickly. "Where is the Morgan stallion, Father?" she asked in a strained voice, and turned to scan the rolling mesa.

Mormon Tucker drew a deep breath and snapped his strong white teeth. "Killing himself back there in the brush trying to buck a saddle from his back," he growled. "We better ride fast, Reynolds. I don't want to lose that stud."

The cowboy was in the saddle like a flash. His blue eyes picked out the deep imprints where the big horse had bolted to freedom, and he loped away without waiting for Mormon Tucker and his daughter. He shook his tight-twist rope loose when he entered a deep wash between high banks, and a moment later he was staring at another set of tracks made by a shod horse.

Without knowing why, he replaced his rope and reached for the rifle in the saddle-boot. Then he sent the roan through the sandy wash at a slow walk until he rounded a shoulder of red sandstone. A deep savage curse growled from his throat when he swung down from the saddle and moved warily toward a great shadowy huddle lying in the deep sand.

"It's murder," he muttered huskily, and raised his head to scan the sky-line. "And I'd like to come up with the killer!"

The cowboy could see at a glance that the stallion was dead. A pool of crimson had formed under the big head, and the saddle was a litter of leather shreds where it hung by the stout cinches under the belly of the horse. The tracks of the shod horse led up through the wash, and Reynolds was staring at them when Mormon Tucker and his daughter galloped in from the other end.

Mormon Tucker threw his bulk from the saddle with shuddering growls booming from his bearded throat. His big hands were clenched into bony knobs when he stopped beside the dead stallion and traced the bullet hole with eyes that suddenly flamed into burning coals of fury. The girl shuddered silently, and Roaming Reynolds wisely stepped back and waited for the big Mormon to speak.

Mormon Tucker weighed better than two hundred pounds, and now he stood with feet wide apart, and his knuckles cracked with the effort he was making to control himself. He stepped back at last and opened the fingers of his right hand. Pointed to something that was twisted in the forelock of the stallion's mane where it hung down between the glossy ears.

"You see it, Betty?" he whispered. "You see it up there near the Morgan's ears?"

The girl stifled a sob and turned away. "See what?" the cowboy asked quietly.

"Eagle Dupree has been here," and the Mormon's voice roared with a booming whisper of anger and hate. "That's his mark yonder, Reynolds. Take a good look so you will know it in the future."

Roaming Reynolds leaned forward from the hips to stare at a broken feather. He shook his head when he recognized it. An eagle feather from the king of all birds. Golden brown with touches of soft grey, but the quill was broken to make the feather sag over in an L.

"So that's the mark of Eagle Dupree," Reynolds said softly. "He might fly too high one of these days."

"He wanted the Morgan," and Mormon Tucker spoke from between clenched teeth. Only his will power controlled the terrible rage in his heart. "When he couldn't get the stallion for his own, he killed it to keep anyone else from having it. That is the way of Eagle Dupree!"

The cowboy glanced at Betty Tucker and stiffened when the girl began to tremble. Mormon Tucker followed his gaze and nodded slowly. The girl crept close to him and stared into his bearded face with frightened eyes.

"Can't we leave here and go back to Salt Lake City?" she whispered. "We can't beat them, Father!"

Mormon Tucker shook himself angrily, and his dark eyes blazed afresh. "That's why I hired Roaming Reynolds," he began harshly, and then lowered his voice. "I will kill him and all his gang if he dares to touch you," he promised solemnly. "I do not fear him and all his feathers!"

"But you know what he threatened," the girl pleaded, and pressed her hands against her swelling breasts. "Oh! If I were only a man!"

Roaming Reynolds watched the girl, and his face changed to a hard mask. Flame smouldered in his wide blue eyes while the corners of his mouth tightened and dimpled with little ridges of muscle.

"What did he threaten?" and his voice was metallic.

Mormon Tucker turned slowly and looked the cowboy up and down. "Said he was going to marry my daughter, or else—" He broke off suddenly and pointed at the broken feather in the stallion's mane.

"I'd admire to meet Eagle Dupree," Reynolds said slowly, and rubbed the handle of his sixgun. "What for kind of a looking jasper is this outlaw Ramrod?"

Mormon Tucker shook his head gravely. "Eagle Dupree would kill you, Reynolds," he answered positively. "Tall upstanding figure of a man with very dark eyes. Folks call him handsome, but he has the look of the Devil himself. Dupree is the fastest gunman in the Triangle, and he is wanted in all three states that border the Strip!"

The tall cowboy shrugged carelessly, but his tanned face was as craggy as the peaks in Zion

17

Park off in the Utah distances. Only his blue eyes showed the interest he felt in the man who signed his name with the feather of the king eagle.

"Where at can I find this hombre who kills anything he can't take for his own?" he asked softly.

Mormon Tucker shook his head. "I didn't hire you to get killed," he muttered. "Best leave Eagle Dupree alone."

"You hired my guns," Reynolds answered sharply. "I'm a gun-fighter, and I don't pretend to be anything else aside from cow work!"

Mormon Tucker sagged as the fierce anger left him. "Let's ride," he said slowly, and moved toward his horse. "Shoot to kill if anyone comes toward us, because we are deep in outlaw country. That way we will have an even chance, and I can tell you more about Eagle Dupree while we are heading back for home."

Roaming Reynolds scowled and watched the girl. Betty Tucker stayed close to her father and swung her dark head to study the sides of the wash. Then she mounted her sorrel and caught the cowboy's eyes upon her.

"He would kill you," she whispered.

The tall cowboy shrugged his broad shoulders and holstered his rifle in the scabbard under his left fender. A mocking smile curbed his lips when he laughed softly and shook his head.

"I take a heap of killing, Miss Betty," he

answered carelessly. "But if I was you I'd stay close to home or get myself fully dressed."

The girl flushed and fumbled at the buttons of her wool shirt. Roaming Reynolds continued to smile that hard grin that dimpled the corners of his lips. The girl lowered her eyes and stared at the strong brown hands caressing the grip of the long-barrelled sixgun.

"I thought you meant—?" she whispered.

"I meant to get dressed like a man," the cowboy interrupted bluntly. "Right now we are right in the middle of the Outlaw Strip where the only law is what men pack in their holsters!"

"I hired you to do the fighting," Mormon Tucker boomed softly. "Now let's point our horses toward the M T!"

CHAPTER II

Mormon Tucker rode out of the wash and swept his arm in a wide circle. The girl rode close enough to rub stirrups while Roaming Reynolds stayed just far enough in the rear to watch the back trail.

"They call this the Strip," Tucker began bitterly, and shook his big head when he turned for a last look at the Morgan stallion. "South there is the canyon of the Colorado River; the Grand Canyon. To the north just above my place on the Virgin River is Zion Park. Over west is Nevada, and sometimes I think the Lord made this place as an addition to hell!"

"But you love it, Father," the girl reminded softly. "You said it was just the kind of a place you have always dreamed about. I have seen you watching the sunsets on the Vermilion Cliffs as though it was a picture painted by some great artist."

"Painted by the greatest artist of them all," the big Mormon answered solemnly.

"Some of the best grazing I ever saw, Boss," Roaming Reynolds remarked quietly. "Good feed all year around."

"Yes," and Mormon Tucker sighed deeply. "It is natural horse country, and my business is raising horses. That Morgan was improving our strain, and we look for a good colt crop."

"Plenty of water for desert country," Reynolds added. "You ought to do well here unless the heavy snows cut off the green feed."

"I have done well," and the big Mormon squared his shoulders proudly. "My men snare the wild mares back in the hills; thousands of them running on the high plateaux. We bred to blooded stallions I imported, and last year we foaled nearly four hundred colts."

Roaming Reynolds nodded. "I had one of yore geldings in my string down on the Heart outfit," he answered. "Likewise old Trap Duncan used considerable of yore M T stock on his Diamond Bar cattle spread. That's how come me to ride up this away to see did you need a good riding hand breaking some of those colts for work."

"I've heard about you, Reynolds," Tucker mumbled, and stroked his black beard. "And like you admitted yourself, you are a gun-fighter. I have men who can ride well enough, but they don't carry firearms."

"And you lost plenty of stock," the tall cowboy reminded quietly.

Mormon Tucker slumped dejectedly in the saddle. "We Mormons are men of peace, Reynolds," he answered slowly. "Our riding stock is all gentle broke like you know, but the last year we have been raising horses for these owl-hoot buckaroos."

"Meaning this outlaw gang of Eagle Dupree's," the cowboy grunted. "What about the law up this way, Boss?"

Tucker laughed shortly. "Look at this country," he said bitterly. "Mountains on every side for criminals to hide. They know every hogback and coulee, and what law there is stays close to the towns. Like you mentioned to Betty, every man makes his own law up here in the Strip!"

"That's fair enough," Reynolds drawled, and tapped the gun on his leg. "How many men you got riding on the M T pay-roll?"

"Six," and the Mormon's face was sullen. "But I told you that we are all men of peace. Fighting is foreign to our natures!"

Roaming Reynolds nodded and glanced at the girl. "You take them white-tailed mule deer over in the Kaibab forest," he answered musingly. "They run like all get-out when something scares them at a water-hole. They ain't nothing in the world more peaceable than them critters, but I see a pack of wolves jump a band down in a deer-yard one time when the snows was heavy."

The girl watched his tanned face intently, and her dark eyes sparkled with eager interest. "Poor deer," she said softly. "I suppose they were all killed when the wolf-pack attacked."

Reynolds smiled and shook his head. "There

were a lot of does and fawns in that bunch," he answered thoughtfully. "They couldn't run on account of the heavy drifts, and when the fight was all over I counted eight wolves all dead and tromped to shreds. Deer might be plumb peaceful, but they can shore get their hackles up when their young are in danger!"

Mormon Tucker raised his big head slowly and glanced at the cowboy. Roaming Reynolds stared straight ahead with his eyes turned on the Vermilion Cliffs far in the distance. The girl rode closer to her father, and Tucker snorted angrily.

"By the Prophet," he intoned in his deep voice, and clenched his square fists. "I believe you have given me the answer, Roaming Reynolds!"

Roaming smiled then and turned his head to stare for a long moment into the dark eyes above the heavy black beard. Again his right hand was rubbing the grip of his sixgun, and the Mormon nodded slowly and took a deep breath.

"It is war," he declared solemnly. "Eagle Dupree started it when he shot the Morgan stallion. Like you just now stated, even the deer will fight to protect their young!"

The girl stared at the two hard-faced men and shivered. The face of the gun-fighting buckaroo was etched with battle-lines while a deep smouldering fire flamed briefly in his wide blue eyes. The jaw of Mormon Tucker was thrust out pugnaciously to match the light glowing deep in his sombre dark eyes.

"Send me away, Father," she pleaded earnestly. "We have many old friends in Salt Lake City who will be glad to have me for a long visit!"

"You'd never reach Salt Lake City now," Roaming Reynolds answered coldly. "Not after what I've heard about Eagle Dupree!"

"But I could try," the girl insisted, and gripped her father's left arm. "What do you think, Father?"

Mormon Tucker frowned and turned his head slowly to scan all the wild country around them. Then he locked glances with his daughter and shook his head from side to side while his lips set grimly.

"Like Reynolds pointed out, you couldn't make it," he muttered bitterly. "You know why they call this country the Strip."

The same hard smile creased his tanned face when Roaming Reynolds reached to the saddle-bags behind the cantle of his scarred saddle. He fumbled for a moment in the left-hand pocket while the girl stared intently. He withdrew his hand with a cartridge belt and holster; passed it to the girl and pointed to his own waist.

"Buckle this on, Miss Betty," he said casually. "That old Peacemaker is the mate to the one I use. Five shells in the cylinder with the hammer riding on an empty, and if you don't know how to use it, I will be more than glad to teach you."

The girl glanced at her father and took the heavy belt. Cinched it around her trim waist and tied the holdback low on her shapely thigh. Then she slid the heavy sixgun several times to loosen it of hang while her dark eyes scanned the desert wastes.

Roaming Reynolds nodded with quiet satisfaction while he watched each separate move. He knew guns and the people who handled them, and some of the battle-light left his eyes when the girl tried the single action while she stared out across the high desert.

A jack rabbit broke from cover and leaped across a low clump of sage-brush. Metal flashed suddenly in Betty Tucker's right hand with a booming roar. The girl caught the bucking gun with thumb earing back the hammer on the recoil when the rabbit doubled up in mid-air and fell thirty feet away. Being gun-shy, the two M T horses bucked and started to run, but the Mormon checked them expertly.

Roaming Reynolds smiled and turned to his new boss. "I was you, I'd quit fretting," he said dryly. "There's one Mormon knows how to bust a cap, and from where I sit it looks like there is going to be a good season on wolves."

Mormon Tucker was staring at his daughter with eyes that were wide and incredulous.

"Where did you learn to shoot like that?" he demanded sternly.

The girl flushed and bit her lip. "I learned at school," she stammered. "We shot at targets on the rifle range, but I knew you did not approve of firearms, so I said nothing about it."

"You mean you deceived your father?" and the big man stared at his daughter as if she were a stranger.

"Not that, Father," the girl answered quickly. "I just had a chance to learn, and after all we were only shooting at targets. Do you care very much?"

"You take a curly wolf or a man now," Roaming Reynolds interrupted swiftly, and his voice was dry and hard. "They ain't near so hard to hit as that jack yonder. I reckon you know what to do if you ever come up on any of that Dupree gang, Miss Betty!"

Mormon Tucker frowned. "A woman's place is in the home," he said heavily. "It ill befits a young girl to fight like a savage, and if it comes to fighting, my men will do it."

"Now you take them deer over in the Kaibab," Reynolds drawled meaningly. "They was right there in their own yard, and they had five or six big bucks with them. But you should have seen them does cutting up wolves with their sharp hooves when they went on the prod."

Mormon Tucker frowned sternly. "That will do,

Reynolds," he said evenly. "Even Eagle Dupree would not dare to come to the M T Ranch, if I understand your meaning correctly. We Mormons teach our women the ways of peace and gentleness, and after this Betty will remain close to home where her mother can watch over her."

Roaming Reynolds smiled. "I'd like to be there to see her mother if Eagle Dupree rode into the M T," he remarked softly. "There ain't nothing in the world can fight like a mother protecting her young!"

"My wife represents all that is peaceable and gentle," Mormon Tucker answered with dignity, and turned to regard his daughter with stern disapproval. "Unbuckle that belt, Betty!"

His deep voice spelled parental authority, and the girl reached for the heavy buckle without argument. Roaming Reynolds frowned with sudden anger and reached out with his left hand to seize the girl's fumbling fingers.

"Leave it," he barked sharply. "You better have one and not need it, than to need one bad and not have it close to yore hand. Let that gun ride on yore leg, gal!"

Mormon Tucker seemed to swell up when his heavy voice crackled like rolling thunder. His was a nature that could not tolerate interference, and his dark eyes flashed dangerously while he stared at Roaming Reynolds. The girl sat stiffly in the saddle between the two men and waited for the outcome.

"I said to leave it ride on yore leg!"

Roaming Reynolds tightened his jaw stubbornly and locked glances with Mormon Tucker. His lean body jerked suddenly in the saddle when he drove his spurs to his horse and slammed into the sorrel gelding under Betty Tucker. Her horse screamed and went down just as the cowboy raced past and scraped her from the saddle with his rigid left arm.

The stampede threw Mormon Tucker's horse to the side just as a rifle cracked in the distance. Roaming Reynolds reined in behind an outcropping of rocks and let the girl slide to the ground. He was beside her with Winchester in hand while his roan trotted to the rear, and his voice bellowed at the big man in the clearing. "Off that hoss, Mormon! Get down behind these rocks on the double quick!"

Mormon Tucker scowled with anger and turned his big barrel-chested bay. The rifle cracked again and kicked him from the saddle just as he reached cover. Roaming Reynolds leaped out in a crouching run and dragged the heavy body behind the rocks when a volley of shots flattened out from the opposite ridge. The girl was watching him with dark eyes wide and unafraid, and the cowboy smiled grimly and picked up his Winchester.

"I aim to tally for that gunnie," he muttered under his breath. "The bush-whackin' son!"

Without haste he levered a shell into the breech and took careful aim at the ridge two hundred yards away. He pressed trigger with a steady slow squeeze when a rifle spoke; smiled coldly when a man jerked into view and tumbled down the face of the rocky cliff. Bullets stirred dust in front of his position, and he answered the shots as fast as he could work the lever.

"You killed him," the girl whispered, and pressed a hand against the swell of her breast. "You killed him for what he did to Father!"

A hoarse growl sounded behind the pair while the cowboy was reloading the magazine, and he laid the hot rifle aside when the sound of hooves rattled from the opposite ridge and faded away. Mormon Tucker was on his knees taking off his long black coat when the cowboy turned. Betty Tucker was beside him tearing the sleeve from his fine linen shirt.

"Just nicked me," the big Mormon growled hoarsely. "Will you accept my hand and my apology, young man?"

Roaming Reynolds stared before a wide smile spread across his craggy, powder-grimed face. Then he dropped the rifle and reached across to grip the big man hard.

"Glad to touch skin with you, Boss," he chuckled. "I liked to scared Miss Betty to death,

29

but it just so happened that my eye caught the shine of the sun on that rifle barrel before that feller pressed trigger. He was aiming at you, and he couldn't have missed."

His eyes wandered to the wide shoulders and great deep chest. Mormon Tucker was a mighty man of bone and muscle, and his bearded face was grave when he glanced at his daughter. The girl was tying a bandage around his huge bicep, and her jaw was set and determined when she spoke to her father. Low and throaty with suppressed strength.

"I'm carrying Roaming's spare gun on my leg from now on. I have never disobeyed you before, Father, but this is one time I insist on using my own judgment."

Mormon Tucker nodded absently and continued to stare at the tall cowboy. "It means fight to the finish now, Betty," he muttered. "I don't know too much about fighting, but I can take orders as well as give them. Roaming Reynolds is boss on the M T when powder starts to burn!"

His deep voice was quiet and steady, and his dark eyes were unwinking when he made his statement. Reynolds nodded with satisfaction and levered to his feet with a grim smile.

"From now on every man on the M T spread gets himself fully dressed," and he glanced at the Mormon's generous waist-line. "That means a sixgun on yore leg, and a carbine in the saddle-boot under yore saddle-fender. And I said that applies to every man drawing riding pay."

Mormon Tucker nodded agreement and pulled on his long black coat. "I'll see that all our men get dressed," he answered soberly. "Now we better ride back to the Virgin River where we belong."

The girl looked at the two men and calculated the difference in their weights. Roaming Reynolds would weigh a hundred and sixty-five; at least forty pounds less than Mormon Tucker. The cowboy caught her glance and mounted his rangy roan. Then he kicked the left stirrup loose and held it toward the girl.

"You will have to ride double with me," he remarked casually, like one cowhand would talk to another. "They killed yore sorrel out yonder, and my hoss can carry double better than that chunky bay yore dad is using."

Mormon Tucker frowned and then smiled ruefully. "Nothing else to do, daughter," he agreed reluctantly. "But I want you to know that we Mormons don't encourage that sort of thing with our girls, Reynolds!"

The cowboy shrugged carelessly. "I don't have no truck with women-folks," he drawled. "Miss Betty is just the same as any other hand to me."

The girl flushed and swung up behind him. Tightened her fingers in his belt and jerked spitefully while she whispered just behind his ear—

31

"Thanks for the compliment, cowboy. I won't bother you very long . . . gun-fighter!"

She scratched the roan with her spur; held steady when the big horse leaped ahead like a startled deer. The cowboy lurched in the saddle and caught his balance when the girl steadied him. Then he rowelled on the other side and grinned slyly when the roan started bucking. Betty Tucker held tightly with both arms around his swelling chest until the roan straightened out and started to lope.

"You brute," she gasped, and loosened her arms. "Can't you control your own horse?"

The cowboy thrilled uneasily to the closeness of her warm body, and it was a moment before he trusted himself to speak. The girl smiled from the shelter of his broad back, and gazed admiringly at the sturdy column of his neck.

"My spur kinda slipped," he answered lamely. "Something must have scared the roan when you slid on behind, cause I never knowed him to act that away before. You just hang on and rattle if he sets in to bucking, pard."

"I can ride if you can," the girl answered, and jerked the broad belt. "Sorry I have to bother you like this."

"No trouble at all," he grunted, and eased his shoulders away from the swell of her breasts.

They rode in silence for more than an hour, and the cowboy stared with interest when they splashed through the shallow ford of the Virgin River. Broad pastures of rich green grass stretched back into the rolling hills, and the ranch buildings were cool and white in the very centre.

Mormon Tucker spurred up and took the lead when they climbed out on the sloping bank. "Welcome to the M T, Reynolds," he called cordially, and once more his deep voice was calm and peaceful. "We hope you are going to like it here well enough to stay awhile."

"I doubt it," Betty Tucker whispered just loud enough for the cowboy to hear. "Thanks for the ride, cowboy, and I hope I have not troubled you and your horse too much."

"No trouble to speak of after the first little sneak," Reynolds answered with a grin. "Can I help you down, or can you make it by yore lonesome?"

The girl knuckled his back angrily and released her hold on his belt. "Don't put yourself out any, Mister gun-fighter," she muttered, and slid to the ground. "I only rode with you because I had to."

CHAPTER III

Roaming Reynolds gazed at the green fields of grain surrounding the ranch buildings. Shook his head doubtfully when he saw a dozen separate pastures under stake-and-rider fences, but his head nodded quickly with understanding when he saw the bands of mares and their colts. Mormon Tucker might be short on the ways of fighting men, but there was no doubt about his ability as a hoss-breeder.

"Everything shore looks peaceful enough here," he told Tucker. "But I don't see any of the hands you mentioned."

"I'll call the men," Tucker answered, and walked over to a wagon tyre suspended from a stout chain.

The cowboy watched with interest when the Mormon struck the tyre three times with a short iron bar. Men came from the adjoining pastures and corrals, and Reynolds nodded with satisfaction when he saw them riding on well-trained mountain horses. A button of sixteen was working in a corral not more than a hundred yards away, but the boy ran for his horse and came riding across the yard in place of walking.

"That sliver has the ear-marks of a cowhand," Reynolds remarked to Tucker. "Texas feller from the double-rigged kak he's straddling."

"We call him Texas Joe," Tucker chuckled. "Wild as a long-horn, but he has the makings of a good hand, and he is easy on horse-flesh. Joe, this is Roaming Reynolds, a new hand I hired this morning."

"Howdy, Roaming," the boy drawled, and grinned impudently when he offered his hand. "When you leave the old Diamond Bar?"

The tall cowboy gripped hard and answered the infectious grin. "Last week, Tex," he answered, as one man would greet an equal. "You've growed considerable since I saw you last. I'd say the change done you good."

"Got restless in the feet," the boy answered quietly. "Just geared my tops and drawed my time one day, and rode over the hill to see what was on the other side."

"There's plenty to see, and lots of hills," Reynolds agreed. "You won't stay here very long."

Five bearded men loped up and dismounted. They gathered around Mormon Tucker while their serious eyes studied the tall cowboy from high heels to high hat. All were young men in their early twenties, but they wore the sombre clothing of the Utah Mormons to match their bearded unsmiling faces.

"I want you to meet Roaming Reynolds," Tucker began in his deep voice. "Reynolds is fighting boss on the M T from now on until we clean out that gang headed by Eagle Dupree. They declared war this morning and Reynolds proved himself to me. Talk to them some, Reynolds."

The cowboy studied each bearded face and allowed his eyes to wander down to their flat hips. Tall deep-chested fellows with tanned faces and rope-burned hands. Not a man in the group was carrying a gun, and Reynolds frowned while his right hand rubbed the handle of his old Peacemaker forty-five.

"From now on all you men get yoreselves fully dressed," he said quietly, but his voice carried an edge that was unmistakable. "That means a sixgun on yore legs, and a rifle under yore fender when you have riding business away from the spread. Eagle Dupree has done declared war on yore boss, and it's time you was learning to fight for the iron that pays you yore wages."

Sullen eyes glared back at him resentfully. Full lips tightened behind silky beards that had never known a razor. Four of the riders turned to glance at one of their companions, who stood a half-head taller than Mormon Tucker. Authority sat on his broad shoulders when he frowned at the other men and then spoke sternly to Roaming Reynolds in a deep quiet voice.

"I'm against it," and the frown deepened on the big man's face while he stared at the gun on Betty Tucker's right leg.

The girl flushed and avoided his gaze while she glanced at the tall cowboy. Mormon Tucker watched the antagonism between the two men and spoke softly to Roaming Reynolds.

"That's Brigham Smith, my foreman. Perhaps you had better explain to him why Betty is wearing your gun."

"Yes," the big man said slowly. "I'm waiting to learn the meaning of such a war-like display."

Roaming Reynolds squared his shoulders, and a frown twitched the corners of his mouth. Mormon Tucker had introduced him as fighting boss, and he came to the point without hesitation.

"Eagle Dupree swore he would marry Miss Tucker," and he faced the big Mormon squarely. "Like you know, Dupree takes what he wants, or kills what he can't take. He tried to kill one of us not more than two hours back, and he lost a man in the trying. You'll wear a sixgun, Smith!"

Brigham Smith stared steadily at the cowboy, and the fingers of his right hand played with his silky beard. His face wore the stern serious look of the Deacon, and his brown eyes glowed with a strange fanatical light. Then he stepped quickly forward and lifted the heavy sixgun from the worn holster on the girl's leg. Stepped back again without changing expression and held the handle of the gun toward Roaming Reynolds.

"You are a stranger up here," and his deep voice vibrated like a deep-toned bell. "We are men of peace, Reynolds, but we can take care of our women without your help. I return your weapon!"

"You get one like it and strap it on yore leg," Reynolds drawled softly. "That's an order, Smith!"

"I return your weapon," and Brigham Smith thrust the gun at the cowboy with a heavy frown.

Roaming Reynolds took the gun and reversed it in his hand. Then he stepped forward and re-holstered it on the girl's leg. His blue eyes were unsmiling when he turned to face Brigham Smith while the other Mormons watched in silence. The young Mormon set his full lips and shook his big head.

"I am in charge of the men here on the M T," he said slowly. "They do what I tell them to do, and I will not submit to any challenge of my authority."

"There always has to be a first time in everything," Reynolds answered carelessly. "I'm the fighting boss of this crew, and I don't set myself up as a man of peace."

Brigham Smith towered a full three inches above six feet. He stepped forward suddenly and gripped the cowboy by both arms before Roaming Reynolds could step back. Lifted him easily and set him aside while his brown eyes reflected the controlled anger in his heart.

"Weapons are the works of the devil," and his

heavy voice boomed solemnly. "Return that gun to this stranger, Betty Tucker!"

The girl turned quickly and stared at him while her breath caught against her throat. Her dark eyes swung across to study the face of Roaming Reynolds, and she waited for him to speak.

"Leave it be!" and the cowboy's voice barked like a rifle. "Eagle Dupree ain't rodding any Sunday School spread, Smith. I put that gun there and it rides where it is!"

Brigham Smith drew a deep breath and tightened his lips. "I resent your interference, Reynolds," he said quietly. "I have spoken to Betty's father for her hand according to our custom. He has accepted me as her suitor, and I will not tolerate any interference from a gun-fighter stranger who rides among us to destroy our peace. Remove that weapon at once, Betty!"

"Leave it ride," and Roaming Reynolds stared at the tall Mormon coldly. "I might be all that you say, but I'm giving the orders when it comes to fighting hardware!"

The young Mormon moved with the speed of a mountain cat. His flat hand caught the cowboy on the cheek and rocked him back on his high heels with the force of the blow. Reynolds caught his balance with right hand slapping down to his scabbard like a flash of heat lightning. He gun covered Brigham Smith while angry fires leaped high in the blue eyes behind the menacing gun.

"Don't shoot, Roaming!"

The cowboy smiled frostily when Betty Tucker shouted with a note of pleading in her throaty voice. Brigham Smith flushed angrily and knotted his huge fists while the light of battle glowed in his brown eyes.

"Put up that gun," he ordered sternly. "I won't tell you again, stranger!"

The cowboy reversed the gun in his hand and stepped close to Texas Joe. A quick thrust and the long barrel slid down the band of the button's Levi's with the worn handle tilting out. Like a flash Roaming Reynolds stepped forward and struck Smith a stinging blow full across the mouth.

"You still a man of peace?" he asked icily.

Brigham Smith lost his composure and charged like an angry bull. Roaming Reynolds caught him with a left coming in; followed through with a driving right to the jaw that numbed his arm to the elbow. Then he shifted back with his left cocked for a follow-up.

The young Mormon stopped suddenly while his big frame shivered under the blow. His eyes closed when he fell forward on his face, and Roaming Reynolds caught him and eased the big man to the ground. His tanned face was as calm as ever when he turned to the gaping crew and spoke in his deep drawling voice.

"You fellers stampede to the bunkhouse and

strap on yore hardware pronto. Eagle Dupree and that gang of owl-hoot buckaroos don't do their fighting with their fists. Fly at it unless some gent figgers he wants to start an argument!"

The men looked at him and back at the still figure of their young foreman. Then they shook their heads silently and moved away with thoughtful expressions on their bearded faces. Roaming Reynolds smiled then and walked over to take his gun from Texas Joe.

"Sorry I had it to do," he muttered.

He holstered the gun smoothly while his eyes studied the man on the ground. Betty Tucker and her father shifted uncertainly, and then the girl came forward and held out her hand.

"Thanks for not using your gun, Roaming," she said earnestly. "Brigham is a Deacon in the church, but he is the bravest man on the M T. Or he was until you came."

Reynolds held her hand and glanced down at the gun on her leg. "You will have to fight for you and him both," he answered dryly. "That feller would die before he would strap on a cutter."

The girl shook her head and gently released her hand. "I'm afraid for him now," she whispered.

"Brigham is my foreman," Mormon Tucker interrupted, and his deep voice carried a note of worry. "He is a mighty man and slow to wrath, but when he thinks a principle is involved, he would face death and destruction with a smile."

"He might face both," Reynolds answered significantly. "Gun-fighters don't settle a ruckus with their fists, and the Deacon makes a mighty big target for a gent on the shoot!"

Mormon Tucker nodded his big head. "I fear for him," he muttered, and his voice raised. "Brigham man-handled Hip High Hardy several months ago. Beat him almost to a pulp right on the street in Red Horse."

"That gent who uses the flip-draw?" and the cowboy's eyes widened. "He beat that gun-slammer up with his fists in town?"

Mormon Tucker nodded with a sigh. "Hip High couldn't stand on his feet, but the Deacon refuses to carry a gun in spite of the outlaw's threats to kill him the next time they meet. You met Hardy this morning, and you can judge for yourself."

The cowboy shrugged carelessly. "Every man lives his own life the way he figgers best," he answered lightly. "And some of them die mighty young out here in these parts when they get too mule-headed to change their ways."

"They will kill him," the girl murmured, and turned her pretty face to hide the terror in her dark eyes. "Brigham wouldn't have a chance against the guns of that killer!"

"He won't change," Mormon Tucker sighed heavily, and then his eyes lighted up when the four hands returned slowly from the bunkhouse with cartridge belts strapped around their lean waists.

"Glad to see you fellows showed good sense," he praised quietly. "The first law of life is self-preservation, and I'm telling you all to take good care of yourselves."

Texas Joe eased toward Roaming Reynolds and nudged him with a bony elbow. Pointed at the man on the ground, and Brigham Smith stirred restlessly when all eyes turned to watch him. Roaming Reynolds tightened his lips and hooked his thumbs in his gunbelt while he balanced easily on the soles of his hand-made boots.

Brigham Smith sat up and shook his head while his eyes blinked rapidly. Then he levered slowly up on his powerful legs and stared at the circle of faces. For a long moment he studied the tall cowboy while he swayed unsteadily. Turned abruptly without speaking and walked across to a flowing water-trough.

No one spoke when he dipped his head beneath the cold water and held it for a long moment. He whooshed like a great bear when he came up for air. His big right hand reached for the blue bandanna around his throat, and he dried his face and beard carefully while his head nodded slowly back and forth.

"Watch him, Roaming," Texas Joe whispered softly. "He aims to take you shore as sin!"

Brigham Smith tucked the bandanna in his

43

hip pocket and shook his head to clear away the webs of fog. Then he turned squarely and walked straight up to Roaming Reynolds with the same fanatical light glowing in his brown eyes.

"Keep back, Deacon!"

Brigham Smith ignored the warning snapped from the cowboy's stiff lips. Long arms swinging loosely at his sides while he came on with heavy measured tread, and a resolute determination etched in the lines of his ruddy, bearded face.

Roaming Reynolds stared his unbelief and took a backward step. His right hand flipped down to his scabbard and drew the gun with a movement incredibly swift. The long barrel spiked out when he cradled his wrist against his ribs with thumb on the hammer.

Brigham Smith kept coming until his big swelling chest touched the muzzle. Only his brown eyes told of the blazing fires leaping high in his heart while he breasted the sixgun and stared at the cowboy. Roaming Reynolds felt that absolute fearlessness, but his face was hard when he warned the bigger man gruffly.

"You start to make a move and I'll drop hammer shore as hell!"

He eared back the hammer and held it ready to slip under his thumb. Brigham Smith ignored the threat while he leaned against the gun. He took a deep breath and opened his full lips to show strong white teeth set doggedly together.

"He who lives by the sword shall die by the sword," he recited sternly. "Put up your gun and learn the ways of peace if you intend to dwell among us. The meek shall inherit the earth!"

The cowboy stepped back a pace and held his gun steady. "I don't know much about the Scriptures," he answered gruffly. "But it says something about Pride going before a fall, and it likewise says that the stiff neck shall be bowed!"

Brigham Smith nodded his head slowly and held his position.

"Blessed are the peaceful," he intoned soberly. "I told you to put up that weapon of the devil!"

Roaming Reynolds made a little jabbing motion with his Colt. "Stay back, Smith," he muttered. "You better stick to yore job of work," and his voice held the trace of a sneer. "I'll stick to mine like always!"

Brigham Smith shook his head and stepped forward. Calm and deliberately, he lowered his right hand and reached for the spiking gun. The cowboy took three backward steps with a puzzled look in his cold blue eyes. The Mormon followed him step by step, and his big jaw thrust out stubbornly while his hand reached for the gun.

"Stand hitched! You make another step and I'll burn powder!"

Brigham Smith balanced on his big boots. "You won't shoot," he said softly, and stepped in fast.

Roaming Reynolds snapped his teeth and made

a quick decision. He stepped back another step while his thumb lowered the heavy hammer. Then he leaped forward to meet the advancing Mormon with the gun arching high. The long barrel slapped down viciously to buffalo Brigham Smith on the left temple to stop that inexorable advance. This time he side-stepped when the big man buckled his knees and sagged to the ground like a pole-axed steer.

"He was right when he said I wouldn't shoot," he remarked to Mormon Tucker. "But the man don't live who can take my gun when I got it in my hand. You tell Smith I'll kill him the next time he makes a play like that last one!"

Mormon Tucker frowned and shifted his big feet. Betty Tucker was watching the cowboy with admiration shining in her dark eyes. The other riders were fingering the handles of their weapons with eyes glancing from their foreman to the new gun-fighter who had twice demonstrated his fighting ability.

Roaming Reynolds turned on them and allowed a slow smile to curl the corners of his hard mouth. "You gents figger out where you stand yet?" he asked harshly.

They glared sullenly and turned their faces away from the challenge in his blue eyes. Mormon Tucker sucked in a great draught of air and stepped out with his right hand held high.

"It's war," and his deep voice rang with

certainty. "Brigham Smith is a splendid man in times of peace, but now we must fight fire with fire. No one doubts his courage, but he showed poor judgment in not reading Reynolds the way Reynolds read him."

"He might have killed the Deacon," a young rider muttered. "Best you talk some more, Boss!"

"I'll talk," Tucker answered firmly. "You men will take your orders from Reynolds when it comes to fighting. You, Reynolds, will take your orders from Brigham Smith when it comes to all work on the ranch!"

"He's a heap of a man, but you better try and talk some sense into his head," the cowboy grunted. "I'll take orders like a good hand in the breaking tank, but him taking orders from me is something else again."

"He'll lever up on his hind legs and try to booger you the minute he rouses around," Texas Joe cut in suddenly. "The Deacon don't know the meaning of quit!"

Roaming Reynolds scowled and studied the unconscious man. "I don't booger worth a hoot," he muttered harshly. "And I don't want to drop hammer on a gent that packs the sand he does."

Betty Tucker came to Reynolds and laid her hand on his left arm. He stared into her brown eyes for a moment and waited for her to speak while his fingers curled around the grip of his

47

gun. Mormon Tucker frowned and shook his wide shoulders.

"Thanks for not killing Brigham," the girl said softly. "I knew you wouldn't, because you are as brave as he is. You had to do what you did, and some day he will thank you for it."

Texas Joe laughed behind his grimy hand. "Not the Deacon," he said in his changing voice. "He never was knowed to change his mind once he set it on something."

The cowboy nodded confirmation when he spoke to the girl. "Better look after yore man now," he said carelessly. "He might have a headache when he rouses round, and it might be well to tell him not to go on the prod like he done before. I aim to take care of myself."

The girl dropped her hand and bit her lip. The light left her pretty face when the cowboy walked away, and she stared when he stopped to speak to Texas Joe. She could see the hero-worship in the wide grey eyes of the boy, and for some reason the two seemed very much alike.

CHAPTER IV

"Thanks for warning me, feller," the tall cowboy said softly, and slapped Texas Joe on the shoulder.

"Nice cold-cockin', Roamin'," the boy praised carelessly, and stuck out his grimy hand. "You can count on me to side you all the way down the river!"

Roaming Reynolds smiled and shook hands gravely. "Knew it all the time, pard," he answered soberly. "I'd rather have you at my back than any man on the M T spread."

"You wouldn't fool a waddy?" and Texas Joe searched the cowboy's face for some sign of hoorawing. "You wouldn't spin a windy that away, would you, Roamin'?"

"Listen, Tex," and Reynolds looked the boy squarely in the eye. "You know as much about Eagle Dupree and his owl-hoot buckaroos as I do. They mean to get this spread, and Dupree wants the gal. How long would it take them to get both if we were all men of peace and acted like Brigham Smith preaches?"

"An hour at the outside," the boy answered gravely, and tried to keep his changing voice deep and low. "That Betty gal is a likely filly, Roamin'. I've travelled some, and I never see another like her."

"Yeah," but the cowboy showed his lack of interest. "Women is out of my line, and I'm hired to smoke my guns. You know these hills and draws pretty well around here?"

"Knows all of them," the boy answered confidently. "I wrangle the cavvy when they are turned out to graze, but I'm not always going to be a jingler. You got something on yore mind, pard?"

"Like as not I will be riding with you," Reynolds remarked casually. "That away we can sort of keep cases on those outlaws over in Rainbow Canyon. Unless I miss my guess, Hip High Hardy is going to keep the promise he made the Deacon."

"They ain't a man borned what can stand up to a gun and it smokin'," Texas Joe muttered and shook his tousled head. "A forty-five slug will knock you down no matter where it hits you, and the Deacon makes quite a target."

"He'd make a fighting man," Reynolds sighed. "Quick on his feet, and he don't know how to back up."

Joe clutched his arm and whispered huskily. "Looky yonder, Roaming. The Deacon is coming out of his dreams."

The tall cowboy turned quickly with his hand close to his gun. Betty Tucker was bathing the big foreman's head with cold water from the trough, with a maternal expression on her gentle face. Brigham Smith sat up slowly and pushed the cloth away with his left hand. Raised up like a man in a dream and glared around the yard until his slitted eyes located Roaming Reynolds.

"I'll teach him the ways of peace," he muttered, and started slowly forward.

Mormon Tucker stepped in front of Smith to bar the way. Both big hands on the Deacon's muscular chest while he used his bulk in an effort to halt that slow advance. Brigham Smith raised his head with that same peculiar look glowing deep in his brown eyes.

"Hold up and do some thinking, Deacon," Tucker advised softly. "Better not try any more foolishness with Roaming Reynolds."

"I'll take his gun and save his life," Smith muttered hoarsely. "We are men of peace, and he will have to become one to dwell among us!"

"Better for you to change and become a fighting man like Goliath," Mormon Tucker answered clearly. "And likewise Samson who slew the Philistines with the jawbone of an ass!"

"The stranger uses firearms," Smith muttered. "It is my duty to teach him the error of his ways. Step aside, Tucker!"

Roaming Reynolds spread his boots wide and frowned when the foreman shook loose and started for him. Betty Tucker ran in front of Smith and blocked him off again. Her voice was low and pleading when she grasped his arm and held tightly.

"Please don't be so stubborn, Brigham. He came here to help us, and you know that he will never allow you to touch his gun!"

"I'll take it if I have to try seventy times seven," and the big man set his lips and glared at the cowboy over her shoulder. "He is an Apostle of death and destruction, and my duty is plain!"

Roaming Reynolds frowned while he studied the magnificent frame of the stubborn Mormon. The Deacon looked to be about twenty-six or seven, and his mighty shoulders tapered down to a lean waist topping powerful long legs. His weight would be in the neighbourhood of two hundred pounds, but the Deacon seemed entirely unconscious of his body. Big fists that seemed capable of felling a bull hung on his muscular arms and knotted into mauls, while his brown eyes bored into the craggy fighting face of the watching cowboy.

"Can't you see, Brigham?" the girl pleaded huskily. "He is just as stubborn as you are, and you each have your own work to do. Roaming Reynolds will never allow you to touch his gun!"

Brigham Smith shook his big head and pushed the girl gently aside, but with a strength that was irresistible. Big hands swinging at his sides, he started for the cowboy with square jaw jutting out like a shoulder of rock. His full lips moved silently, and his eyes never left the scowling face of Roaming Reynolds.

Texas Joe shifted his feet and growled under his breath. "Better change yore mind, Deacon," but his voice broke on a high shrill note. "You ain't doin' nothing but buying yoreself grief!"

Roaming Reynolds crouched forward with sparks gleaming in his narrowed blue eyes. His knuckles smarted and ached from the blows he had pounded against the hard flesh of his stubborn opponent. The long-barrelled sixgun leaped to his right hand like a beam of flashing light, but Brigham Smith ignored the threat and continued that slow measured advance.

"Slow down, Deacon! The third time might use up all yore luck!"

The cowboy's rasping voice cut the still air like a knife while he centred his sights with thumb dogging back the hammer of his spiking gun. Brigham Smith shuddered involuntarily, but his stride remained the same. Mormon Tucker sucked his breath in noisily and gripped his fists while his dark eyes stared at the Deacon intently.

He sighed when the tall cowboy made a sudden decision. Roaming Reynolds broke ground and holstered his gun with a smooth flip of his wrist. Then he vaulted to the saddle on the rangy roan and squared the animal around with a touch of the reins. Brigham Smith stepped aside then with his eyes boring steadfastly into the face of the gun-fighter, after which he continued to advance with a faint smile curling his lips.

Roaming Reynolds neck-reined the roan and walked the big horse forward until the broad chest of the animal touched the Deacon. Step by step he pushed the big man back to the spot where Mormon Tucker was standing.

"He stepped back, and he will step back again," Reynolds growled savagely. "I can't gun down an unarmed man, even if he is a damn fool!"

He wheeled the roan and cantered across the yard just as the Deacon recovered from his surprise and leaped forward with both big hands gripping for a hold. Texas Joe gigged his horse between the two to cut the Deacon off, and then he spurred after Roaming Reynolds.

"You'd have to kill him to change his mind," he growled angrily. "That big jigger don't know when he's up again something that is bigger than him and his funny ideas."

Roaming Reynolds shook his head, and his deep voice was regretful when he voiced his thoughts. "If he was only a fighting man!"

"He is a fighting man," the boy growled. "Only the stubborn jughead ain't found it out yet. The Deacon ain't afraid of nothing on earth, but some day that big carcass of his will stop all the lead some notch-whittlin' son can pump out of his gun!"

Brigham Smith started across the yard with the same purposeful stride. Mormon Tucker growled deep in his throat and charged his foreman like an angry bull. His muscled shoulder hit the Deacon high and spun him around, and Brigham Smith tensed his muscles to meet the attack.

"You too, Tucker," he said quietly. "And after I have finished I will continue my work!"

Betty Tucker stepped between the two men and threw her arms around the Deacon. "Father is wounded," she almost shouted. "He was shot in the shoulder when the outlaws attacked us!"

Brigham Smith underwent a sudden change. He released himself from the girl and stepped toward Mormon Tucker with both hands extended. The expression on his face changed to one of sincere regard, and his deep voice was as soft as the mellow tones of a muted bell.

"I didn't know, Mormon. Are you hurt bad?"

"I would have been killed had it not been for Roaming Reynolds," Tucker answered as softly. "Those outlaws hid on a distant hill and ambushed us when we rode out of that big wash where we found the Morgan stallion. Another bullet killed Betty's horse."

"And she rode back with that gun-fighter," Smith muttered bitterly. "She was holding on to him with both arms when I saw you coming through the corrals."

Mormon Tucker spread his hands and shrugged his shoulders. "What could she do?" he asked. "Would you have her walk when the outlaw pack were trying to kill us?"

Brigham Smith nodded soberly. "Yes," he answered. "I would rather see her dead than sullied by the touch of one who lives by his guns!"

"Have a care, Deacon," Tucker warned, and his eyes glowed with an angry fire. "Betty is my only child, and I think more of her than I do of all the horses on the M T. Roaming Reynolds is a just and upright man, and I would trust everything I have to him!"

"Your daughter?" and the Deacon gasped with amazement mirrored on his bearded face. "You would trust Betty to a gun-fighter?"

"Any place," Mormon Tucker answered firmly. "I believe in the signs as much as you do, and Roaming Reynolds was sent to us!"

"What does it profit a man to gain the whole world and lose his soul?" Smith asked solemnly.

"Sometimes a man's soul ain't so very big," Tucker answered tartly. "I have an idea that your own might grow a lot bigger when you know that cowboy better. His mind is as clean as river sand. Not only that, but you forget the Scriptures in your anger!"

"I forget the Book?"

"You forget! I come not to bring you peace, but a sword. Now do you remember?"

"The sword of righteousness," the Deacon answered stubbornly. "And that is given only to the chosen. The stranger knocked me down with his gun!"

"If an enemy smite thee, turn to him the other cheek," Mormon Tucker intoned sternly.

Brigham Smith gasped and stepped back, and the light of battle faded from his dark eyes. "You are right," he whispered hoarsely. Then he turned slowly and stared after the two cowboys in the distance, and once more his big hands clenched tightly. "But I did turn the other cheek," he growled. "And he smote me again!"

"You said something about seventy times seven," Mormon Tucker suggested. "And it will be that many times if you continue with your mad intentions!"

"It will be that many times," Brigham Smith admitted quietly. "What a man he would make if he would lay aside his weapons of destruction and pursue the ways of peace!"

"Back there in the wash when he first found the stallion," and the voice of Mormon Tucker rumbled softly. "He was fighting back the tears when Betty and I rode up. He had a chance to kill Hip High Hardy and Canuck Avery, but he allowed them to ride away in peace."

"Hip High Hardy," and the Deacon changed the subject. "I want to meet him again."

Mormon Tucker sighed and shook his head. "Hardy will kill you, Deacon," he warned. "Unless you use your head and strap on a gun like the rest of us. No man can use his hands against the shocking, stabbing lead of outlaw guns!"

"Goliath did not use a gun," Smith muttered.

"And he didn't fight his head and use his fists," Tucker snorted. "He picked himself out a handful of big rocks, and Goliath wasn't too proud to fight!"

Brigham Smith smiled grimly and rubbed his temple. "Are you saying that I was too proud to fight?" he asked quietly.

"But you are a man of peace," and Mormon Tucker smiled broadly. "You forget your logic, Deacon."

The smile fled from the face of the big Mormon while he stroked his black silky beard. "I succumbed to the temptations of anger," he whispered. "I saw my duty as a Deacon of the Church, and I tried to do it."

"You mean you would do anything to fulfil your duty?" Tucker asked carelessly.

Brigham Smith straightened proudly. "Anything," he answered sternly.

"Roaming Reynolds is that same way," Tucker said quickly. "Only he calls it fighting for the iron that pays him his wages. In some ways you and he are very much alike. Better think it over, Deacon!"

Brigham Smith set his lips and turned to the girl. His eyes flashed with anger when he saw the gun on her leg. Betty Tucker drew away and stood close to her father.

"I told you to remove that gun!"

58

The Deacon's voice rumbled like thunder when he roared at the girl. Betty Tucker stared at him and dropped her strong fingers to grip the worn handle.

"And I intend to carry it until this trouble is over," she answered in her throaty voice. "Don't you dare to glare at me that way, Brigham Smith!"

The Deacon started forward with hand reaching out. Mormon Tucker met him halfway and stared into the angry brown eyes. The two big bearded men stood chest to chest in a clash of wills that threatened to explode into physical violence.

"You are working for the M T, Deacon. You forget that you take your orders from me!"

Brigham Smith sighed and drooped his big shoulders. "I forgot," he muttered. "But you forget that Betty is my promised wife!"

"The betrothal has not been announced," Tucker said sternly. "You have even forgotten our customs, Deacon!"

Brigham Smith dropped his jaw and stared at the stern face of his employer. His face showed the torment raging deep within him, and his big hands gripped hard while he tried to gather his rioting thoughts. Then he nodded his head and extended his right hand.

"I forgot," he repeated humbly. "I have no authority over Betty until the betrothal has been announced. I wanted her to come to me unsullied."

Betty Tucker leaped forward and pounded her fists against his broad chest. "Don't you dare say such things about me," she cried. "And don't you talk that way about a man who is not present to refute your insinuations!"

Brigham Smith stood steady as a rock and stared at the girl without moving a muscle. "You were holding on to him with your arms," he accused sternly. "Another man besides your promised husband has known the nearness of your body."

"Take that back!"

Betty Tucker slapped down for her holster and jammed the sixgun against the great swelling chest of the Deacon. He smiled bitterly and pushed the gun away with his left hand.

"You wouldn't use it on me," he said softly, and smiled down into her blazing eyes. "You know our laws, Betty. I am powerless to speak now, but after we are betrothed you will obey me in everything."

The girl curled her lip and stepped back to holster the gun. "A woman can always change her mind," she answered darkly, and turned to stare after the two riders in the far distance. "I might change mine before this terrible trouble is all settled!"

"Betty!" and the Deacon's voice expressed his

stunned surprise. "Do you realize what you are saying?"

"I said that I might change my mind," the girl repeated clearly. "Every girl likes to feel the security that comes when she knows that her man will fight for her. Prayers and sermons don't help much when a wolf like Eagle Dupree is stalking the badlands. You know what he promised!"

"He said he would marry Betty," Morgan Tucker interrupted hoarsely. "He said he wanted that Morgan stallion, and when we got there we found a broken feather twisted in the stallion's mane!"

"An eagle feather," the girl whispered, and shuddered violently.

"He won't come here," Smith answered confidently. "And you can stay home until after the law does its duty!"

"The law," Tucker muttered bitterly. "Up here in the Strip the only law is what men carry in their holsters. Roaming Reynolds is the only law we can depend on to help us out of our trouble!"

"And Roaming Reynolds is a fighting man," Betty added. "Any woman would feel secure under his protection!"

Brigham Smith frowned and turned to Tucker. "You told him to take orders from me about the work," he began. "There are a dozen colts to be gentled, and a buckaroo never wears a gun in the breaking-pen."

Mormon Tucker stared for a long moment. "Meaning you are going to order him to break these colts?" he asked softly. "And then carry out your plans when he is without his gun?"

"Did you ever know me to quit?" the Deacon asked softly.

"I'll warn him," Betty Tucker cried hotly. "And not only that, but Texas Joe promised to side his pard all the way down the river. That boy won't hold his temper in, and I'm warning you, Brigham!"

"Texas Joe is just a boy," Smith answered lightly. "He is not yet seventeen."

"Texas Joe is man-size when he has a gun in his hand," the girl answered sharply. "He would kill you if you took advantage of Reynolds after they shook hands and became pards!"

Brigham Smith flushed with anger. "As foreman of the M T, I will discharge him," he said bluntly. "I intend to maintain discipline among the men under my care!"

"I hired Joe," Mormon Tucker interrupted quietly. "And I'll do the firing if necessary. Right now we need every man we have, and especially those who can handle a gun. You forget yourself, Brigham!"

Brigham Smith stared at his employer and clenched his strong teeth. "You have changed, Tucker," he said slowly. "You are no longer a man of peace."

"Did you ever see a pack of wolves attack a band of deer when the snows were high?" Mormon Tucker asked softly.

"Several times," Smith answered. "But we are not animals."

"I am when it comes down to protecting my young," Mormon Tucker snapped. "And you will be if you want to live long enough to carry out the plans you had in mind."

Brigham Smith sighed and turned away. "I will gentle those colts myself," he said quietly. "Your gun-fighter escaped while you kept me talking, but tomorrow is another day!"

CHAPTER V

Rainbow Canyon glowed in the morning mist like a half-circle of frozen colour. Accessible only through a twisting maze of tortuous passages carved through the *malpais*; the hardened burned rock of a terrific upheaval when the world was young. High above and to the west stood the sentinel peaks of Zion Park, sculptured like the pillars of some giant cathedral.

Forming a background towered the Vermilion Cliffs, and these were etched boldly against the sky-line, blood-red and massive where Rainbow Canyon came to a blind end to make an impregnable retreat for the outlaw band of Eagle Dupree. Blooded horses grazed contentedly in natural pastures where the blue-stem grass grew saddle-high along the margins of ice-cold streams fed by mountain springs.

Canuck Avery and Hip High Hardy rounded a shoulder of rock in a narrow pass and stopped their horses to study a scattering of huts at the far end of a little valley. The wide-shouldered gunman sighed softly and shrugged with relief.

"The boss ain't here," he whispered hoarsely, as though in fear that his voice might carry to the settlement. "You know how he takes on when a man falls down on his job."

"That tall gun-hawk," Avery answered slowly. "Eagle will forget about the stud when we tell him about that blighter. Blimey if I ever see a man so blinkin' fast with his 'ands!"

Hip High Hardy brightened visibly and headed his horse toward the cluster of buildings. "I ain't through with that jigger," he muttered. "He taken up for old Mormon Tucker when we had the game right in our hands."

Canuck Avery ground-hitched his mount at a pole corral and swung to the ground to strip his gear. His narrowed eyes lifted to the back trail and fastened on a horseman just coming through the pass. Then his right hand unloosed his rope while he whispered sharply to his thick-set pard.

"We better rope us out fresh hawsses, Hardy. Yonder comes Eagle, and like he says, they ain't no rest for the wicked. Like as not he tells us to ride back and snare that Morgan!"

Hip High Hardy muttered in his throat and jerked his saddle. The two men were saddling fresh horses when a tall man dressed in immaculate broadcloth cantered between the corrals on a black thoroughbred and stood his horse in the narrow lane. Dark eyes in a thin handsome face studied the preparations, and a jerk of the well-shaped head told that he understood.

"Going someplace?" he asked in a soft pleasant voice.

"Howdy, Eagle," Hardy answered nervously.

"Me and Canuck run into a little hard luck, and we knew what you would say. We had that Morgan stallion throwed and hog-tied, but he got away."

Eagle Dupree studied the heavy face for a long moment. "He got away," he prompted at last.

"Yeah," Hardy answered. "Mormon Tucker come faunchin' through the bresh about the time we stretched out the stud and made a three-bone tie. Canuck dabbed a loop on the Mormon and drug him off his hoss."

The tall outlaw leaned forward in his carved saddle. "I saw that Morgan stud," and his voice was low. "Saw him chousing through the tangles with a bucking saddle bolted on his back. You know anything about that?"

Hip High Hardy shifted his big feet and glanced at his pard. "I was going to snap the rough out of him," he muttered.

"And he throwed you," Dupree continued with biting sarcasm. "You let him get away just to satisfy your own vanity!"

Hardy scowled and shook his wide shoulders. "The critter don't live what can throw me," he snarled hoarsely. "The stud had help!"

The tall outlaw stiffened and stared intently. "You better talk some more, Hardy," he said softly. "You said the stallion had help!"

"Me and Canuck bolted that buckin' saddle on the stud," Hardy explained desperately, and lowered his eyes to avoid the piercing gaze that seemed to look right through him. "I climbed aboard while Canuck got ready to throw off his ties, and right then was when this other jigger bought chips and cut down with his Winchester."

Eagle Dupree sat his saddle like a statue. Only his dark eyes glowed with an inner excitement to betray his interest. Hip High Hardy shifted uncomfortably, and Canuck Avery busied himself with the fittings on his scarred saddle.

"This other jigger," Dupree murmured softly. "You recognize him?"

Hardy shook his head. "Never saw him before," he growled. "His slug cut the check-rope to give the Morgan his head. Caught me off balance, and piled me in the bresh before I could get another grip."

"Check-rope, eh?" the tall outlaw almost whispered. "You mean you was taking a handicap to ride the stud?"

"Didn't want to rough him up too much," Hardy muttered. "So we stretched his head high to keep him from bogging between his knees. Right then was when this stranger cut loose with his rifle and spoiled the play."

"And the stallion high-tailed," Dupree said softly. "Being fairly rapid with your tools, you killed this meddling stranger?"

Hip High Hardy squirmed uncomfortably, and Canuck Avery laughed raucously. "Hip High didn't have a chance," he volunteered. "Both his cutters spilled when he joined the bloomin' bird gang."

"He had the drop with that long gun," Hardy muttered. "With the hammer eared back for a follow-up."

Eagle Dupree stroked his thin black moustache. "What for kind of a looking gent was this sudden stranger?" he asked softly.

"Tall jigger about yore size," Hardy answered sourly. "About twenty-four or five, with the damnedest blue eyes I ever see. Black bull-hides and hand-made boots, and he packed about a hundred and sixty-five pounds on his frame."

"Sounds like a gun-fighter," Dupree murmured softly. "How'd he wear his tools?"

"Long-barrelled forty-five Colts tied low on his right leg," and Hardy gave the description glibly to take attention away from himself. "From his rigging and gear he must have been around considerable. Double-cinched rig and tie-hard maguey, and his bridle carried chains like they use further west."

"You think he's the law?" Dupree asked.

Hip High Hardy shook his head. "Not him," he answered positively. "Just a fast gun-slammer hunting practice if I know the signs."

"I'd like to meet him," Dupree whispered.

"Like as not the blighter will look you up,

Boss," Canuck Avery chuckled. "Hip High told him that if he didn't get him, you would."

"I want first chance, Eagle," Hardy mumbled. "For what he done to me back there in the bresh!"

"If he's fast like you say, he would beat your flip draw," the tall outlaw answered coldly. "You got any idea where I could find him?"

Hip High Hardy scowled and glanced at his leader. "Like I told you, we had Mormon Tucker wrapped up in ropes," he muttered. "Like as not this brash stranger tied him loose and heard all about us by now."

Eagle Dupree smiled gently and stretched out his left hand to point at the two fresh horses. "You figger to go some place?" he asked quietly.

"Me and Canuck aims to get that Morgan stud," Hardy muttered. "We always finishes what we starts!"

Eagle Dupree shook his head. "Don't bother," he said softly. "I got the Morgan myself."

Hardy jerked up his big head and stared at the smiling face. "You got the stud?" he repeated in a whisper.

Eagle Dupree nodded. "He was bucking the saddle when I came across him," he explained quietly. "Charged me twice when I tried to rope him, so I left a feather in his mane."

The two men stared at their tall leader and shuddered. "You killed him?" Hardy whispered hoarsely.

"I take what I want," and now Dupree's voice was like the twang of brass. "When I can't take it, I kill and leave my mark!"

"A broken feather," Avery muttered, and turned his head to avoid that piercing gaze. "That Mormon blighter won't take that sitting down."

"Mormon Tucker is a man of peace," Dupree sneered contemptuously. "And his whole crowd on the M T are just like their boss."

"Yeah," Hardy muttered thickly. "But this stranger ain't no man of peace if you ask me. On top of that, he's the kind of a jigger women like."

Eagle Dupree leaned forward and stared at the heavy face. "Meaning Betty Tucker?" he asked softly. "That what yo're trying to say, Hip High?"

"It had to come sometime," Hardy muttered. "You've been gun-boss of the Arizona Strip quite a spell of time. Aside from me, you ain't had much competition."

"Aside from you?" and Eagle Dupree swung to the ground and faced Hardy with his shoulders in a crouch.

"Hold yore hand, Boss," Hardy almost shouted. "You're faster than me with yore tools, and we both knows it. You took me wrong, Eagle!"

"Might be well for you and me to settle this right now," the tall outlaw insisted quietly. "There isn't room enough in the Strip for two gun-bosses."

Hip High Hardy licked his thick lips and shifted

his feet. "I can't match you, Eagle," he said desperately. "I might get a shot away, but you'd get me first. Let it ride like that, Boss!"

Eagle Dupree smiled coldly. "You wouldn't get a shot away," he declared bluntly. "You wouldn't get yore guns out of leather, and now is a good time to prove it!"

Several men from the cabins had strolled up to the corrals and were leaning against the bars. Rough, bearded men with the marks of the owl-hoot trails etched indelibly upon them. Smouldering eyes that watched each move of the two men with a blood-lust that was unmistakable.

"You pack two guns, Hardy," and the tall outlaw stared at his victim. "You never saw a man in yore life that could handle two guns at the same time, and make them both do what he wanted them to do!"

Hip High Hardy glared angrily and squared his shoulders. "Wes Hardin could," he growled. "And he could put 'em where he called 'em!"

"He couldn't," Dupree contradicted flatly. "Wes Hardin carried that extra gun for a spare, and he did most of his work with his meat-cutter."

"I can work both hands," Hardy muttered. "You got no call to bait me in front of the boys!"

Eagle Dupree reached to his left vest pocket and his long fingers played with a feather. The grey feather of the king eagle, and Hip High

Hardy glared at it with the courage of desperation glowing deep in his narrowed eyes.

"So you are fast with both hands," the tall outlaw sneered. "And you can place your shots where you call them."

Hip High Hardy nodded his head and balanced on his big boots. He knew Eagle Dupree; knew what was behind the quiet contempt so plainly written on the darkly handsome face of his chief. There was no place in the gang for a coward, and down in his heart Hardy was not convinced.

"Like you said," he muttered, and watched the tall outlaw closely.

"I don't like that silver buckle on yore hat," Dupree said suddenly. "It hurts my eyes when the sun hits it."

Hip High Hardy stared and sucked in his breath. "Damn you, Eagle," he snarled, and his hands flipped down to the tilted grips of his twin guns.

Eagle Dupree twitched his right shoulder in an incredible movement of blinding speed. The fingers of his left hand played with the feather when pale flame ripped out from his right hand like a flash of lightning. Hip High Hardy jerked his big head and crashed to earth before his hands could flip the guns loose from his holsters, and the smoking forty-five was holstered deep in leather before the two-gun man struck earth and bounced on his shoulders.

"Gawd!" Canuck Avery whispered the word

hoarsely and pointed at Hardy's battered black Stetson.

Every man in the silent crowd followed his pointing finger and shuddered unconsciously. The silver buckle was missing from the leather hatband, and while they watched, Hip High Hardy rolled over and came up groggily to his knees. His eyes held the stunned look of a stricken deer, and his left hand went to his hat and rubbed his head.

Thick fingers removed the hat and fumbled with the band. Pale blue eyes cleared somewhat to stare at the leather band where the silver buckle had rode. Eyes that dropped to the tilted handles of the twin guns riding high on his hips, and Hardy shivered and closed his eyes.

"Shoot," he muttered hoarsely. "Yo're the best, Eagle!"

"I knew it all the time," Dupree answered softly. "Didn't want to kill you, Hardy. So I just cut that buckle loose, but my hand throwed off a trifle and creased yore skull. Might have been a speck of dust in the barrel of my cutter, but you ain't hurt any to speak of."

Hip High Hardy levered unsteadily to his feet and rubbed the lump on the side of his head. "You can count on me from now on out, Chief," he muttered thickly. "You could have killed me, and you throwed off yore shot. My cutters never cleared leather!"

Eagle Dupree smiled and stepped closer to Hardy. His left hand removed the feather from his pocket and tucked it under the leather hatband.

"Keep it for a souvenir," he chuckled, and clapped Hardy on the shoulder. "There ain't room in this pack for a coward, and you ain't one, Hip High. Touch skin, and forget it!"

He smiled as he held out his right hand, and the beaten gunman seized the hand and gripped hard. "Yo're the boss of the Strip, Eagle," he shouted hoarsely. "And I'll take it personal to the gent what says different!"

His blood-shot eyes darted around the ring of faces and challenged each man in the group. Faces were turned hurriedly away while rope-burned hands raised high away from gun-butts. Hardy sneered nastily and staggered over to the horse-trough where he dipped his head beneath the cold water. Wiped his brutal face on his neck-rag, and then his eyes fastened on the feather in his hat.

He took the eagle feather from the band and broke it with his thick fingers. Placed it carefully in the inside pocket of his greasy vest and shrugged his wide shoulders back.

"You dang right. I'll keep that feather," he said quietly. "And someday I'll put it in that stranger's hat when he gets through kicking. There's one jigger I can fade with an iron!"

"Hardy," and the voice of Eagle Dupree was sharp.

"Yeah, Boss!"

"No man uses my mark except me. Is that clear?"

Hardy stared and dropped his eyes. "I get yuh, Boss," he muttered. "I won't tag him with yore private mark."

"This M T outfit," the tall outlaw said harshly. "I aim to break it like a straw in spite of all the gun-fighting strangers in the Strip. I want that spread, and I want the girl, and I aim to take both!"

"Right behind you, Boss," Hardy answered promptly. "I owe that roamin' cowboy a couple for what he done to me!"

"Same here," and Canuck Avery moistened his thumb and whetted the keen edge of his skinning knife. "I'm saving something for the Deacon when I catch him right!"

"He liked to beat you to death with his maulies the last time you and him met head-on," and Hip High Hardy grinned. "They just ain't no quit to that big jigger, and you better use a gun."

"You men listen to me," Eagle Dupree said sharply. "I want to gather every head of stock we can get a rope on. We're making a drive to Red Horse before old Mormon Tucker gets organized, and I'm making arrangements to ship."

"Then we starts all over again," Hardy

75

chuckled. "Mormon Tucker is raising hosses for us, and all we got to do is break 'em for work."

"You start the men out to ride circle," Dupree answered. "Cut out the mares and round up the young stock. We're making a drive to town to-morrow."

He mounted his thoroughbred and waited until Hip High Hardy had given orders to the men. His right hand flicked down and drew his sixgun; punched the spent shell from the cylinder and shoved a fresh one through the loading gate with a thoughtful frown on his thin face. When the men had ridden away, he called to Canuck Avery and Hardy.

"This stranger," he began softly. "You figger him to be just a saddle tramp?"

Hardy shook his head. "Not him," he answered positively. "That jigger has been around considerable from the cut of his riggin' and gear. Talks like a Texan, and I'd say he was tophand with hosses and cattle."

"He's got an eye, Boss," Avery added sharply.

"His gun," the tall outlaw whispered. "How does he wear his hardware?"

"Moulded holster tied low on his right leg," Hardy answered promptly. "Handle tilted out for a fast draw, and his cutter shines like silk. I'd say he was a dead shot from the way he cut that check-rope with his Winchester."

Eagle Dupree shrugged carelessly. "Not many

men are good with both rifle and hand-gun," he deprecated. "But he might make us trouble if we let him stay."

"That's right," Hardy agreed quickly. "Me and Canuck will ride gun-sign on him and smoke him down."

Eagle Dupree frowned and shook his head. "Might be we could use him," he muttered. "With another fast gun-hand, the three of us could keep the Strip all to ourselves."

Hip High Hardy shook his big head. "Not him, Eagle," he muttered. "You can see it in his face. Craggy and hard when he makes fighting talk, and he'd want to be boss. Better let me take him his needin's!"

Again the outlaw shook his head. "You and Canuck ride out and see what you can find out about this stranger," he said crisply. "Find out who he is and where he comes from. I want to have a talk with him before he gets in too deep."

Hip High Hardy stared and rubbed the grips of his guns. "Yo're the boss," he admitted reluctantly. "But that tall cowboy is bringing us grief unless I misread the sign. He thinks a heap of hoss-flesh, and you done killed the Morgan stallion and left yore mark where everybody could see it."

"You mean this stranger might take exception?" and the dark eyes of Eagle Dupree glowed with a curious gleam.

"He's bound to do it if he found the stud back there," Hardy answered. "I thought there for a time he was going to rub out me and Canuck for what we done to that stud. He's bound to follow them tracks, and he won't miss that feather. That jigger can see everything with one good look!"

Eagle Dupree smiled happily. "Line out and cut his backtrail," he ordered softly. "Find out all you can about him, and report back to me before you make a play. And Hardy . . ."

"Yeah, Boss!"

"Don't forget to keep that feather for a little reminder!"

CHAPTER VI

The first fingers of dawn were plucking at the eyelids of Roaming Reynolds when Texas Joe shook the big cowboy by the shoulder. "Rouse up, Roamin'," he whispered. "You and me is riding for the big Augur."

"Rising right up, pard," and Reynolds slid from his bunk and reached for his Stetson. Texas Joe grinned and voiced his thoughts.

"Funny how a cowhand always puts his hat on the first thing when he wakes up, and takes it off last when he turns in of a night."

"Being his weakest point, that's where he's most like to catch cold," the tall cowboy chuckled. "We eating before we pound leather?"

"Cooky has a snack all ready," the half-grown boy answered. "Cowboy coffee you can float a hoss shoe in, with all the fixin's. Drag on yore foot-gear and let's make tracks."

Roaming Reynolds followed in silence when Texas Joe led the way to the cook-shack, and neither spoke again until they had roped and saddled horses for the day's work. The tall cowboy breathed deeply of the high desert air while he rode the river trail with his young pard, and Texas Joe finally explained the reason for the early morning departure.

"The boss wants you to keep away from the Deacon until he cools down," and he watched his companion closely. "Red Hoss is the nearest town on the Virgin River, and Mormon Tucker wants you to make arrangements for a shipment of trained cow ponies. He sent me along to show you where to go."

"The Deacon," Reynolds murmured. "You mean Brigham Smith," and he nodded his head slowly. "That's right good figgerin', button. He shore got himself all steamed up."

Texas Joe swallowed noisily and straightened his back. He was old enough to make a hand on the M T, and young enough to be natural. Tall for his age with the awkward leanness of a rangy colt, and as full of untamed spirit. Now he fingered the grip of his gun while a troubled look settled in his light blue eyes.

"Might be better this away," he muttered. "If the Deacon met any of those owl-hoot buckaroos, chances are he'd stop lead. He claims to be a man of peace, but when he gets his mad up he don't care who he fights . . . with his fists."

"No wonder the boss didn't want to send him to town," Reynolds answered with a nod. "There's too much of him for a good gunnie to miss."

"Red Hoss is a bad town, pard," Joe announced in his changing voice. "We're like to run across Eagle Dupree hanging around the hoss buyers when we come to the rail siding."

Roaming Reynolds glanced up quickly. "The boss didn't make no mention of that," he drawled slowly, but his blue eyes sparkled with anticipation. "I thought Eagle Dupree stayed close to Rainbow Canyon out near the cliffs?"

The boy scowled fiercely. "Eagle Dupree goes where he damn pleases," he muttered. "They ain't much law up this way, and what there is never got any proof on that hoss thief. I'd shake my gun loose before we rides in, if I was you."

Roaming Reynolds automatically freed his sixgun of riding crimp and smiled when he caught the boy watching him. They were nearing the little shipping town that sprawled in the shadow of Zion Park; a cattle and mining town with one main street winding between great boulders as big as houses. Saloons and stores under the board awnings on both sides of the street, with hard-faced men eyeing them from under wide-brimmed hats.

"Salty looking outfit," Reynolds murmured under his breath. "Every man packing one or a pair of hog-legs, and that's law enough in any man's country."

"Fair enough for working hands, but they don't rate enough speed to auger with Dupree and his pack," Texas Joe muttered. "What you want to do first?"

"We'll see the Agent first," Reynolds answered quietly. "Lead on to the depot, Joe."

Texas Joe kept to the middle of the dusty street and pointed for the sprawling depot and loading chutes at the far end. Swung down and ground-hitched his horse like an old-timer in front of the office where a little man in black sleeves was checking car numbers.

"Howdy, Mister Peters," he addressed the agent. "Wants you to meet up with Roaming Reynolds; gun-boss on the M T."

The little agent looked startled when he swung around. "Howdy, Reynolds," he squeaked. "I reckon Mormon Tucker wanted to make shore his cars was spotted on the siding. They just now come in, and I was making out the way-bills."

The cowboy nodded and glanced at the cars. "You see a ghost or somethin'?" he asked softly.

"Mebbe you better come on inside and sign for the cars," Peters suggested nervously. "You can load out any time within forty-eight hours."

The cowboy swung down from his saddle and followed the little agent into the office. Reached for his tally pencil and signed his name to the paper Peters pushed toward him. Then he glanced up at the agent with a slow smile on his tanned face.

"All right, pard," he murmured. "What you got on yore mind that's got you all worked up into a lather?"

"He's right around the corner," the agent whispered hoarsely. "He took a good look at you

82

when the button popped off about you being gun-boss on the M T."

"Yeah?" Reynolds drawled softly. "Give this jigger a name, Peters. Sounds plumb interesting to me."

"Eagle Dupree," and Peters sucked his breath in noisily. "The fastest gunhawk in the whole Arizona Strip!"

Roaming Reynolds straightened slowly and stared at the flushed face of the little agent. "Well, I'll be seeing you to-morrow," he answered loudly. "When we bring in that load of saddle-stock for shipping."

He turned the knob and stepped out on the low platform with a thoughtful expression in his blue eyes. Texas Joe was standing stiff as a poker near the two horses with a scowl on his thin face. A tall slender man was leaning against the depot with a gold toothpick between his white teeth where he could command the entire platform.

Roaming Reynolds stamped across the platform with spur chains jingling, but his keen eyes took in the expensive clothing and hand-made boots of the tall stranger. Then he came abreast of Texas Joe and reached for his trailing whangs.

"All set, Joe," he told the boy. "You get the mail yet?"

Texas Joe held his stiff pose like a pointer dog. "I ain't moved a step," he whispered hoarsely. "Yonder stands Eagle Dupree!"

"I ain't never met the gent," Reynolds answered carelessly. "Let's you and me ride, pard."

"Just a minute, cowboy," and the tall man glided forward like a shadow. "Being new in these parts, might be I should introduce myself. Eagle Dupree is my handle."

The cowboy turned slowly and acknowledged the introduction with a nod of the head. "Howdy, Dupree," he drawled. "I sets up to grub when they holler Roaming Reynolds. I've heard some about you."

His blue eyes were studying the outlaw carefully without giving offence. He was conscious of piercing brown eyes that seemed to bore into a man's brain. Black hair curled at the temples, with a long hawkish nose curving down to meet thin lips set in a straight line. Smooth-shaven except for the little black moustache emphasizing a face tanned the colour of saddle-leather. Small slender hands on incredibly long arms that showed unusual muscular development even through the broadcloth sleeves of the long coat.

"New gun-boss on the M T, eh?" Dupree repeated thoughtfully. "Looks like Mormon Tucker has been losing some stock."

"They never had no gun-boss before," Texas Joe interrupted hotly. "And the old man knows who has been rustling his hosses!"

Eagle Dupree smiled coldly and shrugged his slender shoulders. "You haven't lived long, son," he said slowly. "It might be smart for you to keep your mouth shut until you get your growth."

"I do a man's work, and I draw a man's pay," the boy snapped, and flushed angrily when his deep voice broke suddenly to end on a high crescendo. "Down Texas way they make cottonwood fruit out of rustlers wherever they find the varmints!"

Eagle Dupree stared steadily at the boy without speaking, but his eyes flashed with a strange fire until Texas Joe swallowed and dropped his gaze. The tall outlaw curled his lips in a sneer and turned his eyes upon Reynolds, who was watching the little play while his head nodded imperceptibly. As though he were checking his findings over in his own mind.

"So you are gun-boss on the M T?"

Roaming Reynolds nodded again. "I signed on to draw fighting pay," he admitted frankly. "In between times I ride the first rough string in the breaking tank. What's yore own business, Dupree?"

A slow smile of admiration spread across the outlaw's dark face. A long-barrelled Peacemaker Colt with a silver inlay crusting the shining metal snugged tightly against his right thigh with the tie-backs thonged low. Ivory handle yellowed with age, and smooth from long care and usage.

"I deal in horses," he answered softly. "I run a little spread over in Rainbow Canyon near the Vermilion Cliffs. It's a beautiful place at sunset if you're ever riding by and can find your way in."

"I'll drop in and see you sometime," and the cowboy smiled slowly. "You never can tell where a band of hosses will stray when they got on the loose, and Joe here jingles the cavvy."

He lowered his lids lazily and waited for Dupree to answer. The tall outlaw smiled easily and then chuckled with amusement. Texas Joe regarded him with a scowl of hatred on his young face while his fingers gripped the handle of his old single action. Eagle Dupree spoke quickly when the boy cleared his throat.

"I could use another good hand on my place if you are not satisfied where you are," he murmured. "That goes for young Joe also."

Texas Joe snarled like a cat and arched his back. "I might be a button like you say, but I earn my pay honest and ride 'em straight up," he shouted angrily. "I ain't talkin' none out of turn when I say that the same thing goes for Roamin'!"

The outlaw raised his eyes in surprise. "Only your tender years stand between you and a grave in Boot Hill," he said gently, and hooked his right thumb in the belt above his gun. "I'd kill a man for saying what you just said!"

Texas Joe growled in his throat, but once more his eyes dropped before that piercing stare. Eagle Dupree smiled with his lips and turned his eyes back to Roaming Reynolds. The cowboy stood with legs wide apart, and his head leaned a little forward on his chest while he stared thoughtfully at the cruel face of the man on the platform.

"A man wouldn't say it unless he had proof," Reynolds remarked casually. "And if he had the proof, he would do all his talking with a cutter, and it a-smokin'!"

Dupree nodded while a smile lighted his dark face. "And after that he would be past talking," he almost whispered.

The cowboy reached to his vest pocket with his left hand. Dark eyes watched him intently for a hide-out gun, but Reynolds smiled and withdrew his thumb and forefinger slowly. Held a crumpled feather in his hand while his blue eyes locked glances with Eagle Dupree.

"Hoss thieves stole a stud from Mormon Tucker the day I rode in," he said conversationally. "Big Morgan chestnut, and some polecat shot the stallion when he couldn't dab his twine for a catch. I found this here feather twisted in the mane right up above the bullet-hole."

"Too bad," Dupree murmured, and shrugged carelessly while his dark eyes stared at the cowboy's craggy face. "You got any idea who shot the Morgan?"

The cowboy stared for a moment in silence, and his fingers returned the feather to his pocket. He balanced easily on the soles of his bench-made boots while he shook his head a time or two.

"I haven't any proof," he said at last.

"And if you had the proof?" Dupree asked softly.

"I'd let my cutter do my talking for me!"

Roaming Reynolds muttered the words savagely without raising his deep voice. His blue eyes were cold and frosty to make his craggy face a mask of pale determination. Nothing moved except those bright blue eyes which somehow seemed to chill the outlaw.

"Perhaps you have a suspicion," he said softly, and shifted his weight on the soles of his polished boots.

"I don't shoot a man on suspicion," and the cowboy rapped the words harshly. "Like Hip High Hardy might have told you."

"Ah," and the outlaw narrowed his dark eyes. "So you talked with Hip High Hardy!"

Roaming Reynolds knew that it was coming, and he crouched forward with right hand shadowing his gun. Then he noticed a change of expression in the eyes of the outlaw, and he relaxed his muscles when Dupree swept off the black Stetson with a graceful flourish.

"This is a pleasant surprise, Miss Betty," and Dupree bowed low from his waist. "I had some other matters to attend, but they can wait until another time."

The girl nodded slightly and came close to Roaming Reynolds. The cowboy was regarding her sternly, and the frosty light still glowed in his blue eyes to make his tanned face hard and ruthless. When he spoke, his deep voice was edgy with tension.

"Why did you follow me to town, Miss Betty?"

The girl flushed and glanced at Eagle Dupree. "Father sent me in to tell you to be careful when you come back," the girl whispered. "Brigham is looking for you."

"Ha," and Dupree smiled mockingly. "So you have had trouble with the Deacon, that mighty man of peace!"

"Bridle yore tongue!" The cowboy glared at the outlaw when he bit the words off between tightly clenched teeth. "What went on between Smith and me is none of yore business!"

Eagle Dupree shrugged gracefully. "Pardon," he said softly. "I forgot that there was a lady present. My mistake."

"You run along, Miss Betty," Reynolds growled irritably. "I have a few little things to do in town before I can leave," and he stared coldly at Eagle Dupree.

"I will wait," the girl answered quickly. "I have some things to tell you while we ride back to the M T. I can show you most of the range we use, and point out the landmarks."

Roaming Reynolds sighed and stepped back to his horse. "Be seein' you another time, Dupree," he said shortly. "Like you mentioned one time, there's a lady present, and our talk can wait a spell."

"Any time," and the tall outlaw smiled pleasantly. "You can find me back there in Rainbow Canyon if you and yore pard changes yore minds."

"That's right," the cowboy agreed softly, and matched the smile with one of his own. "But right now I'm hunting for hoss thieves, and I want to have more than suspicions when I come up with them and do my talking."

Betty Tucker shrank back and held one hand over her lips. Texas Joe shifted his worn boots and bit his lip to stop the trembling that quivered his mouth. His hand half pulled his old gun when Eagle Dupree twitched his right shoulder. Then the outlaw shrugged erect and forced a smile to bloodless lips when he saw the girl staring at him with stark fear in her dark eyes.

"You sure you haven't something to do down the street?" he asked quietly. "Like getting the mail, or buying some pretty ribbons?"

"We can get the mail on the way home," and the girl whispered the words. "Father warned me not to ride alone."

"You will have no worries as long as the new gun-boss is with you," and Dupree smiled engagingly. "He carries plenty of sand, and he isn't the kind of man to hide behind a woman."

"I can say the same for you, Dupree," Reynolds

murmured. "We will finish our *wawa* some other time."

"That would be better," the outlaw agreed, and raised his hat to the girl. "Good morning, my dear."

He turned his back and walked to the corner entirely at ease. Roaming Reynolds scowled and shook himself impatiently. Stepped aboard his horse with teeth tightly clenched, and then he too forced a smile when he saw the girl watching him with a hurt look in her wide brown eyes.

"Get yore hoss, Betty," and his deep voice was soft. "We better be getting back to the M T, and you can show me the landmarks while we ride."

"I showed you most of them," Texas Joe grumbled. "That feller meant to cut down on you shore as sin."

"There's a time and a place for everything," the tall cowboy said sternly. "Might be better for you to listen more and talk less until you get the velvet off yore horns, button."

"Any jigger what packs a gun is man-size," the boy snarled angrily. "I ain't much on the talk, but I can read the sign when it's as clear as fresh mud."

"You ain't much on the think, either," Reynolds muttered. "Seems to me I hear somebody say several times that there was a lady present. Seems like I hear that you was raised up part way down in Texas!"

Texas Joe twisted uneasily and dropped his eyes. "I had it comin', pard," he growled hoarsely. "Beggin' yore pardon, Ma'am."

The girl reached over and patted his hand with a smile. "You were doing the best you could, Joe," she praised quietly. "Until Roaming came to the M T, you were the only fighting man we had. We won't ever forget it."

"I better stop here at the Post Office and get the mail," the boy mumbled, and slid from his saddle. "And I got to get me some makin's to smoke."

The girl turned to Roaming Reynolds when Texas Joe disappeared inside the old building. "Please, cowboy," she pleaded softly. "Don't fight with Eagle Dupree. He is the fastest gunman up here, and he will kill you if you press him too far."

The tall cowboy smiled frostily. "I take a heap of killing that away, Miss Betty," he drawled, but his eyes sparkled with an inner happiness. "I won't make gun-talk to any of these owl-hoot buckaroos until I have something definite to talk about. When I do . . . ?" and his calloused palm rubbed the handle of his gun.

The girl shuddered and came closer. "Promise me," she begged. "Promise me you won't look for trouble."

"Yore father hired me to look for trouble," Reynolds grunted, and avoided her serious brown eyes. "Sorry I can't promise what you want."

"But he has a big gang," the girl whispered. "They are all killers, and you are the first one who has ever challenged their rule up here."

"Yonder comes Joe through the door," the cowboy answered carelessly. "We can talk on the way home if it's all the same to you."

CHAPTER VII

Mormon Tucker frowned when he looked across the big yard from the front room he used as an office. Brigham Smith was riding down the lane on his big chestnut gelding, and the Deacon's face was heavy with moodiness. His dark eyes burned with a fanatical light while he followed the tracks made by the horse of Roaming Reynolds and Texas Joe.

"They rode with the sun," he muttered solemnly. "But they are still in darkness, and it is my duty to make them see the light!"

Mormon Tucker watched the slowly-moving lips of his big foreman and shook his head. Then he tightened his lips and called in his deep booming voice:

"Betty! Come quickly, daughter!"

He arranged the papers neatly on his desk while he waited; turned to the deep-chested girl when she ran into the room with a question in her brown eyes. The heavy gunbelt was still buckled around her trim hips, and Tucker shook his head and sighed.

"Look through the window, girl," he said heavily.

Betty Tucker came close to the big window and stared at Brigham Smith. "He never forgets," she whispered. "And he never quits."

"Get your horse ready and ride to town," Mormon Tucker ordered sternly. "Tell Reynolds that the Deacon is looking for him, and to avoid trouble. Brigham is a gentleman, so you stay and ride back with Reynolds. There will be no trouble as long as you are present."

"But Roaming," the girl said slowly. "You know what will happen if the Deacon tries to take his gun!"

"Roaming Reynolds is also a gentleman," Mormon Tucker answered promptly. "I'd trust my life and all my women-folks in his care. Go quickly and do as I say!"

Betty Tucker ran lightly from the room and raced for the corrals. Roped and saddled her horse like a man, and then she was spurring through the trees down by the creek, taking a short-cut that would lead into the lower river road.

Mormon Tucker waited until she was out of sight. Then he mounted his big bay and rode down the lane to overtake the foreman. Lines of worry creased his florid face, and he tugged at the heavy black beard while his eyes watched the road. When he came out from under the cottonwoods he spurred his horse and rode well forward to ease his heavy bulk in the saddle.

Brigham Smith was a serious young man who followed his convictions stubbornly without fear or favour. Being a man of peace, and a Deacon in the church, he was opposed to weapons and the

95

men who used them. Mormon Tucker knew that his foreman would follow Roaming Reynolds until he had accomplished his purpose.

Just what this purpose was, Mormon Tucker was not quite sure. He had sighed with relief when the cowboy had retreated rather than have more trouble with the Deacon, but he also knew that Reynolds feared neither man nor beast. He was still puzzling over the problem when he heard voices around the bend in the twisting road.

He stopped his horse and swung lightly to the ground in spite of his bulk. Crept through the brush near the river bed, and his jaw tightened when he saw Brigham Smith sitting his saddle with both hands on his broad hips. Canuck Avery was holding the drop with a forty-five Colt in his left hand, and his Cockney brogue contrasted strangely with the deep voice of the Deacon.

"I'm telling you to ride on, Marty," Canuck snarled through his nose, and his pale little eyes glittered angrily. "Fer tuppence I'd smoke you down right where yuh sits!"

"You are an outlaw, and a man of violence, Avery," the Deacon answered in his deep bass voice. "Lay aside your gun and leave the country while there is yet time. I am a man of peace, but I warn you to go while you can."

The rustler sneered and cocked his head to one side. "Bless my soul if the blighter ain't cracked," he chuckled. "Daffy as a loon, no less, and fancy him telling me what to do."

The Deacon frowned and set his lips stubbornly. Then he gigged his horse forward and rode toward the startled rustler with his right hand extended. Gripped the heavy gun and jerked it from the outlaw's hand, and Canuck Avery snarled curses and whirled his horse aside to avoid collision with the big chestnut.

The Deacon threw the gun in the water and spurred his horse to ride the gunman down. Canuck Avery skinned back his lips like a trapped fox and jerked his right arm down. Pale flame lanced out from his hand twice in rapid succession, and he neck-reined his horse with lips curling back over long yellowed teeth.

"You would have it, blimey," he growled.

Brigham Smith jerked back in the saddle and then gripped his belly. Sagging in the middle, he kicked with his spurs and rode in to come to grips. Canuck Avery stared for a moment before his right hand whipped to the back of his neck. Then he flashed a thin-bladed knife and rode forward to meet the wounded man.

"If hot lead won't stop yuh, cold steel will," he growled savagely, and murder stared from his piggish eyes.

Mormon Tucker leaped out of the brush roaring like a bear. The rustler wheeled his horse and spurred away with terror in his pale eyes, and

Tucker caught the Deacon's horse by the bridle reins and held fast.

"He shot you, Brigham," he growled softly. "Are you hurt bad, man?"

Brigham Smith tried to straighten his body; stifled a groan and sank forward again. "I have business in town, Tucker," he grunted hoarsely. "Turn my bridle loose so that I can do my duty."

"Your duty and your business is at home in bed," Tucker answered sternly. "You are bleeding bad, Brigham."

"Reynolds has brought war to the M T," the big man answered doggedly. "I will strip him of his guns just as I did Canuck Avery!"

Beads of perspiration stood out on his tanned forehead while he clutched the saddle-horn and glared at Mormon Tucker. Tucker returned the stare and shook his big head.

"And you got shot twice," he grunted. "I'm telling you never to try that with Roaming Reynolds. He carries forty-fives, and Canuck Avery shot you with a thirty-two derringer. Now I'm taking you home, and I don't intend to argue."

Brigham Smith did not answer. Little pools of crimson were forming in the dust under his stirrups. His head was sagging low on his great chest, and his eyes were closed tightly against the weakness that swept over him like a flood. Mormon Tucker led the horse back to the bend in the road where he mounted his bay and started for the M T.

Brigham Smith murmured softly and balanced in the saddle from long practice. "I must do my duty," he repeated over and over, and Mormon Tucker quickened his pace.

His heavy voice shouted for help when he rode into the yard between the corrals. Two bearded buckaroos ran from the breaking pen and helped him lower the big foreman to the ground. They staggered under the wounded man's weight when they brought him up the stairs and into the big house where they laid him on a low couch. Mormon Tucker turned to his wife and gave his orders calmly.

"Get the front room ready, Ma. Have the women prepare plenty of hot water and bandages. We will carry him yonder when you are ready."

Ma Tucker was a comely woman of forty with a sweet rounded face. Deep of bosom like her daughter, and pity shone in her brown eyes when she watched Brigham Smith shaking his head while he kept his eyes tightly closed.

"Will he live, Father?" she asked softly.

"Canuck Avery shot him twice through the belly," Mormon Tucker answered simply. "We will do all we can. Go now and make ready."

"You want a doctor, Boss?"

Mormon Tucker nodded at the cowboy. "Get to Doctor Turner as quick as you can. Send

Roaming Reynolds to me as soon as he returns from town."

Brigham Smith was unconscious when they carried him to the side room and laid him gently on the big four-poster. Mormon Tucker helped the women undress the moaning foreman, and he waited in his office until the Doctor came racing across the yard with a black satchel across his knees.

"The Deacon," he barked. "Shot like he is, the chances are that he has bled out. Where is he?"

Mormon Tucker pointed to the group of women back by the door. Tucker was seated behind his desk when Roaming Reynolds dropped from his saddle and came bounding up the stairs.

"What happened, Boss?" the cowboy barked, and his blue eyes were wide and alert while his right hand hovered close to his gun.

"It's the Deacon," Tucker answered softly. "He was out looking for you when he met Canuck Avery down by the river. He took a gun away from the outlaw, but Avery shook a hide-out down his sleeve and shot Brigham twice through the belly."

The cowboy shook his head slowly, and his face was grave. "The law wouldn't hold Canuck for that, even if they caught him," he drawled quietly. "You think the Deacon will make it through?"

"Doctor Turner is in there with him," Tucker

answered softly. "Might as well discuss this thing now. The Deacon was riding in to meet you, Reynolds. I'm mighty glad you didn't meet him first," and he glanced at the heavy gun on the cowboy's leg.

Roaming Reynolds stared through the window with flame smouldering deep in his eyes. Then he shook his square shoulders and faced around to stare at the big bearded Mormon without winking.

"I wouldn't have shot him, Tucker," he said stiffly. "But I wouldn't have allowed him to take my cutters either. I can't say just what would have happened, and my fists are still sore from that last ruckus with the Deacon. I've seen men get sense knocked into their heads with the handle of a gun several times."

Mormon Tucker nodded his understanding. "The Deacon is a brave man, Reynolds," he murmured softly. "And I hired your guns. Both of you working for me and my interests, and I admire to see you two make out to be friends," and he sighed heavily.

Roaming Reynolds nodded slowly. He got the meaning behind Mormon Tucker's words, and his face was thoughtful while he listened to sounds from the sick-room. He was still nodding when he rose to his feet and slipped the heavy gun in his scabbard to ease the riding crimp.

"I like the Deacon," he growled under his

breath. "Never met a rannihan like him in all my born days, and I'll square up for him whether he likes it or not!"

Mormon Tucker held out his hand and smiled. "I knew you would, Reynolds. Good luck to you, and we don't have to tell Brigham right now."

The cowboy mounted his horse and rode out to meet Betty Tucker and Texas Joe coming toward the house. The girl stopped him with a silent question in her brown eyes. Reynolds jerked his thumb toward the side room in the front and spoke in a low voice.

"Brigham Smith needs you in there, Betty. The Doctor is there with him now. Him and yore Ma."

"But you," the girl whispered, and caught his arm. "Where are you going, Roaming?"

"Just riding," he answered evasively. "Joe and me has to look after some stock up in the north pasture. We won't be long."

"I am going with you," the girl muttered stubbornly, and gripped the handle of her gun. "You are riding gun-sign, Roaming. I can see it in your face, and I'm going to make a hand this time."

"You can't tell much about a feller's face," the cowboy answered lightly. "Not only that, but the Deacon needs you now more than me and Joe does. See you come grub-time."

"But you might meet Eagle Dupree," and the girl's hand trembled on his arm.

Roaming Reynolds smiled with his lips. "I'd admire to meet Dupree," he answered softly, but his voice was cold and twangy. "You keep that sixgun buckled on, and stay close to the ranch. Now don't you start in for to worry, Betty."

He touched his horse with a spur and rode down the lane with Texas Joe right behind. The button pulled up alongside and pointed to a clump of trees about a mile ahead.

"That's where the Deacon met Canuck Avery," he said, and tried to keep his changing voice low. "I can handle that feller, Roamin'."

The cowboy smiled and shook his head. "He gets a chance, pard," he grunted softly. "What would you do if some big feller rode you down and tried to take yore iron out of yore gun-hook?"

Texas Joe squirmed in the saddle and scratched his sandy head. "Reckon I'd buffalo him between the hawns th' way you done," he answered slowly. "But Canuck Avery is rustlin' stock along with the rest of them owl-hoot buckaroos."

The cowboy nodded silently and followed the tracks in the soft earth. Canuck Avery was keeping close to the river, and Reynolds growled with satisfaction and pointed to a horseshoe in the short grass. Several shiny nails glittered in the bright sun, and they could see a speck in the trail up ahead.

"He's cast a shoe," Texas Joe whooped. "That's him about a mile up ahead. Like as not he will fort up in them rocks to make a stand where the river makes a bend."

"Mind what I said if we come up on him," Reynolds warned sternly. "He gets a chance to tell his side of the ruckus, and after that he gets a white man's chance to defend himself one more time."

"The Deacon didn't have no gun," Texas Joe muttered, and fingered the trigger of his old Colt.

"It was the Deacon's fault if he wasn't dressed proper," Reynolds barked sharply. "Runnin' up agin' a jigger he knowed was all primed for a kill!"

He swerved over toward the trees and increased the pace along the river-bank. They could see the horse limping badly up ahead, and they gained rapidly before the outlaw turned and saw them coming. He tried to spur his horse into a run, but the animal stumbled and fell heavily to its knees. Avery scrambled up and raised his hands when the two riders bore swiftly toward him.

Roaming Reynolds fanned out to the right with Texas Joe swinging to the left. Canuck Avery faced them biting his lower lip, and then his high-pitched voice broke the silence.

"It was self-defence, s'help me," he shouted. "He meant to bloody well kill me with his bare maulies. You'd have done the same thing in my place, mateys!"

Reynolds swung down from the saddle and

faced the cowering rustler. His gun was in his holster, but Texas Joe had his gun half out of leather while he glared savagely at the prisoner.

"About that Morgan stallion," the cowboy drawled softly. "You and Hip High Hardy rustled that stud, and I caught you with the goods. Now you talk straight while I listen right close."

"Hardy wanted to ride him, is all," Avery whined. "That's hit, matey. We was just going to give that stud a ride to settle a bet."

"Yo're a liar," Texas Joe snapped viciously. "You rustlers knocked the old man cold and tied him up so he couldn't so much as move a finger. Then yore killin' boss shot that stud because he couldn't dab his twine on him back there in that sandy wash!"

The rustler turned slowly to face the boy. His thin face twisted with anger, and his lips drew back to show long canine teeth at each side of his mouth. Then he shook his right arm suddenly and went into a crouch.

Roaming Reynolds flipped his right hand down in a sweeping pull. His gun roared and bucked up in his hand, and Canuck Avery screamed like a wounded horse and shook his bloody fingers. The derringer was knocked twenty feet away, where it buried itself in the sand, and Texas Joe stared with his gun half out of the worn scabbard.

"Don't shoot," the prisoner whimpered. "I'm entitled to a trial, I am!"

105

Roaming Reynolds smiled coldly. "You'll get it," he promised grimly. "From men who don't know how to lie or cheat. But first we better pull the shoes off that cayuse of yores."

Texas Joe caught the tired horse and led it close. Roaming Reynolds reached to his saddlebags and produced a pair of pliers which he threw to the boy. Texas Joe pulled the three shoes, and then he planted himself before the prisoner with both hands on his hips.

"Been me I'd have drilled you plumb centre," he sneered. "Yo're lucky you only lost yore stinger in that little brush. I never did cotton none to a gent what would pack a hide-out up his sleeve!"

Canuck Avery stared at the joint of his trigger finger. "I'd have had you if it hadn't been for yore pard," he growled hoarsely. "You had yore cutter half out of leather, and it was stickin' there when the smoke cleared off."

"You tried to run another sneak, Mister," the boy sneered. "Now you stand hitched while I take yore hardware. My gun is out of leather now, and I'm itchin' to have you make a funny pass!"

His eyes blazed with excitement when he reached out his left hand to empty Avery's holster. Roaming Reynolds watched with a smile twitching the corners of his mouth, but the boy lifted the gun and stuck it down in the band of his

Levi's. Then he stepped back and glanced at the tall cowboy.

"Him," he sniffed. "How about stretchin' his neck on the end of a grass rope?"

"We ain't the law," Reynolds answered with a frown. "Put him on his hoss and take the reins. I promised him a trial, and he's going to get one that will curl his toes!"

Canuck Avery pulled the neckerchief from around his throat and wrapped it around his wounded hand. He shivered slightly when he raised his eyes and saw Reynolds watching him. After which he walked to his horse and climbed the saddle without a word. Texas Joe followed behind, and then he holstered his gun with a grunt and mounted his own horse. Gathered up the lead reins with a jerk and turned to Reynolds.

"Line out for home," the cowboy ordered softly. "I'll bring up the rear just in case Hip High Hardy gets an idea to ride in and side his pard."

"You couldn't have cut 'er if Hip High was here," Avery snarled. "There's two men got you faded with a cutter right here in the Strip, and Hardy is one of them!"

"He fast?" Reynolds asked carelessly.

"Fast? Listen, feller. Hip High could get both guns out and dot yore eyes before you slapped wood. And some day he will do it, s'help me!"

"You had the same idea," the tall cowboy drawled. "Where at is yore pard right now?"

"I ain't talkin'," Avery mumbled. "You will find out about him sooner than you figger. Where you blighters taking me?"

"To the M T," Reynolds answered quietly. "You said you wanted a trial."

"Them Mormons ain't the law here in the Strip," Avery howled. "You got to take me back to Red Hawss."

"You stay at the M T until the sheriff comes to get you," Reynolds answered sharply. "Who's this second gent what has me faded with my tools?"

"Eagle Duprce, that's who," the prisoner snarled. "Eagle will square up if it takes him the rest of his bloody life!"

"Yeah," the cowboy grunted carelessly. "Line out for the M T, button," he said to Texas Joe. "We promised to be back for grub, and we don't want no one to worry."

CHAPTER VIII

Betty Tucker hushed her protests when Roaming Reynolds cantered out of the yard with Texas Joe at his heels. Her brown eyes sparkled with a light that was actuated partly by anger against Canuck Avery, added to admiration for the tall young cowboy who had signed the M T payroll to do battle with the horse thieves.

The girl sighed softly and walked her horse to a corral where she stripped the riding gear and turned the animal in. Her pretty face was thoughtful when she benched her saddle to air-dry, and her right hand caressed the grip of Roaming Reynolds' gun. Then she turned toward the big house.

Mormon Tucker looked up from his papers and nodded his big head. "You did your work well, daughter," he said approvingly. "It might have been fatal if Brigham had met Reynolds. As it is, he lies grievously wounded, but the man has the constitution of a bear."

"Father," and the girl's tone was low. "It happened this morning."

Mormon Tucker straightened up and peered from under bushy brows. "Yes," he agreed. "Down in the river bed beyond the bend."

The girl waved a hand. "Not that," she answered

irritably. "Roaming met Eagle Dupree back there in Red Horse. They were talking when I reached the depot, and I am sure they would have fought with their guns if I had been a minute later."

"What's that?" and Mormon Tucker half rose to his feet. "Reynolds met Eagle Dupree after what happened to the Morgan stallion?"

The girl nodded. "They were crouching toward each other like mad dogs," she explained with a shudder. "Then Dupree saw me and took off his hat. Roaming asked me to do some errands down the street, and I refused. So we rode home together."

Mormon Tucker stared thoughtfully and shook his big head. "Sometimes I doubt the wisdom of hiring Reynolds and his guns," he said softly, and then his big shoulders straightened. "But it had to be done," he added vigorously. "Dupree and his outlaws were stealing us blind!"

The girl patted the gun on her leg and stared at her father. "You have not obeyed his orders, Father," she said quietly. "Every man was to get himself fully dressed. A sixgun on his leg, and a rifle under the saddle-fender when he went riding."

"Nonsense," Tucker snorted. "Why should I be wearing a gun right here in my own home?"

"Why shouldn't you?" the girl parried. "Canuck Avery met Brigham not more than a mile from here."

"Go to him," Tucker answered quietly, and began to finger the papers on his desk. "I must finish my work!"

The girl came around the desk and laid her smooth cheek against his black beard. "You like Roaming Reynolds, don't you, Father?" she whispered.

"Eh?" and Tucker jerked erect. "Of course I do, daughter. He is a young man of character and force, but now we must think of Brigham. He has been like a son to me."

"That is because he has been with you longer than Roaming," the girl answered softly. "When he has been here a year or two . . ."

The Mormon chuckled. "Not him," he scoffed. "That Roaming cowboy won't stay in any one place a year or two."

The girl turned away with a soft sigh. "I was hoping he would," she said in a little voice. "And you were hoping the same."

Mormon Tucker frowned sternly. "Don't forget that we are Mormons, daughter," he warned. "We have our own ideas about the fitness of things, and Brigham Smith is a Deacon of our Church!"

"He never allows anyone to forget that," the girl answered wearily. "And he could be so different."

"He will be different when he is well," Tucker assured her. "Little things bring about great changes, and Brigham will be a different man when he finds his feet again. Go to him now, Betty."

Betty Tucker turned away and knuckled the tears from her eyes. She moved slowly down the big hall and stopped at the door of the room where Brigham Smith was fighting for his life. Ma Tucker glanced up and came to her feet when the girl opened the door and came in, and then she was holding her daughter against her breast.

"There, daughter," she crooned. "He will get well, and you must be brave."

"Roaming," the girl sobbed softly. "Everyone wants to kill him. He met Hardy and Canuck when he first came here, and to-day he met Eagle Dupree. Even Brigham was hunting for him."

Ma Tucker smiled gently and cupped a hand under the girl's chin. "Here now, Betty," she chided gently. "Your worries should be for Brigham. He was shot twice by that sneaking Avery man. The Doctor just left, and he gave Brigham an even chance if he keeps quiet, and has good care."

"I will nurse him, Mother," and the girl dried her eyes. "If he only was a fighting man," she added in a whisper, and approached the bed.

Brigham Smith opened his eyes and turned his head. For a long moment he stared up at the girl, and then a wistful smile curled his full lips under the silky black beard. His right hand reached out and gently patted the girl's arm, and Betty Tucker felt her heart jump when she recognized the longing for affection and comfort.

"Betty," he whispered, and his deep voice was subdued by weakness. "I knew you would come."

"Brigham," and the girl stroked his feverish brow to hide the desire in his pleading brown eyes. "You must fight very hard to get well now, Brigham."

His eyes clouded for a moment at the formality in her tone. "Just Brigham?" he asked softly. "Everyone calls me Brigham."

The girl continued to stroke his head and glanced at her mother. The wounded man followed her gaze and was satisfied. Mormon girls did not make an open exhibition of their feelings before their elders. Schooled from infancy to repression until after the nuptials had been announced, and Brigham Smith remembered that he was a Deacon.

"Later perhaps," he murmured, and smiled through the pain that twisted his bearded lips. "It is enough that you are near me."

A scraping noise sounded from the side window, but the three in the sick-room were absorbed in their own problem. Ma Tucker was the first to turn, and she stifled a scream when she saw a wide-shouldered man slip down from the sill and plant his big boots firmly on the floor. Her hand went to her lips when she saw the menacing sixgun cocked back for a shot, and then a snarling voice jerked the eyes of Betty Tucker and Brigham Smith toward the intruder.

"She won't be near you long, Deacon. Any of you makes a peep, I'm pressing trigger!"

"Hip High Hardy!"

Betty Tucker breathed the words through parted lips while her hand pressed down on the wounded man's head to restrain him. Brigham Smith was trying to sit up, and the burly outlaw smiled sneeringly and swivelled his gun to cover the pair.

"In the flesh," he muttered. "Walk over this way, gal, and don't try to cut no rusty on me. I'm taking yore gun first off!"

Betty Tucker levered erect and approached the outlaw like a person in a dream. Ma Tucker took a step and held Brigham Smith down while Hardy lifted the girl's gun and stuck it down in the band of his dungarees. Then the outlaw jerked a piggin' string from around his waist and flipped a small loop open with his left hand.

"Hands behind yuh, sister," he croaked hoarsely. "Anybody starts through that door, you better warn them to stay out. I'll kill the three of you if you raise an alarm."

Brigham Smith was breathing heavily while his dark eyes smouldered with the old fanatical fire. His great chest rose and fell like a pair of bellows, and his lips twisted with an inner rage that brought a rush of blood to his head.

"Don't touch her, Hardy," he whispered in his deep bass voice. "I'll kill you with my hands unless you depart at once and leave us in peace!"

Hip High Hardy scowled and centred his gun on the wounded man. "I'll touch her," he muttered hoarsely. "And you won't kill no one, me bucko. I'm holdin' a handful of forty-fives; not thirty-twos like Canuck got you with."

"Into the valley of death," the Deacon muttered, and strained against the hands that held him to his bed. "Step over here, Betty!"

"Hands behind yuh," Hardy growled savagely. "Or I'll kill the Deacon and yore Ma, and take you nohow. Eagle Dupree wants you, and Eagle takes what he wants!"

Betty Tucker caught her breath and stared at Brigham Smith. Her rounded breasts rose and fell with the effort she was making to solve the problem, and then she sighed and reached her two hands behind her back.

Hip High Hardy snared both wrists with his loop and made a pair of swift wraps and a tie. He pushed the girl to one side just as Brigham Smith rose up from his bed and tossed the heavy covers aside. The bare muscular torso of the wounded man gleamed like marble in the fading rays of the setting sun; as white as the surgical bandages that circled his lean abdomen to hold the medicinal compresses.

Not a sound came from his straight lips as his

feet found the smooth floor and balanced when he pushed his towering bulk erect. Hip High Hardy sucked in his breath and jabbed viciously with the muzzle of his gun.

"Back!" he barked. "Down, before I smoke yuh down!"

No expression on the big bearded face of the Deacon as he caught his balance and started his slow advance with both hands reaching toward the gunman. Hip High Hardy dropped his jaw and stared his unbelief. Then he lowered the hammer under his calloused thumb while a cruel grin spread over his stubbled face.

Ma Tucker stood on the other side of the bed like a woman in a dream. Something had paralyzed her muscles; had robbed her of the ability to make a sound. Betty Tucker was staring with her brown eyes wide with terror and fear for the wounded man. Brigham Smith advanced slowly like an irrepressible force that cannot be halted.

"Stop!"

Hardy was crouching forward now while his little eyes stared at the slowly advancing giant. Two hundred and forty pounds of unconquerable purpose looming six-feet-four above him like some misty figure from the past when cave-men fought to the death for the women of their choice.

The outlaw wheezed and backed away while the red killer-light flamed hotly in his eyes, and made the saliva drool from the corners of his gaping mouth. Then he leaped forward like a mountain cat that has been cornered by a grizzly. The gun in his fist rose swiftly and crashed down on the head of the Deacon with a sodden thud, and the big man buckled his knees and began to sink.

Brigham Smith shook himself like a dog coming out of water and straightened up. Onward he came like a slowly surging tide, and the outlaw side-stepped and brought the gun thudding down like a club. The Deacon shivered like a stricken pine and sank slowly to the floor as his dark eyes slowly closed. He did not fall. Just buckled his knees and coiled slowly to the floor under a crashing weight that shut off the power of his indomitable brain.

Hip High Hardy skinned back his teeth and grinned like a killing lobo. His gun jerked around to cover Ma Tucker; motioned to the bed with a savage jerk of the head that was unmistakable.

"Scream," he sneered softly. "And Mormon Tucker will be a he-widow!"

The older woman shook herself and came slowly to the bed. "I won't scream," she said quietly. "But there will be a vengeance."

"Tear one of those sheets," the outlaw ordered, and now his voice was quiet. "Then turn over until I tie up yore hands!"

Betty Tucker watched in fascinated silence

while her mother tore a sheet and rolled over on the bed. Hip High Hardy took a strip and made a quick tie to fasten the plump wrists behind her back. Then he took another strip and made a crude gag which he bound around her mouth.

"You've killed the Deacon," Betty Tucker said softly, but the outlaw turned swiftly at the venom in her throaty voice.

"And if I did?" he sneered.

"There is one who is not a man of peace," the girl answered quietly. "He swore an oath to take up for Brigham, and he never breaks a promise."

Hip High Hardy scowled. "Meaning this Roaming Reynolds jigger?" he asked hoarsely.

The girl nodded. "He started out after Canuck Avery," she almost whispered. "And he never fails!"

"He got Canuck," the outlaw growled. "But he won't keep him long when he finds out that I got you. That's how come me to let yore old lady live. It's you agin' Canuck, and they better not do my pard any hurt!"

Betty Tucker stared at the outlaw and glanced at her mother on the bed. Ma Tucker had rolled over and was making a mute appeal with her dark eyes. Kicked her foot slightly, and the girl drew a deep breath and looked away. The older woman's feet were free, and the outlaw might forget.

Hardy laughed softly. "I left her legs loose on purpose," he grunted. "But if she makes a move

118

before ten minutes, I'll slip back here and let her have a slug. Yuh savvy, old woman?"

Ma Tucker shuddered and nodded her head. Mormon Tucker should be at his desk not more than thirty feet away, but the house was constructed solidly of heavy logs, and was almost sound-proof. The outlaw read her thoughts and slid across the room to the door.

"If Mormon comes through there, that makes you a widow," he whispered hoarsely, and his rough voice boomed softly like a gust of wind in the evergreens. "I'm locking this door to make it a little harder for you."

He turned the key in the lock and withdrew it. Stuck it down in a vest pocket with a grin and turned back to the girl. Betty Tucker drew herself up proudly and faced him without a trace of fear in her pretty rounded face.

"Do with me what you will," she said softly. "But if you hurt Mother, I'll kill you with my own hands!"

"Eagle likes 'em with plenty of spirit," Hardy answered carelessly. "Reckon you and me better high-tail out of here. Get over there and straddle that window sill!"

He pushed the girl toward the window and waited while she threw her right leg across. Long shapely legs clad in rough Levi's that fitted her tightly from hips to knees. Little hand-made boots peeping from under the high cuffs like the foot-gear of any working buckaroo. Then the girl brought her left leg over and waited.

"Give us ten minutes if you want to see the gal again, old lady," he snarled at Ma Tucker. "I'm killin' her first if any of yore peaceful crew gets their hackles up and goes on the prod!"

Betty Tucker was staring at the face of Brigham Smith. The big man was sprawled on the floor near the bed, and his scalp was bleeding from the blows that had felled him. Then the girl saw the gentle rise and fall of his gleaming white chest, and she turned to her mother to hide her discovery.

"Wait ten minutes, Mother," she murmured softly. "Then you climb out the window and let Father know."

Ma Tucker nodded her head and closed her eyes. Hip High Hardy stepped across the sill and dropped to the ground five feet below. He reached up with his left hand and pulled the girl down beside him; caught her against his burly chest when she slipped in the soft loam.

"Gawd!" he muttered, and held her tightly for a moment. "If Eagle wasn't the boss—"

"But he is," the girl said soberly, and tried to free herself. "He would kill you if you harmed me, and we both know it. You wouldn't have a chance against him."

Hip High Hardy snarled when a mental picture flashed across his mind. A picture of the time when Eagle Dupree had wished a gun in his hand to beat the flip-draw Hardy was so proud of. His left hand released the girl and jerked to his vest pocket to finger the crumpled feather he would always keep for a souvenir.

For a moment he held the feather uncertainly in his thick fingers while his little eyes glared at the body of Brigham Smith across the sill. Dupree had told him never to use his personal mark, and the wide-shouldered outlaw tucked the eagle feather back in his pocket with a muttered curse.

"C'mon," he growled, and gripped the girl by the arm. "I got hosses hid out here in the bresh, and you and me is making tracks!"

Betty Tucker allowed herself to be led through the tangled vines that shaded the big house. She was sure that she heard the beat of horses hooves, but no one was in sight when Hardy guided her through a hedge of cypress and pulled the slip-knots in the hair-ropes that tethered a pair of horses.

"M T stock," the outlaw sneered. "The best in the country, and now you lift yore boot to the oxbow while I give you a boost."

Betty Tucker bit her lip and placed her small boot in the stirrup. Hardy stooped and placed a shoulder under her hip; lifted her easily to the saddle and waited until she had found the other stirrup. Then he mounted his own horse and gathered up the lead reins in his left hand. Not

121

until then did he holster the heavy sixgun in the hand-shaped scabbard on his right hip.

Betty Tucker turned in the saddle and watched the window until the brush cut off her view. Back in the sick-room, Ma Tucker stared at the window and strained at the sheet that held her wrists. She swayed back and forth until her weight pitched her upright on the edge of the bed, and she crept across the floor on her knees to keep her head below the level of the sill.

Her eyes fell on the white chest of Brigham Smith and held for a long moment. "He lives," she moaned through the gag.

A curl of smoke in the old stone fireplace made her shoulders snap back. Then she was sliding across the room on her knees while her brown eyes studied the ash-covered coals. A time or two she shook her head doubtfully, and then her lips set in a straight stubborn line.

Turning her back, she reached her hands out behind her and felt cautiously. A live ember touched her fingers and scorched her flesh. Ma Tucker jerked slightly and turned her wrists. Held them so until the odour of burning cloth came to her nostrils. The flesh began to scorch, but the mother of Betty Tucker held her position until a sudden flash of flame told her that the cloth was burning. Then she wrenched with her strong shoulders and beat out the flames when her hands came free.

No thought of the burns on her wrists when she tore the gag from her mouth and hastened to the side of Brigham Smith. His eyes were closed with long lashes lying on his cheek. Her right hand reached up and explored the wounds on his scalp with tender searching fingers. Then she leaned over and listened to the beat of his heart.

"Thank God, he lives," she murmured, and she tried to raise his heavy shoulders to the bed.

Brigham Smith lay perfectly still with only his gentle breathing to tell that he lived. The dead weight was too great for even the strength of the buxom woman, and she allowed his shoulders to slip to the floor when her eyes fastened to the bandage around his abdomen. The starchy whiteness of the hand-loomed cloth was stained and soggy with crimson stripes that waved in the folds like a mocking banner.

"Oh," the woman moaned. "The compresses have slipped. Mormon! Mormon Tucker!"

Screaming the name of her husband, she found her feet and staggered toward the window. Plunged through it in her excitement and terror, to hit the ground in a rolling tangle of legs and arms. Her head struck the root of an evergreen, and she crumpled in a heap when a curtain of darkness blotted out the fading light.

CHAPTER IX

Roaming Reynolds glanced up when he saw the evergreen lane leading to the M T Horse spread. Texas Joe was leading the horse of Canuck Avery with a youthful scowl of hatred on his fuzzy, unshaved cheeks. The tall cowboy spoke gruffly and rode up to take the lead reins.

"Lope in and get Mormon Tucker," he murmured. "Tell him to come down to the granary right away."

"Yuh can't do this slinkin' thing to me," Avery whined. "I wants a fair trial by my peers."

"You'll get it," Reynolds answered grimly. "Every man on the M T is yore better. Now you grab a holt of yoreself and be a man if you can."

Texas Joe rubbed the grip of his gun and sidled his rangy roan off side. "Bust him a couple of licks, Roamin'," he growled. "Just to teach that dang furriner some savvy."

"High tail," Reynolds snapped. "And bridle yore loose jaw if you want to pard up with me!"

Texas Joe hit his horse with the hooks and rocketed across the big yard. Scattered gravel when he lit off a-running, and mounted the porch steps three at a time. Slid to a stop before the flat top desk where Mormon Tucker was making figures on a paper.

"Roamin' wants for you to stampede to the granary right off," he growled savagely. "Him and me done brought in a jigger what goes by the handle of Canuck Avery. He wants a fair trial!"

"Eh? You say you and Roaming caught Avery?"

"Yuh heard me," the boy growled. "Roamin' is herdin' him up there toward that old fort you done built!"

Mormon Tucker kicked his heavy chair back and levered upright on his thick muscular legs. Reached for his black flat-crowned Stetson and smiled slowly at the scowling boy.

"It is well," he answered quietly, and gripped Texas Joe man to man. "Canuck Avery will get a fair trial that will assure both justice and law. Lead on, buckaroo."

Texas Joe turned away to hide the grin of pleasure on his thin tanned face. Straight across the big yards between the corrals with his right hand gripping the handle of his gun. He stopped at the door of the Grain house and waited for the big Mormon to precede him.

Built of heavy logs and adobe sod, the big granary on the M T resembled a frontier fort. Row after row of sacked barley and oats lined the walls for winter feeding against the storms from the north when pastures were buried deep beneath heavy snows. Barrels of water stood in each corner to be used for fighting fire, or for drinking in case of a siege.

125

Mormon Tucker took his seat behind a little table and laid his flat-crowned beaver on the floor. The chores of the day were finished, and the red sun was sinking in the west to paint the cathedral peaks of Zion Park with vivid colouring. The hush that always precedes the twilight hour made the big room sombrely silent while Mormon Tucker raised his head and glanced around.

The five young riders of the M T were seated on benches at one side of the room, their bearded faces grave and serious. Serious faces that had never known the touch of a razor blade. Smouldering eyes alert and watchful, and not a man among them spoke.

Spur-chains tinkled musically and gradually sounded louder when Roaming Reynolds led his prisoner from the barn to the council chamber. Texas Joe brought up the rear with his grimy hand clamped to the handle of his old gun. Canuck Avery bit his lips while his little eyes darted in every direction for some possible avenue of escape. He knew these Mormons and their ways.

The young Mormons drew deep breaths when the tall cowboy pushed the cowering outlaw through the great double doors. Texas Joe took his stand as guard, and his young face was as serious as the rest when he watched Reynolds place the prisoner in front of the table.

Mormon Tucker stared at Avery for a long

moment while his brown eyes probed the mean face. He had the air of a man who is trying hard to find some good to offset the evil in his fellow man. At last he sighed deeply and shook his big head as though to acknowledge defeat. His deep voice was a rumbling whisper when he began to speak.

"Brigham Smith lies grievously wounded and close to death, Canuck Avery. Reynolds claims that your act was justified in part, but that is for the outside law to decide. The fact remains that you were trespassing on M T range at the time, and your people have not been friendly to mine."

"She's always been open country up here," Avery muttered. "Was a time when a gent could ride where he wanted to, and no questions asked."

Mormon Tucker nodded his big head. "I remember that time well," he agreed. "And I remember when outlaws and rustlers rode into the Strip to rob honest men who were too busy to learn the ways of fighting men."

"You got no business in this country if you don't know how to fight," Avery answered argumentatively. "Everybody up here expects to fight to hold what he wants!"

Mormon Tucker shook his head sadly. "We Mormons are men of peace," he said slowly. "We also try to be just and honest, but when we are aroused to anger, we learn to fight fire with fire," and he glanced at Roaming Reynolds.

127

"Him," Canuck Avery muttered. "He ain't no man of peace by a long shot, but Eagle Dupree will show him something about fight he never heard tell of in all his borned days!"

Roaming Reynolds raised his head, and his blue eyes were glowing with the fires of anticipation. "Is that a promise?" he asked softly.

"Yo're bloody well right," the prisoner shouted, and his face showed that he was glad to shift the conversation away from himself. "Eagle is gun-boss up here in the Strip, and he said there wasn't enough room for two!"

"Something in what he says," the tall cowboy agreed quietly. "You got any idea where I could find that *buscadero* after we have made medicine with you?"

Mormon Tucker frowned and hammered on the table with his big fist. "You will restrain yourself, Reynolds," he said sternly. "We did not meet here to arrange the terms for a personal combat."

"Like you said, Boss," and Reynolds flushed under his heavy tan. "Reckon I forgot myself and spoke out of turn," but the fingers of his right hand caressed the worn grip of his sixgun.

"About this trespassing," Tucker continued, and fixed the prisoner with an unwinking stare of severity. "Were you alone when you came out to the M T just to take a ride?"

"You didn't see no one else with me, did you?" Avery growled.

"I didn't," Tucker admitted. "But it was the first time I ever saw you alone. Usually you are in the company of that blackguard known as Hip High Hardy!"

Canuck Avery split his thin lips with a sneer. "The Deacon would be dead right now if Hardy had been rubbin' stirrups with me," he muttered. "The man don't live what could ride Hip High down and take a cutter from his hand!"

"It has been done," Roaming Reynolds interrupted thinly. "And I've seen guns shot right out of the fists of a gent what tried to trigger two at the same time!"

"Order!"

Mormon Tucker glared at the tall cowboy and then turned to Canuck Avery with stern disapproval on his florid face. He breathed deeply to show the effort he was making to control his own temper, and the younger Mormons sat forward and watched without moving their bearded lips.

"He started it," Canuck Avery whined. "He started it when he rode in here and throwed down on me and Hardy."

Mormon Tucker relaxed as though he had found his answer. "He did not start it," he contradicted slowly. "You and Hardy started it when you roped me from my horse, and the real purpose of this arraignment is to question you about your part in the stealing of the Morgan stallion. What have you to say?"

Canuck Avery realized that he had made a mistake. He wet his thin lips and shrugged sullenly, and Roaming Reynolds shifted on the soles of his boots and turned his head slightly to listen.

"We didn't steal the stud," Avery snapped. "All I did was help Hip High Hardy drive him out on the mesa. Hardy wanted to ride him, and after that we aimed to turn him loose and let him run. Me and Hardy had a wager between us."

"You lie," Tucker contradicted flatly. "You were stealing the Morgan, and you committed assault against my person when I rode up to claim my property!"

"You got me and Hardy wrong, guv'nor," the prisoner answered in an aggrieved tone. "Like Hardy was tellin' me, either him nor me stood a chance again' you if you went on the peck and tied into us with yore maulies. Hardy didn't want to use a gun on you, so we done the next best thing to keep you from getting hurted bad."

"You and Hardy meant to kill me," and the Mormon's voice was edgy with threat. "You would have carried out your intentions if Roaming Reynolds had not come along to stop you."

"He started all the trouble," Avery answered sullenly. "When he cut down on me and Hip High with his Winchester!"

"I shot the check-rope you was using on the stud," Reynolds corrected softly. "I never learned

130

to throw off my shots, and Hardy wouldn't be doing what he is doing now if I had aimed to smoke him down!"

"Yuh see, Guv'nor?" Avery shouted triumphantly. "You fellers is all men of peace, and this gun-slammer rides in here looking for smoke-trouble. He's like all the rest of them blighters when they hears as how there is another fast gun-dog ridin' the same range!"

"It won't do, Avery," Tucker answered heavily. "I personally accuse you and your partner of stealing the Morgan stud."

"Tain't so, s'help me," Avery protested. "Me and Hardy had hot words about him riding the stud, and we was settling a wager like I told you."

Mormon Tucker waved his hand as if to dismiss the subject. "Is it not true that Eagle Dupree breeds horses back in Rainbow Canyon?" he asked quietly.

"Shore he does," and the prisoner's face lighted up with a new ray of hope. "You fellers got him all wrong when you pegged him for a rustler. He sells hoss-flesh the same as you do."

"Your boss has made threats against me and mine," Tucker said coldly. "He boasts openly that he takes what he wants, or kills what he can't take!"

"I never heard him say that," Avery mumbled, and glanced at the craggy face of Roaming Reynolds. "Worst thing about Eagle is that he knows he is the fastest gun-slammer in the Arizona Strip."

Reynolds reacted instantly. "He is not! No man can do his best work when he knows that he is wrong!"

"Mebbe yo're the fastest?" Avery taunted.

Roaming Reynolds changed in a flash. "I am," he almost whispered, and crouched toward the prisoner with flame glowing deep in his narrowed blue eyes. "I won't leave here until I have proved it to yore boss!"

"You won't ever leave here," Avery answered positively. "I see him shade Hip High one day, and Hardy could beat you without half trying. Eagle let Hip High start, and he beat him to the shot before Hardy's guns had cleared leather!"

"Looks to me like Dupree was playing a shore thing," Reynolds answered bluntly. "Him and Hardy was both wrong, and two wrongs never yet made a right, or settled an augerment."

Canuck Avery smiled and balanced on his scuffed boots. Once more he had turned the talk away from himself, and he turned his head to glance at Mormon Tucker. The big leader was watching the men along the wall in sombre silence, and the prisoner followed his gaze automatically.

One of the young Mormons rose slowly and came forward with a rope in his hand. He stood apart from the little group around the table, and his hands built a small loop while he stared coldly at Canuck Avery. The rustler cringed back with the colour draining from his face, and his voice was a squeaking whisper when he appealed to Roaming Reynolds.

"You promised me a fair trial, cowboy! You can't hang a pore blighter for doin' what he had to do. Now can yuh, matey?"

Roaming Reynolds stared at him without smiling. "You mean you were obeying orders when you and Hardy rustled the stallion?" he asked softly, and swayed gently while he waited for Avery's answer.

"S'help me," Avery whined. "Hip High Hardy would have shot me down like a bloomin' partridge on the wing if I had give him any loose lip!"

"Shore he would," the cowboy agreed. "And you meant to take the Morgan stallion over to Rainbow Canyon for Eagle Dupree!"

"I didn't say that," Avery muttered sullenly. "Hip High was set on riding him and winning my money for himself."

Roaming Reynolds shook his head slowly and looked suggestively at the man with the rope. "You lie again, Avery," he said flatly. "Now you take a good look at that maguey and make up yore mind!"

Avery swivelled his head and glanced at the rope. "That's it," he almost shouted. "Eagle had

133

some blooded mares he wanted to breed back there in Rainbow!"

Reynolds nodded and glanced at Mormon Tucker, and the big man returned the nod. "We lost a band of twelve mares last week," Tucker said quietly. "We read the sign plain in the dirt, and they pointed toward Rainbow Canyon. It was Brigham Smith who persuaded me to stay away from the Canyon, because Dupree and his gang were all armed, and ready to kill!"

"All he wanted was to breed his own mares," Avery snarled. "Eagle bought that band up in Utah."

"He wanted to breed the Morgan to my mares," Tucker contradicted, and two bright spots of colour flamed on his cheeks. "Better tell the truth for the good of your soul, Avery."

Canuck Avery sulked until the young Mormon flipped his right hand. The finicky loop circled the rustler's scrawny neck and tightened to take up the slack. Roaming Reynolds half-turned and called to Texas Joe.

"Open the doors, Tex. We aim to hang this rustler on a bent limb unless he comes through and tells the truth!"

Texas Joe grinned and opened the double doors. Canuck Avery waited until daylight showed, and the sneer faded from his face when he saw the deepening shadows of twilight.

"I'll talk," he shouted, and the perspiration of

terror stood out on his face. "Eagle wanted that stud to breed those mares you spoke about. He'll slit me bloomin' gullet for welchin', but that's the truth, mateys, s'help me!"

"Mebbe he's just saying that to save his own skin," Reynolds suggested softly. "That jigger would rather lie for credit, than tell the truth for cash."

"It's the whole truth, I tell yuh," Avery shouted desperately. "I ain't fitten to die!"

"Are you willing to sign a statement to that effect?" and Mormon Tucker leaned forward to probe the face of the rustler with his sombre brown eyes. "I have the paper all drawn up and ready."

"I'd never live if I signed that paper," Avery snarled wolfishly, and curled his lips to show long yellowed fangs. "Eagle Dupree would shoot me down like a dirty yeller dawg!"

"But yo're a prisoner," Reynolds reminded him. "You will get another trial by the law, and anything you say will be used against Eagle Dupree. Better think it over, yuh sneaking rustler!"

"He'd kill me, I tell yuh," Avery shouted hoarsely. "I wouldn't live long enough to take the oath!"

"You won't live very long if you don't sign," Reynolds interrupted softly. "That's a new rope around yore skinny neck. Wouldn't take long for it to cut off yore wind."

135

The young Mormon twitched the rope suggestively, and Canuck Avery turned to face Mormon Tucker with a plea in his piggish eyes. Tucker frowned sternly and pointed to the paper on the table in front of him.

"You heard what Reynolds said, Avery. And we are not forgetting that Brigham Smith lies close to the valley of the shadows. Look out the door, Avery. The shadows are getting deeper down there under that lane of trees."

"I'll get a fair trial?" Avery whispered hoarsely. "You'll give me pertection in case Eagle Dupree finds out what I done?"

Mormon Tucker nodded his big head gravely. "We will hold you here for the sheriff," he promised. "Yonder is the paper and pen."

Canuck Avery reached up and felt of the rope. The young Mormon twitched it tight, and the prisoner swallowed hard and reached for the pen. He scrawled his name hastily without reading the paper, and then he straightened slowly and turned to Mormon Tucker with his lips quivering.

"The rope," he whispered. "Tell him to take the damn thing offen me, guv'nor!"

"Remove the rope, Bruce," Tucker said quietly. "We won't need it any more. You may take your place with the others."

The young Mormon flipped the noose expertly, and Canuck Avery sighed shudderingly while he rubbed his neck. Then he straightened up when some of the colour returned to his angular face. Mormon Tucker levered to his feet and came around the table.

"You will be held until an officer of the law comes for you," he said sternly. "I have wanted to get evidence on Hardy and Eagle Dupree for more than a year, and Reynolds said that you would betray your partners to save your own worthless life."

"It was a trick," Avery snarled, and spat like a cornered cat. "You'll pay for what you done to me, and that paper won't be worth nothin' in court!"

Mormon Tucker smiled and waved his thick arm. "I have all these witnesses," he said quietly. "And Roaming Reynolds proved that he knew how to read the stature of a man."

"Dupree will settle with that gun-passin' meddler," Avery cried furiously. "They ain't room up here for the two of them, and Eagle is the best!"

Mormon Tucker frowned. "Take him back to that cell in the barn, Reynolds," he ordered quietly. "He will be safe there until the law comes for him."

Canuck Avery jerked suddenly and sprawled face forward across the table. Fully a second later, the flat crash of a heavy rifle echoed from the distance. Roaming Reynolds ran to the door and stared into the shadows down the long lane;

shook his head when hoof-beats drummed from the ford in the river.

"They killed Canuck because they knew he would talk to save his neck," he remarked carelessly, and then he stepped back and shut the heavy doors. "They got Canuck right between the shoulders."

Mormon Tucker was examining the body. Avery had slipped to the floor, and now his glassy eyes were staring sightlessly at the timbered roof of the granary. The cowboy shrugged and turned to Tucker with a frown of disappointment mirrored in his eyes.

"No use trying to catch the killer," he said quietly. "But after this we will place a guard at the end of the lane in case Eagle Dupree brings us more grief. He would burn the M T to the ground if he knew we had that paper to use against him in court."

Mormon Tucker reached for the paper and folded it neatly. Tucked it in an inside pocket with a nod of his big head. He reached down for his beaver and pulled it down on his head, and Roaming Reynolds stepped up to him and pointed to his right leg.

"I told you to get yoreself dressed, Mormon. After this you strap on yore hardware and keep it close to yore hand. Eagle Dupree has declared war, and you see for yourself what that means!"

Brown eyes smouldered briefly, and then Tucker nodded soberly. "You are the boss when fighting starts, Reynolds," he answered soberly. "I'll get myself dressed like you ordered."

He whirled on his heel when a woman screamed out in the yard. Texas Joe threw the double doors open, and Ma Tucker ran into the granary with tears streaming down her comely face. Mormon Tucker took her in his big arms and soothed her until she became more quiet.

"Now, Mother," he murmured. "Tell me all about it!"

CHAPTER X

Ma Tucker caught her breath and tried to still her quivering lips. "Betty!" she gasped chokingly. "He took Betty with him!"

Roaming Reynolds leaped forward like an uncoiling spring. "Easy, Ma," he counselled, but his deep voice was harsh. "Who was it got Betty?"

Ma Tucker fought for control and held tightly to her husband. Every man in the room waited breathlessly until she had quieted enough to speak. Sobs racked her plump form and gradually subsided.

"It was that man called Hardy! He came through the window in the Deacon's room while we were talking to Brigham. He had a big gun in his hand, and he threatened to kill all three of us if we made a sound!"

Mormon Tucker trembled with anger. "And me sitting at my desk out in the hall," he muttered hoarsely.

"Without a gun on yore leg," Reynolds accused bitterly. "He would have killed you too!"

Mormon Tucker flushed with guilt and soothed his wife. Roaming Reynolds came forward and touched her on the shoulder.

"Brigham Smith?" and his low voice cut like a knife. "Is the Deacon all right, Ma?"

"He is alive," the woman whispered sobbingly. "Hardy took Betty's gun and tied her hands behind her back. Brigham got right up out of bed and started for Hardy, and the outlaw hit him on the head twice with his gun. Brigham fell on the floor with his head bleeding, and he is still unconscious!"

"Wife," and the voice of Mormon Tucker was gravely accusing. "Why did you wait all this time to tell us?"

"He tied me up with sheets," Ma Tucker sobbed. "He put a gag in my mouth and told me to wait ten minutes or he would kill Betty," and she held out her hands.

Mormon Tucker leaned forward and muttered in his beard. "Burned," he whispered. "He did that, Mother?"

Ma Tucker shook her head. "I did it," she answered with a shudder. "Hardy locked the door and took the key. There were some coals smouldering in the fireplace. I burned the sheets loose."

"My dear," and the big Mormon held her close against his massive chest. "Can you tell us the rest?"

Ma Tucker sighed tremulously and straightened her shoulders. "I started for the window when I saw Brigham," she whispered. "Lying on the floor by the bed, but I couldn't lift him. The compresses slipped and he is bleeding badly from his old wounds!"

"Betty?" Roaming Reynolds barked sharply. "Tell us about her."

"Hardy forced her to climb through the window," Ma Tucker continued wearily. "He said he was taking her to Eagle Dupree. I waited until they were out of sight, and then I climbed through the window. I fell and hit my head on a root, and I must have fainted until I heard that rifle shot just now!"

Roaming Reynolds leaned forward eagerly. "You saw the dry-gulcher?" he asked tensely.

Ma Tucker shook her head. "I didn't see him," she answered. "But the shot came from the river ford, and Hardy went that way with Betty."

Her eyes wandered across the room and widened when she saw the body of Canuck Avery. "He did that?" she whispered.

Mormon Tucker nodded his head. "Avery had just signed a confession," he explained. "Texas Joe opened the doors for Reynolds to take the prisoner away, but that shot came and killed the traitor."

"My girl," Ma Tucker moaned. "The terrible beasts!"

Mormon Tucker tightened his full lips. His calm face belied the passion that was surging through him like liquid fire. He walked over to the table and opened a drawer, and when he straightened up his big hands were buckling a gunbelt around his hips.

"Let us go to the Deacon," he said quietly, and led the way from the granary.

Roaming Reynolds and Texas Joe were right behind him when he pushed into the side-room. Brigham Smith was lying on the floor between the window and the bed, and he opened his eyes when they picked him up and placed him back in bed. He tried to rise when he saw the cowboy, but Mormon Tucker held him down by the shoulders.

"Easy, Deacon," he whispered. "Reynolds is a friend of yours, so don't strain yourself any more than you have to."

"Unhand me, Mormon," and the wounded man roared like an angry bull. "He brought war to the M T, and I'll take his weapons away from him with my bare hands!"

Roaming Reynolds stiffened and then relaxed. "Not for a while you won't," he said softly. "Looks like you'd learn some sense after all this ruckus!"

Brigham Smith struggled to arise, and the cowboy backed toward the door. "Mebbe I better leave the room," he muttered. "You stay here with him, Boss; you and Ma. Texas Joe and I will start after them raiders right off, but don't let the other men leave the ranch until we get back."

He was gone before Mormon Tucker could answer. The Mormon riders were muttering angrily outside the big house, and the tall cowboy stopped long enough to give his orders. They

143

eyed him sulkily while their hands gripped the guns on their legs.

"You fellers stay right here and guard the ranch," Reynolds said gruffly. "Eagle Dupree has a big gang, and he just might take a notion to raid the place if we all ride gun-sign after that killer of his."

A tall young buckaroo stepped out from the group. "They call me Utah Young," he said slowly. "I'm not waiting here for you or anybody else!"

Not more than twenty-three, and his silky black beard had never known a razor. Tall and broad-shouldered, with the serious face that marked all his fellows. Now his eyes sparkled with righteous anger.

"We fight for our women," he snapped. "You can't tell us what to do when our Betty is in danger!"

"I'm tellin' you," and the voice of Reynolds was hard as flint. "I'll take care of Betty, and don't you jiggers forget that there are other women here on the M T. You better stay here and fight for them, account of they shore will need help. Any augerments, feller?"

The tall Mormon dropped his eyes and nodded. "Reckon yo're right, cowboy," he admitted gruffly. "Me and the boys will stay here like you said. Good luck to you and the button on yore hunt. But Roamin'?"

"Yeah?"

"You got to get Betty before Hip High Hardy reaches Rainbow Canyon. Eagle Dupree will be waiting back there," and Utah shuddered. "I'll tell you a short-cut if you will make me a promise!"

"Spill it quick, feller," Reynolds snapped. "You wouldn't ask if it wasn't fair!"

"Take the trail up back of the granary," Utah directed soberly, and his eyes watched the face of Roaming Reynolds. "Texas Joe can show you where it cuts across the river about six miles this side of the Vermilion Cliffs."

"I know the place," Joe cut in eagerly. "Six miles will cut down an hour's lead unless a hoss was moving plenty rapid."

"That's good figgering, button," the tall Mormon agreed. "And it might cut down more than that if a feller had to lead another hoss."

"Got yuh," Reynolds grunted at Utah. "That promise you spoke about just now?"

"Kill Hip High Hardy before you come back to the M T!"

The cowboy stiffened and studied the ring of bearded faces. Dark eyes glowed in the deep twilight while they stared at his craggy face. Roaming Reynolds slipped his gun one time while a sudden change passed over him. His blue eyes were narrowed and hard as steel; his mouth a straight gash that told the answer before he put it into words.

"Hip High Hardy is dead, fellers," he rasped, and turned without another word toward the high corrals.

They watched him saddle a deep-chested mountain horse while Texas Joe geared up a rangy bay. The button had not said much since the time Canuck Avery had slumped to the floor back in the granary, but his thin face was older looking by several years. As though he had suddenly grown up to man's estate to take his place by the side of the gun-boss of the M T spread.

His Winchester was snugged down in the saddle-boot, and he was mounted and waiting when Roaming Reynolds stepped across his heavy saddle and waved his hand at the Mormon riders. Jerked his head toward the granary, and touched spur to his bay when Texas Joe thundered across the yard into the deeper shadows where a narrow trail divided a field of growing grain.

"Hit the grit so's we can read sign," he called to Texas Joe. "And keep yore powder dry in case you come to swimming water!"

The boy nodded and gigged his horse in the lead to follow the narrow trail. Ten minutes later they swung down to open a gate; closed it carefully after them to keep the stock from straying into the grain. Then Texas Joe pointed at a gap in the mountains ahead and lined out at a dead run.

"Right behind you," Reynolds barked. "Press on, button!"

They held the mad pace for an hour until Texas Joe held up his hand and reined down to a walk when a heavy fringe of timber sky-lined the ridge above them. The tall cowboy came alongside and asked a question with his eyes.

"It's a stiff climb up there to that hog-back," Joe whispered hoarsely. "Then we drop down to the river and swim our hosses across. That's the place where we wait, Roamin'!"

The cowboy nodded and waved for the go-ahead. Texas Joe took one look at the face above him and shuddered unconsciously. Gone was the easy smile that usually hid the harsh lines around mouth and eyes. Only those cold blue eyes showed any emotion; deep blue that seemed never to wink while they looked right through a man.

Texas Joe held his sweating horse to a fast walk while they climbed the steep slope. Then they were in timber with the rising moon casting long shadows through which they flitted like drifting mists. Deep beds of pine needles covered the ground to muffle all sounds of horses' hooves, and they were still in timber when they reached the bottom of the bosky and paused at the river bank.

"We swim here," the boy whispered, and jumped at the sound of his own voice. "I know the currents, so keep close to my hoss's flank."

He pulled off his rusty boots and dropped his old gun into one of them. Then he rolled them carefully in his leather chaps and fastened the wide belt around his shoulders. Roaming Reynolds was doing the same thing, and a moment later they gigged their horses into the deep waters of Virgin River.

The horses snorted when the cold water closed around them. Then they struck out for the green bank beyond with strong steady strokes. Found the bottom and scrambled out with the sure-footedness that only mountain horses possess. Texas Joe reined in and loosed his latigo to pull his saddle.

"Looks like we got here first, pard," and he tried to make his changing voice soft.

The horses rolled in the lush grass while their riders dried their feet and pulled on chaps and boots. Roaming Reynolds was studying the bottom land to place his landmarks, and he turned to stare at the dripping horses.

"Wet saddles, but we can't take any chances," he grunted. "We better gear them loose and picket them back yonder in that thicket, pard."

Texas Joe smiled in the darkness. To be the pard of a man like the gun-boss was beyond his wildest dream of maturity. He took the hair *mecates* and led the two horses back into a clearing beyond the brush screen, and when he returned Roaming Reynolds was checking the loads in his gun.

"Wanted to tell you, Roamin'," he began softly. "This Hip High Hardy uses a flip-draw in case you didn't know. Packs his hardware with the butts pitched out like as if he was going to work the old cross-draw. But he don't."

"I heard something about it," the tall cowboy murmured. "Keep on talking, Joe."

"He wears his belt high on his hips," Joe continued. "Hooks both thumbs in his belt so's his palms ain't but three-four inches above the handles. All as he does is drop his hands and flip his wrists, and he usually figgers on having a jigger close enough for hip-shooting. Don't throw yore shots off none, feller."

Roaming Reynolds smiled coldly in the darkness. "You just keep a picture of the Deacon on yore mind, button," he said coldly. "I like that big buckaroo in spite of his stubbornness. Mormon and his wife don't think Brigham will beat the old man with the sickle, but you couldn't kill that feller unless you cut off his head and hid it from him. If he was only a fighting man!"

Texas Joe echoed the deep sigh and came closer. His grimy right hand touched Reynolds until the cowboy raised his head and stared at the thin tanned face.

"Out with it, pard."

"You can think about the Deacon," Joe

149

muttered. "Me, I'm keeping my mind on the prettiest gal I ever see in all my travels."

Roaming Reynolds straightened slightly. "Meaning Betty Tucker," he said softly. "I was trying not to think too much about her."

"She's thinking a lot about you right now," Joe answered gruffly. "I could see it when she looked at you, and old Mormon saw it too. Not only that, but the Deacon is jealous of you."

Roaming Reynolds shrugged angrily. "I got a mind to slap you over the skull with a gun," he growled. "I don't think that away about no gal, and I want you to keep that in mind from now on out."

"Might be you don't," Joe answered doggedly. "But that ain't keeping Betty from thinking that away about you."

"Now you listen to me, button," Reynolds clipped harshly. "I'm nothing but a wandering gun-passer and I knows it. I can't stay put long in one place on account of hearing about some fast gun-hawk what thinks he is tops with his tools. It wouldn't be decent for me to get ideas about a gal who was raised among men of peace!"

Texas Joe stared back into the glowing eyes and shrugged his thin shoulders. "Yo're cloudin' the sign, pard," he said with a slight sneer. "I was talkin' about what Betty was thinking; not you. Yuh can't keep her from thinking what's on her mind, and she keeps comparing the Deacon agin' you."

Roaming Reynolds clicked his strong white teeth and turned abruptly toward the river. "This here lower trail," and his voice was as harsh as his features when he changed the subject. "You say it comes out yonder to meet up with the short-cut we taken?"

"Keep on foolin' yoreself," the boy sneered softly. "You see that dry bench down yonder in the moonlight?"

"What about it?"

"That there is the river trail," Joe answered. "Comes right past here and leads on close to Rainbow Canyon where Eagle Dupree rods his owl-hoot spread. Mebbe yo're still thinking about the Deacon!"

Roaming Reynolds turned swiftly. His left hand closed like a vice on the right arm of the startled boy, and Texas Joe sucked in his breath and tried to jerk free. The tall cowboy held him easily and stared with his smoky blue eyes.

"One more peep out of you about Betty Tucker," he warned harshly. "And right then is when you and me quits parding up!"

"Don't be a damn fool, Roamin'," the boy snarled. "Now you just use yore head for something else besides a place to hang yore old John B."

Reynolds loosened his grip and watched the

151

twisting features. "Sorry, button," he murmured. "Spell it out."

"Ma Tucker said as how that dang outlaw had Betty tied up," the boy muttered. "Him leadin' her hoss through the tangles, and you fixin' to call his hand. Aw right feller; yo're a gun-hand, but what about the gal when powder begins to burn?"

Roaming Reynolds stopped breathing for a moment as the meaning of it all flashed across his brain. He extended his right hand while a shamed smile curled his straight lips and spread across his face.

"Saying I'm sorry again, pard," he murmured softly. "You got to keep her hoss from boogering in case me and Hardy decides to bust a couple of caps. She wouldn't have a chance among the timber and brush if her hoss went on a stampede."

Texas Joe swelled with pride and swallowed noisily until he was sure he had control of his changing voice. "I'd go to hell for yuh, Roamin'," he muttered hoarsely. "I didn't mean for to ruffle you till yuh got yore hackles up, but I wanted you to think about that pore gal-chip coming through the tangles with Hip High Hardy. Ma whispered to me to look out for Betty, account she knew you was gunning for that barn-shouldered killer."

Roaming Reynolds was staring at the gravelled bench by the water's edge. His hard face was thoughtful while he studied the problem, and

Texas Joe rubbed the grip of his gun and waited.

"You stay back, Joe," the tall cowboy said at last. "Be ready to grab Betty's hoss when I give you the high sign. I made several promises back there by the granary, and I aim to keep them regardless. Yo're acting as pick-up, and I don't want you cuttin' in on my play!"

Texas Joe nodded when he saw the little ridges of muscle edging up to make the cowboy's jaws jut out like granite. Then he turned his head and listened intently for some vagrant sound that came from down on the winding river trail.

"Listen," he muttered sharply. "You hear anything, Roamin'?"

Roaming Reynolds cocked his head and tuned his ear to the sounds of the night. "Two hosses comin' slow," he whispered softly.

"Couldn't be no one else but Hip High," Joe grated, and tried to keep the tremble from his voice.

"Get back in the shadows," Reynolds muttered. "Just in case of."

"In case of what?"

"Might be some of Dupree's crew riding down to Rainbow," the tall cowboy warned. "Ma wasn't shore it was Hardy what killed Canuck Avery. If it's somebody else, we got to take them without shooting, on account of the gal."

Texas Joe shook his head. "We can't cut 'er that away," he answered positively. "If it's some of them other riders of Dupree's, best we have our cutters in our hands!"

"In the brush," Reynolds growled harshly. "And remember I said no shooting. Hardy would back-track shore as sin, and we got to think about Betty!"

Texas Joe merged with the shadows and grinned. " 'At's what I told you right along," he answered. "Now that you got that all settled in yore mind, spell out yore orders and I'll try to make you a hand."

"Me and you is slidin' down there to the bench," Reynolds explained in a whisper. "Then you stay in the rear to cover my back in case I need help. We got to stop those jiggers without shooting, and in case one of us goes down, the other one burns the hooves off his hoss getting down that river trail after Hardy and the gal!"

"Wait a minute, pard," Joe said suddenly. "There was only one shot fired at Canuck, and I hear two hosses. That tell you anything?"

Reynolds growled in his throat. "Not for shore," he muttered. "There could be two of them outlaws, because they always ride in pairs."

"It could be, but it ain't," Joe muttered angrily. "Mebbe so my ears is better than yores, but keen yore ear and see do you recognize that voice down on the trail!"

Roaming Reynolds leaned forward to listen. "Yo're right again, pard," he answered contritely.

"That voice belongs to Hip High Hardy. Now you ease back there where you can get Betty's hoss on the run when I make my play. And remember the Deacon layin' back there on the M T. Him and Betty was as good as promised!"

CHAPTER XI

Betty Tucker strained at the rawhide thong that bound her hands to the horn of her saddle. Cold, stark fear tugged at her heart to leave her weak and trembling when she glanced at the huge shoulders and powerful back of her captor. She steeled herself and set her jaw stubbornly when Hip High Hardy turned in the saddle. He was like some great predatory animal while he feasted on her full figure with hungry, lustful eyes.

"Eagle Dupree takes what he wants," he reminded her with a sneer. "He's been wanting you for quite a while, and he won't have to wait much longer!"

The girl turned her head and bit her lip. She was sure that Brigham Smith was dead, and then the fear in her heart forced a question from her pallid lips. A question that trembled to betray her agitation.

"Whom did you shoot back there in the granary on the M T?"

"Mebbe it was old Mormon Tucker himself," the outlaw answered, and his heavy shoulders twitched with sadistic amusement when the girl shuddered violently. "Then again it might have been that salty gun-slick, Roamin' Reynolds."

The girl clenched her teeth and squared her

shoulders. "You wouldn't dare face Reynolds unless you had the advantage," she said huskily. "You are the kind that would only shoot a man in the back. You prowl in the darkness like a mangy wolf!"

"I'll meet that buckaroo some day," Hardy growled viciously. "And when I do, it will be me who whittles!"

The girl smiled with relief. "Then it wasn't Roaming Reynolds you shot," she said quickly.

Hip High Hardy glared at her savagely. "Smart, ain't yuh?" he growled thickly. "But that ain't telling you who stopped my slug back there where they was shore nobody could come up on them!"

Betty Tucker gripped the horn of the saddle. She knew that the big granary was used for a council chamber, and that every man on the ranch would be at the meeting. The outlaw saw the fear in her eyes and grinned.

"Now you ain't so salty, are you?" he taunted. "Roaming Reynolds can't do much by his lonesome."

The girl stared at his heavy face and tried to read what was going on behind the little grey eyes. Then she drew a deep breath and nodded her head.

"They had a prisoner," she almost whispered. "They were going to ask him some questions!"

"It was Canuck Avery," the outlaw almost

shouted. "That yeller-belly was getting ready to tell everything he knowed like a squealing rat. Well, he won't do no talking now!"

Betty Tucker sighed with relief, and watched the cruel face with a sneer of contempt curling her full red lips. Her father and Roaming Reynolds were still alive, and she voiced the thought just to see her captor squirm.

"You can't do this thing, Hardy. Roaming Reynolds will kill you for what you did to Brigham Smith!"

"Huh? Reynolds hates the Deacon as much as I do," the outlaw growled. "Him a man of peace?"

"He was a man of courage," the girl answered slowly, and turned her head to listen to the far-away sound of her own voice. "He faced Canuck Avery empty-handed, and he got up out of bed to meet you."

"The damn fool," Hardy sneered. "You saw what he got both times!"

"But Reynolds is different," the girl reminded. "He won't face you with empty hands!"

The outlaw shrugged carelessly. "He won't face me at all," he grunted. "Besides that, he couldn't track us down in the dark, and it won't be long till we hit Rainbow Canyon."

"But you are afraid of him," the girl continued softly. "You know down in your heart that Reynolds is the better man."

Hip High Hardy dropped back and thrust his

stubbled face close to the girl. "Eagle Dupree wants everything, but he won't get it," he snarled, and the girl shrank from the ferocity etched in his features. "He can have you, because I never found nothing but trouble when I mixed up with women. After I turn you over to Eagle, I aim to ride out and meet that gun-slingin' cowboy. I'll smoke him down and let him lay where he falls!"

"I'm sorry I won't see you anymore," the girl purred throatily.

"You'll see plenty of me," Hardy grunted. "I run second to Eagle Dupree, and you got good eye-sight!"

The girl shook her head. "Not after you meet Roaming Reynolds," and her deep voice was positive. "I'm telling you, and I am sure of it!"

The outlaw growled in his throat and drew back his arm. "I ought to slap you to sleep," he rasped hoarsely. "I'd do it too, if it wasn't for Eagle Dupree!"

"You mean you fear Dupree?" and the girl faced him with shoulders back.

Hip High Hardy ground his teeth with rage. "Dupree is gun-boss up here in the Strip," he growled. "He's tops on the draw-and-shoot, but I ain't fool enough to play the game his way!"

"I think you will die, Hardy," the girl answered softly. "Either Dupree or Reynolds would kill you if you tried a gunman's sneak, and you know it!"

Hardy glared at her for a moment, and then he spurred ahead and tightened the bridle-reins between them. The girl smiled in the darkness when her horse started to move ahead. She had gained a little time; a space of minutes that might turn the tide of circumstances in her favour. She knew of the crossing between the M T ranch and the Vermilion Cliffs, and her woman's intuition was stronger than fear for herself. Hardy had made her mother promise to wait ten minutes, and if her mother had warned the men in time . . . ?

Hip High Hardy glanced up at the rising moon and turned to the right to meet the river. It would be safer riding in the shadow of the trees, and the horses needed a drink. He reined in on the shelving bank and swung to the ground while his eyes drifted across the river and back to the girl.

"Don't try nothing funny," he warned. "You'd only get yoreself killed if you went chousin' through the tangles with yore hands tied to the nubbin!"

"Thanks," the girl murmured. "The horses are thirsty."

Hardy grunted and loosed the cinches to allow the animals to drink. Then he reached for the makin's while the horses blew the cool water and drank deeply.

"Stand hitched!" a voice snapped from the darkness. "I'm coming to take yore guns!"

The outlaw stiffened and held his hands breast-high. His fingers opened slowly to let the half-rolled quirly spill to the ground. His grey eyes narrowed when he swung slowly around to face the voice, and his flat nostrils flared like a stallion when it scents danger at a water-hole.

The girl sat up straight in the saddle with the light of the moon glinting in her eyes. The outlaw's big chest heaved when Roaming Reynolds stepped out from the shadows holding the drop.

"Don't come any farther, Reynolds," and Hardy spread the fingers of both hands wide. "I'll match my draw again' yore drop!"

The tall cowboy stopped instantly. "Suicide," he sneered softly. "And you ain't ready to die yet!"

"I was just telling the gal that I was comin' to meet you," Hardy answered quietly, but his heavy voice held a pleading note. "She said you gave every man a chance!"

"I told him that he didn't dare face you for an even break," the girl corrected quickly. "He was going to hide in the brush and shoot you down without giving you a chance!"

"I was bringing it to you as soon as I got through doing what I was doing," Hardy growled savagely.

"You've done several things, feller," the cowboy grunted. "Might be just as well for you to think back on some of them!"

"Just before we left the M T," the girl interrupted again. "I saw him shoot Canuck Avery in the back!"

"So it was you?" Reynolds said slowly. "They call that murder, and it's just one more count agin' you."

"Mebbe you want to take a chance," Hardy sneered softly. "Yo're supposed to be fast with yore tools!"

A slim shadow detached itself from the trees and approached the two horses slowly. The girl sighed with relief when Texas Joe cut the rawhide thong and helped her from the high saddle. His eyes were fastened upon the face of Hip High Hardy, and he clicked back the hammer of the gun in his hand when the outlaw turned his head and stared.

"You never saw the day you could beat Roamin'," he spat, and swivelled his head to scan the hard face of Roaming Reynolds. "Remember yore promise, pard," he reminded in his twangy drawl.

The outlaw shifted his big boots and shrugged his wide shoulders. Unlike Canuck Avery, he did not know the meaning of physical fear. His voice was quiet and steady when he turned to face Reynolds with a question.

"I don't booger easy. What was the promise he's yappin' about?"

"Mebbe you recollect Utah Young," the cow-

162

boy replied, and his voice was even and low. "He told me about this short-cut over the hills to cut down yore lead. Utah is kin to Betty yonder, and the Mormons protect their women-folks like you know. Utah asked me to kill you!"

No melodrama; just a calm statement of facts. The girl shuddered at the grim finality of it all. Certain things that been done, and other things would be done about it. These men lived by the gun, and some of them would die the same way.

Hip High Hardy skinned back his thin lips in a leering grin. Here was something he could meet on common ground. Canuck Avery had squealed and he had paid with his life. Utah Young was a Mormon and kin to the girl he had captured for Eagle Dupree. And Utah Young had exacted a promise. The outlaw raised his head and stared at Reynolds.

"And you promised him," he said with a chuckle.

The tall cowboy did not smile. No emotion on his hard face except for the smoky blue between narrowed eye-lids. His jaw was edged with little ridges of muscle that stood out boldly in the moonlight.

"I promised!"

"And the gal was telling me that you gave every man a chance," Hardy continued. "Did she have that part of it right?"

Roaming Reynolds leaned forward from the

163

hips, and his face was like chiselled rock. "That's right," he agreed, and his voice sounded like the flat crack of rifle-fire in the distance. "You talked yoreself into a tight back yonder on the trail. We heard you yammerin' five minutes before you showed around the bend!"

Hip High Hardy turned his head and glared at the girl. "Now I know why you baited me," he growled. "Kept me talking so them two could hide-out and grab a sneak!"

"I felt sure they would come," the girl answered steadily. "I was trying to make up for that ten minutes you made Mother wait, and I knew that Texas Joe would hear your voice. He has the keenest hearing in the Strip."

"And I heard you spinning yore windy," Texas Joe sneered. "Tellin' it scarey because you wasn't facin' a man!"

"I'm facing one now," Hardy answered softly. "And waiting for that chance yore pard boasted about."

Roaming Reynolds moved his hand to call attention to the heavy gun. "You attacked a wounded man, Hardy," he said quietly. "You don't know the Mormon breed, and with luck he will live in spite of what you done."

"Too bad," the outlaw sneered, and again he glanced at the girl. "That makes it kinda tough for you, cowboy."

Roaming Reynolds jabbed angrily with the

gun, and then restrained his temper. "It won't work, killer," he sneered faintly. "Right now we are talking about you. You laid hands on the gal yonder, but you didn't do her no hurt to speak of. That right, Betty?" and he waited for her answer.

"That's right, Roaming. He tied my hands to the saddle-horn like you saw. Said he was keeping me for Eagle Dupree."

"Eagle takes what he wants," the outlaw sneered. "The gal won't be no different!"

Roaming Reynolds straightened and stared at the mean face while he tried to control the emotions that raced through his brain. Then he shook himself and addressed Hardy in the same quiet tone.

"I'm talking about you, Hardy. Telling you these things before I kill you, because you got to die. I made a promise, and I never break my word!"

"Quite a preacher, ain't you?" the outlaw sneered. "Stealing the Deacon's thunder!"

"Yeah," the tall cowboy agreed quietly. "I've learned a lot of things from the Deacon in the last few days. That big feller don't know what it means to quit, but we're still talking about you. I never did cotton none to a hoss thief!"

Hardy jerked suddenly erect. "Hard names, Mister," he growled. "But you don't need to pour it on to start gun-smoke!"

Roaming Reynolds nodded slowly. "I said hoss thief," he repeated.

Realization glowed in the outlaw's grey eyes. "So Canuck talked before my slug got him," he taunted. "That makes me out a rustler, so what we waiting for?"

"Just wanted to make shore," Reynolds grunted and holstered the gun on his leg with a flip of his wrist. "I hired out to clean the M T range of rustlers, but I had to get proof. Start smokin' when ready!"

Betty Tucker caught at her throat and clutched Texas Joe by the arm. The button was smiling like a hound that scents the kill after a long chase. No sentiment or mercy in his hard young face, and to show his confidence in the ability of his pard he sheathed his old single-action in the worn scabbard on his thin leg.

Roaming Reynolds was balanced on the thin soles of his hand-made boots. His right hand was hooked in the belt above his gun, and his narrowed eyes were unwinking while he watched the gunman ten short paces away. Hardy deliberately turned his head and stared at Texas Joe and the girl, and he grinned wolfishly when he saw the button with empty hands.

"Better than I expected," he sneered, and his face twisted into a killer's mask of savage cruelty. "All I lose is a little time."

"Yo're losing *all* the time you got," Texas Joe whispered thinly.

Hip High Hardy shrugged and turned to face Reynolds with both hands on his hips. The backs were toward the cowboy with thick fingers touching the reversed butts while he cradled both elbows against his ribs. A smile of confidence spread across the brutal face when he started the famous flip-draw without warning.

The cowboy leaped sideways with his hand plunging down for his gun. Twin blossoms of fire gouted out from the muzzles of Hardy's forty-fives when the killer turned his wrists with an explosive jerk. Roaming Reynolds drew smoothly with the first joint of his thumb dogging back the hammer, and he slipped it when the gunsight lined down under his right eye. Slipped it twice to make the two reports blend together, and Hip High Hardy spread his thick arms wide to flip his guns away when he plunged forward on his face.

The tall cowboy caught the bucking gun on the recoil and crouched forward to watch his enemy. Hardy never moved except for the drumming toes of his big boots that rattled out an emphatic requiem. When the tattoo stopped to leave a strange hush on the river bank, Reynolds cat-footed forward on stiff legs and flipped the body over with his left hand.

For a long moment he studied the staring eyes

as though he were trying to read some hidden message. Then he reached down and covered the brutal face with the battered old black Stetson. Picked up the outlaw's guns and stuck them thoughtfully down in his belt.

"You get him centre, Roamin'?" Texas Joe drawled in his deepest bass.

"Plumb centre, button," the cowboy answered as carelessly. "A promise is a promise. Don't you ever forget it!"

"I won't, pard," the boy grunted. "That jigger had it comin', and he used up all his time."

Betty Tucker turned her back and sobbed with reaction. Texas Joe glanced at her and back to Reynolds. Puckered up his thin face when he leaned over to whisper advice to the cowboy.

"Better smooth her out, pard. She ain't used to seein' hoss thieves get their needin's like us men folks. Better tell her, feller."

Roaming Reynolds scowled and punched the spent shells from his old Peacemaker. Thumbed fresh cartridges through the loading gate while he stared moodily at the shaking shoulders of the sobbing girl.

"You smooth her out, Joe," he growled in a whisper. "She'd buck like a knot-head account of me keeping my promise to Utah Young. I ain't got no idea what to say right now."

Texas Joe hitched up his gunbelt and took a deep breath. Then he high-heeled across the short grass and laid a grimy hand on the girl's shoulder. She shook his grip loose and sniffled through her fingers.

"Don't touch me. You are just a killer like those terrible outlaws. I could see it in your face!"

"It's me, Miss Betty," the boy whispered. "Texas Joe come to tell you how come Roamin' had to rub Hip High out that away."

"He didn't have to kill him," the girl sobbed. "He could have taken his guns when we first rode up. I thought he was fine and strong after he brought Canuck Avery to the M T alive!"

"He *is* fine and strong," the boy defended loyally. "Dag nab you nohow, you buckin' jughead. Roamin' comes out here and risks his life to save you from Eagle Dupree what packs a pocketful of feathers. What do you do? Rares all up and spills him a lot of Sunday School talk. Right now you'd be in Eagle Dupree's clutches if my pard hadn't vowed him a promise!"

The girl dried her eyes and turned to stare at the boy's angry face. His lips were twisted defiantly, and he turned on his heel with a shrug of impatience. Betty Tucker caught his arm and swung him around to face her.

"What did he promise Utah?" she asked in a little voice.

"Utah said he would tell Roamin' a short-cut to the river providing Roamin' made a promise to

169

kill Hip High Hardy. It was the onliest way he could save you in time!"

"But he killed him," the girl protested.

"Hardy was faster than any of them Mormons," Texas Joe sneered. "And every one of them snortin' to give Hardy show-down. He'd have killed the lot and whittled his notches. This away, all them fellers is still alive!"

"Oh! I am so sorry," and the girl ran across the clearing to Reynolds. "Can you ever forgive me, Roaming?"

The cowboy shrugged. "I hired my guns to yore father," he muttered. "And I always keep a promise once I passes my word."

"But he might have killed you," Texas interrupted bluntly. "You let him draw and take first shot!"

"I didn't let him draw first," the cowboy corrected. "They ain't a gunnie living who could beat that flip-draw, but I never saw one yet that could call his shots!"

"So that's how come you to side-slip that away while you was makin' yore draw," the button muttered softly. "Then you started smokin' before he could trigger back for a follow-up!"

"That's reading the sign, button," Reynolds grunted without emotion. "That flip-draw is only good close up. Now we better line out for the M T before Betty's dad starts looking for us."

"Will you forgive me, Roaming?" the girl

asked, and her throaty voice was a soft whisper of pleading.

"You didn't do nothing," the cowboy answered irritably. "Right now yo're needed bad back on the M T. Brigham Smith was out of his head when we fogged away from there."

The girl sighed and nodded slowly. "You are right, as usual," she agreed quietly, and turned away to hide the tears of disappointment in her dark eyes. "If only Brigham was a fighting man," she murmured regretfully.

The cowboy waited until Texas Joe tightened the cinches and led up the horses. The girl was in the saddle when they rode to meet her, and Reynolds waved his hand in the direction that Hardy had taken when he brought the girl to the clearing.

"We'll go back the long way," he decided.

"Roamin', what about Hip High?"

Reynolds glanced at Texas Joe and shrugged indifferently. "Some of them owl-hooted buckaroos will find him before morning," he grunted without feeling. "Let 'em bury their own folks; I didn't sign on to dig any holes!"

The girl shuddered. "That isn't like you," she reproved.

"No, ma'am, it ain't," Reynolds agreed. "But Eagle Dupree is on the loose, and our duty right now is to the living. We better be high-tailing back to the M T!"

CHAPTER XII

The moon was high when the three riders came up the long lane and cantered into the big ranch yard of the M T. Betty Tucker signalled for silence when a yellow square of light plainly marked the window of the room where Brigham Smith had made his gallant effort. Then she came closer to Roaming Reynolds and whispered softly.

"Not yet, Roaming. I want to go to my room and tidy up a bit before he sees me. You and Joe talk to our men while I am gone."

The tall cowboy frowned in the darkness. "The Deacon won't pay no mind to yore clothes to-night," he muttered. "And you keep yore cutter right close to yore hand."

The girl smiled and patted his arm. "It is your gun, Roaming," and she rubbed the worn handle. "I always feel safer when my fingers touch it."

"Them folks will see you," Texas Joe growled. "How you aim to get past 'em?"

"Through the back way," the girl whispered. "Please go out to the barns and talk to the men."

Roaming Reynolds nodded and walked his horse across the big yard in the shadows. He turned his head to watch the girl making her way toward the back of the big house, and Texas Joe came closer, in answer to the nodding head.

"Yo're light on yore feet, button. Cut around back there and watch out for Miss Betty. Don't let her see you, but keep yore eyes peeled."

Texas Joe slid from the saddle and hugged up close to the big house while Reynolds took the bridle reins and led the extra horse across the yard. Betty Tucker was just entering the door of her room when Texas Joe peered through the wide back door. He could hear the murmur of voices coming from the Deacon's room far up the hall, and his thin face was serious when he recognized the deep bass of Mormon Tucker.

Crouching in the shadows, his hand reached out slowly and touched the great brass knob. He stiffened when something hard and round bored into his spine, and he half-turned to stare at the tall figure of the man who had brought all of the trouble to the M T.

"Dupree," he whispered, and tried to stop the trembling that swept over him.

"Hands high, button," the outlaw answered softly. "I take what I want, and I came personal to get it!"

Texas Joe clenched his teeth and shook himself angrily. Then his right hand swept down desperately in an effort to reach his gun. He knew that he could not beat the outlaw to the shot, but he also knew that the roar of guns would bring Roaming Reynolds on the double quick.

A muscular arm rose swiftly behind him. Came

173

clubbing down viciously to smash the battered old Stetson around the ears of the twisting cowboy. Texas Joe buckled his knees and slid against the door without making a sound, and strong hands caught him and dragged him back in the shadows. A moment later the tall figure straightened up and passed through the door with the stealth of a panther.

Not the whisper of sound as he cat-footed down the dimly-lighted hall and paused before the door of Betty Tucker's room. His left hand reached out and fastened on the knob; turned slowly and pushed the door open a crack. Then the intruder stopped to listen, and a slow smile broke the straight line of his lips.

Betty Tucker was bathing her face in a big stone bowl in one corner of the room. The splashing water drowned the slight noise when Eagle Dupree came through the door and closed it gently behind him. He leaned his square shoulders against the oaken panels and waited until the girl reached for a husk towel and buried her face. He coughed gently when she hung up the towel with a sigh, and Betty Tucker jerked erect with the colour rushing to her rosy face.

"You!" she whispered tensely. "You dared to come here?"

"I dare anything, my dear," he answered softly. "And now I must warn you not to raise your voice."

"Leave this house at once or I will scream," the girl answered in a throaty whisper. "You can't escape alive."

The outlaw shrugged carelessly. "Perhaps not," he agreed. "But I can kill the ones you love before they get me. Do you think it is worth it?"

Betty Tucker sighed and dropped her eyes. "What do you want?"

"You!"

The girl shuddered violently. "I would die first," she said slowly. "Whenever I look at you, I think of a killer-wolf creeping through the shadows of night!"

Eagle Dupree frowned while his eyes narrowed with cruelty. Then he crossed the room slowly with gun spiking out from his hand. The girl shrank back until her shoulders touched the wall, and the outlaw advanced slowly and lifted the gun from her holster with his left hand. He tossed it on the low bed while the gun in his right hand came up slowly and pressed against the swelling breast just over the girl's heart.

"Scream," he invited softly. "And I will leave this in your pretty black hair."

His hand went to the pocket of his vest and came away with an eagle feather. Betty Tucker stared at the feather with fear in her brown eyes. The outlaw smiled and circled her waist with his left arm.

"Scream," he repeated softly, and his purring

voice held a challenge he knew would not be accepted. "When you do, you are marking Mormon Tucker and Brigham Smith for death!"

Betty Tucker was tall for a girl, but the outlaw towered above her and stared down into her eyes. She could feel the steely strength of his arm; could feel the throb of racing blood pounding through his veins. The look of fear left her eyes to be replaced by a slow smile that held a suggestion of contempt.

"I won't scream," she said softly. "I won't have to."

Eagle Dupree studied her face. "Meaning . . . ?"

"Roaming Reynolds and Texas Joe came back with me," the girl continued. "I am sure that one of them guarded my door."

The outlaw relaxed with a smile. "Right," he agreed. "That half-grown button was at the back door, but he listened to reason."

Betty Tucker tried to wrench away. "You killed him," she accused breathlessly.

Eagle Dupree tightened his arm and shook his head one time. "I don't kill children," he contradicted softly. "Right now he is sleeping back there in the shrubs. I merely tapped him on the head to save his life."

Betty Tucker took a deep breath and flushed when the outlaw tightened his arm with the fires of desire glowing in his dark eyes. The heavy wool shirt could not hide the beauty of her full figure, and she closed her eyes to shut out the sight of his face.

"You beast," she moaned, and then she jerked back with her eyes opened wide. "You forgot," she said quietly.

The outlaw shook his head. "I didn't forget Roaming Reynolds," he contradicted, and once more his face took on the predatory expression of a hunting wolf. "I have a feather for him if he should blunder across my path."

Betty Tucker shuddered and clenched her hands tightly. "You can't win," she whispered. "You better go while you can."

Eagle Dupree stepped back toward the bed and forced the girl to a seat. "I want to talk first," he murmured. "If you raise your voice . . . ?"

He waved the heavy gun in his hand and sat down beside his trembling prisoner. Now his darkly handsome face was a mask of cruelty while he stared at her and caressed the tiny black moustaches above his full red lips.

"What do you want to know?"

"Canuck Avery," and the outlaw's voice was a silky whisper. "He shot the Deacon, and Roaming Reynolds took Canuck prisoner. Did Canuck talk any before Hardy shut his mouth?"

"I was not there," the girl answered honestly. "I was with Brigham and my mother. The men talked to Avery out in the granary."

"But you know," the outlaw insisted. "I asked

you if Canuck did any talking," and a savage undertone edged his voice to a rough growl.

"Hardy shot him with a rifle," the girl whispered, and closed her eyes. "Hardy came into the Deacon's room and took me prisoner. He nearly killed Brigham!"

"You mean the Deacon tried to stop Hip High?"

"He got right up out of bed," the girl answered proudly. "That beast hit him twice with his gun!"

"Your mother?"

"He tied her up with sheets," the girl whispered with a shudder, and then she straightened her shoulders. "But Mother is safe," she taunted. "I heard her voice in Brigham's room."

"She sent Reynolds after Hardy," Dupree snarled. "There was shooting down by the river. Well?"

"You can't beat Roaming Reynolds," the girl answered confidently. "Yes, there were shots down by the river. Hip High Hardy is dead!"

The outlaw stepped back and tightened his lips. "Reynolds?" he whispered.

The girl glanced at the wavering candle and nodded her head. For a moment her head tilted as though she was listening, but the outlaw was absorbed in his own thoughts. Murmuring voices continued to drift down the hall from the sickroom, and Betty Tucker was no longer trembling when she answered.

"Yes—Reynolds. Hardy boasted of his flip-draw, and he shot first. Reynolds gave him a chance and then he waved his right hand and shot one time."

"Two times," Dupree corrected harshly.

"They sounded like one," the girl murmured. "And Hip High Hardy is dead!"

Eagle Dupree stared at her with anger blazing in his eyes. "For every man I have lost, a Mormon will die," he promised grimly. "As for Hardy, I have no room in my band for failures."

"He was a beast, but he was a brave man," the girl defended quietly, and reached out her hand slowly as though to rest on the bed.

Eagle Dupree leaped forward and grabbed her by the wrist. Twitched the girl to her feet and against his broad chest with one sudden pull, and the gun pressed against her heart when she opened her mouth to scream.

"I ought to kill you," he whispered roughly. "I saw you try to get that gun on the bed. Now you are coming with me unless you want to wear a feather in your hair!"

The girl tried to push herself away with both hands against his chest. Then she shuddered and ceased to struggle when the gun prodded viciously.

"I will go," she whispered. "If you will promise not to shoot any of our people."

Eagle Dupree smiled and loosed his grip. "Not

unless they get in my way," he promised, and started toward the door.

He stopped as suddenly when steps sounded in the hall. His eyes whipped around to the girl when the thud of high heels came closer. Betty Tucker covered her lips with her hand while her brown eyes widened with a stare of fear. Eagle Dupree turned his gun to cover her when he moved closer to the big window.

"Betty," a deep voice whispered. "You all right, gal?"

Eagle Dupree nodded his head and eared back the hammer of his gun. "Quite alright, Roaming," the girl answered. "I will be out in a moment."

"Can I come in for a moment?"

The girl clenched her hands. "No, no," she cried frantically. "I—I am not dressed!"

Eagle Dupree waved his gun and motioned toward the window. The girl shook her head stubbornly and refused to move. They could hear the creak of boot leather in the hall, as though the tall cowboy were undecided.

"Through this window," Dupree whispered. "Or I will kill him when he opens that door!"

"I'll be with you in a moment," the girl called to Reynolds. "Don't come in, Roaming!"

"Where's Joe?" the cowboy demanded roughly. "I sent him to guard yore door!"

"Joe is alright," the girl answered quickly, and

tried to keep the tremble from her voice. "He went to get me some water."

Eagle Dupree was straddling the window-sill with one long leg outside. He stared at the trembling girl and motioned with his gun, but she shook her head stubbornly and refused to move.

"Shoot," she whispered. "And you will be dead before you can find out if you were faster than Roaming Reynolds!"

"I'm coming in, Betty," a hoarse whisper announced from the hall. "Unless you open that door right away!"

Eagle Dupree swung his gun to cover the door while his eyes narrowed. Betty Tucker threw herself suddenly to the floor and rolled under the bed just as a heavy shoulder hit the door. Eagle Dupree swung his leg and dropped from the sill just as the door flew open, and Roaming Reynolds barged into the room with spurred boots shifting for balance.

His blue eyes swept across the bed to the open window, and then the tall cowboy threw himself to the floor beside the bed. He crouched there for a moment until a scraping sound came to his ears, and his left hand clutched a small boot and pulled with a jerk.

"Roaming," a throaty voice protested. "You nearly broke my ankle."

A pair of hands clutched at his arms when the girl pulled herself to her knees beside him. A pair

181

of arms circled his neck and clung to him while sobs shook the girl when she buried her face on his shoulder.

"I was afraid he would kill you," she moaned.

Roaming Reynolds tried to release himself, but the girl tightened her arms and pressed closer. The cowboy covered the window with his gun, and his blue eyes were hard and cold when he jerked a savage question.

"Who was here with you?"

The girl shuddered. "Eagle Dupree," she sobbed. "He threatened to kill us all unless I went with him."

"Joe?" the cowboy almost shouted. "What become of Joe?"

The girl stopped crying and levered to her feet. "Dupree must have hit him with his gun," she answered, and started for the door. "He said Joe was out among the shrubs!"

Roaming Reynolds passed her and leaped through the door. Raced down the hall and through the back door with the girl following closely. His high heels threw gravel when he slid to a stop and jerked his head down to search the bushes close to the house. Then he ran forward and gripped a pair of rusty boots that stuck out from the heavy growth.

"Pard," he muttered huskily. "You alright, Joe?"

He pulled the boy into the moonlight and raised

the limp body in his strong arms. Forgotten was Eagle Dupree and his threats when he stared into the thin tanned face resting on his arm. Then he picked up the boy and carried him back up the hall and into Betty Tucker's room. Laid Joe on the bed while the girl ran to the stone basin and returned with a wet towel.

"Easy," Reynolds warned gruffly. "He might rouse out a-fightin'!"

Betty Tucker bathed the tousled head tenderly. Texas Joe began to slap down for his holster thonged low on his worn chaps. Roaming Reynolds tightened his arms and whispered softly.

"Easy, pard. It's Roamin' holding you, Tex, ole pard!"

Texas Joe stiffened to listen and then tried to sit up. "Blow out that damn candle!" he snarled. "Eagle Dupree is hidin' in the bushes to dry-gulch yuh!"

"He's gone, Joe," the girl answered quietly. "I kept him talking here until Roaming got restless and came to look for you."

Texas Joe rubbed his head and glared at the girl. "You had a gun on yore laig," he snarled. "Whyn't yuh salivate that killer when you had the chance?"

"Easy, button," Reynolds interrupted. "You likewise had a cutter on yore own leg, and I sent you up here to guard Miss Betty."

183

Texas Joe sniffed and dropped his eyes. "I got oncommon good hearin'," he growled. "But I never heard that wolf back there by the door. He had a gun in my back before I could sneeze, and he slapped me to sleep when I made a pass for my cutter. I'm sorry for what I done said, Miss Betty."

The girl smiled and patted his arm. "You did the best you could, Joe," she answered. "He would have taken me away with him if you hadn't been back there by the door."

"I should have got him," the boy muttered. "And you say he come on in here?"

The girl nodded her head slowly. "Mother and Dad are down there with Brigham," she whispered. "They never heard any of the noise, and it's a good thing they didn't. Dupree threatened to kill all of us if I gave warning!"

"Don't know how he got past us," Reynolds muttered.

"He must have come the short-cut from Rainbow Canyon," the girl offered. "He heard the shots down by the river."

"Yeah?" and the tall cowboy loosed the heavy gun in his holster. "Reckon I better try and cut his sign!"

Betty Tucker grabbed his arms and clung tightly. "You mustn't," she cried. "He would hide out there in the shadows and kill you. You must wait until daylight!"

"That's good sense, pard," Texas Joe growled, and walked across the room to plunge his sandy head in the basin of water.

Roaming Reynolds waited until the boy came up for air and dried his face on the husk towel. Betty Tucker still held him by the arms, and he released himself with an impatient jerk. The girl glanced at his craggy face and shrank back holding a hand to her lips.

"Don't look like that," she whispered. "You look just like Eagle Dupree looked when he promised to kill a Mormon for every man he lost!"

"He said that, eh?" and Reynolds allowed a smile to soften his lips. Then he wheeled on Texas Joe and jerked his head toward the door.

"You see any of the men?" he barked.

"You know dang well I never," Joe snarled. "Me layin' out there dead to the world!"

"Let me think," Reynolds muttered. "I never saw hide nor hair of none of the crew since we got back. You reckon they might be up there with the Deacon?"

"Father wouldn't allow that," the girl answered slowly. "Not with Brigham being as sick as he is. Do you think—?"

"Naw," Reynolds growled irritably. "Dupree ain't had time to kill any of them fellers yet. You been in to see the Deacon?"

The girl shook her head. "Like Joe, I haven't

185

had time," she answered. "I came back here to freshen up a bit, and Dupree came in while I was drying my face."

"Got it to do," Reynolds muttered. "We better go up and find out how yore Ma and the Deacon is making out," and he picked up the gun from the bed. "You keep yore hand close to this from now on," he growled, and holstered the heavy weapon in the worn scabbard on her right leg.

"You better stay out of that room, Roamin'," Texas Joe warned in a low whisper. "The Deacon will strip yore hardware shore as sin if you go bargin' in there now."

The tall cowboy stared for a moment while the changing emotions swept across his rugged face. Then he shrugged and shook his head.

"Not to-night he won't," he said confidently. "Lead out, Miss Betty!"

CHAPTER XIII

Mormon Tucker and his wife sat on opposite sides of the big four-poster and watched the bearded face of Brigham Smith. Even in repose there was an austere dignity about the stern features, and in the set of the muscular shoulders and powerful neck. Purposeful and determined so that even unconsciousness could not conceal the character of the real man.

"It has been a long time," Ma Tucker murmured softly. "He hasn't moved, Father."

Even as she spoke the wounded man stirred restlessly and his lips moved to form words that were foreign to his ways of thinking. Ma Tucker glanced at her husband and smiled grimly with her lips.

"Don't touch the girl, Hardy! I'll kill you if you dare to lay hands on Betty!"

"Amen," Mormon Tucker murmured solemnly. "Spoken like a man. Is he conscious, Ma?"

Ma Tucker shook her head slowly and leaned forward to watch the gently-moving lips. "He's out of his head," she whispered. "But sometimes folks change their minds while they sleep when something big enough enters their lives. Be very quiet now, husband."

Silently they stared at the great muscled torso

of Brigham Smith, whom men called the Deacon, skin so white it looked like marble where the black silky beard lay upon his chest. Like a sleeping giant coming out of deep slumber to continue his battles.

He suddenly ceased to twitch and became very still as though gathering his reserve forces. Ma Tucker leaned forward anxiously; caught her breath when she saw his dark eyes regarding her with moody watchfulness. As though he were trying to adjust himself to his surroundings before committing himself. Then he tried to rise to a sitting position, and Mormon Tucker stretched out a big hand and restrained him gently while his deep voice hummed against his lips.

"Easy, Deacon," he murmured, and held the big man down. "Take it easy for a while, son."

Brigham Smith turned his eyes and locked glances with his employer. "Betty?" he asked quietly, and his rumbling voice was surprisingly strong. "Is she safe, Mormon?"

Mormon Tucker nodded his head slowly. "I am sure she is safe, Deacon," he answered confidently. "Don't try to talk now; you received a terrible blow on the head."

The wounded man continued to stare. "Ma and Betty were sitting here with me," he recited carefully, and his face was serious as he pieced things together. "Hip High Hardy came through that window yonder, and he took Betty's gun away from her."

"He did not harm her," Mormon Tucker answered, but his eyes fell before that steady gaze that bored into his very thoughts.

The Deacon sat up in bed in spite of restraining hands. "Look at me, Tucker," and his deep voice vibrated commandingly. "Look me in the eyes and tell me again!"

"You will hurt yourself," Ma Tucker interrupted anxiously. "You must remember your wounds, Brigham. Do lie down again!"

The Deacon shrugged and continued to stare at Mormon Tucker. "Where is Betty?" he demanded sternly.

"I tell you Betty is safe," Tucker muttered, but his eyes wandered toward the window. "She should be coming in most any time now!"

"I asked you where she is," and the Deacon leaned forward.

Mormon Tucker bit his lip and turned to meet that accusing level stare. "Hardy took Betty with him," he confessed frankly. "She had to go to save you and her mother, but I tell you that she is safe!"

Brigham Smith clenched his big fists until the muscles rippled across his chest and arms like thick ropes. He looked like a prehistoric gladiator from an old book, or a grizzly that sweeps all opposition before it. In spite of his wounds, he

189

radiated strength and vitality while he fought to control his natural physical impulses.

"Safe in the hands of Hardy?" and his deep voice boomed accusingly while he stared sternly at Mormon Tucker. "You tell me that she is safe after what Eagle Dupree has promised?"

His hands wandered across the pillow while he tried to marshal his thoughts. His left hand stopped suddenly, and his eyes contracted when he turned his head and glanced at the ends of his exploring fingers.

"By the Prophet," he murmured in a whisper that told of his agitation. "Give to me a sign!"

An eagle feather was tucked under the pillow, and he pulled it out slowly and stared in silence. Mormon and Ma Tucker leaned forward while the breath wheezed noisily in their aching lungs. Only the Deacon was calm as he read the sign for which he had prayed.

"The feather is not broken," he said quietly. "She is still safe, Mormon Tucker!"

"I knew it," Tucker nodded, and drew a deep breath to fill his chest. "I had a feeling that she would return unharmed!"

"Betty would kill herself before she would submit," Ma Tucker whispered, and turned her comely face to hide a tear. "She is a Mormon," she added proudly.

"Hardy took her for Eagle Dupree," Mormon Tucker muttered, and his voice sounded weak and far away while he stared at the window. "He got in while we were holding trial on Canuck Avery in the granary."

The Deacon stared moodily with the lines of thought furrowing his forehead. Calm and quiet, with only the fire in his dark eyes to mark the raging fury in his heart. He turned to look at Ma Tucker when she sighed tremulously.

"Get me my clothes at once," and Brigham Smith started to kick back the hand-loomed sheets.

"You cannot get up now, son," and Ma Tucker pushed him back on the pillows. "Roaming Reynolds started right out after Hardy while you were unconscious. That is why Father said Betty is safe!"

Brigham Smith panted like a spent deer while anger flamed deep in his eyes. "That gun-boss! That wandering killer from the waste-lands!"

Withering scorn and contempt in his deep voice while his hands clenched until the knuckles cracked. Mormon Tucker returned the stare and nodded slowly.

"The gun-boss," he agreed quietly. "He likes you, Deacon. He has helped you several times in spite of your attitude toward him. He could have killed you several times, but he understands you better than you understand yourself. He will bring Betty back to us!"

The Deacon became strangely silent, but his dark eyes glowed like burning coals. He stared at his big hands, turned his eyes down to study the tight bandages on his lean corded belly. Mormon Tucker watched him anxiously; sighed when the big foreman shrugged his shoulders.

"She loves him," he muttered, but his rumbling voice was doubtful. As though he wanted to hear someone else deny the accusation aloud.

Mormon Tucker shook his head. "She admires him, Deacon," he corrected softly. "These outlaws have nearly ruined the M T, and we Mormons did nothing about it. Roaming Reynolds fought fire with fire, and he sold his guns in the cause of Right!"

"I am not a fighting man," and the Deacon closed his eyes. "Betty has shown all of us that she wants someone who will fight for her. I am a man of peace!"

"But you spoke just before you opened your eyes," Mormon Tucker answered softly, and there was a smile on his face. "You spoke the *real* thoughts of your mind, Brigham Smith!"

The Deacon opened his eyes slowly and stared at Mormon Tucker. "I don't understand," he muttered. "What did I say while my mind was beyond my control?"

"You threatened to kill Hip High Hardy if he laid his hands on Betty!"

Brigham Smith nodded calmly. "With my bare

hands," he said grimly. "A Mormon protects his women-folks."

Mormon Tucker sighed and turned away to hide his disappointment. "It cannot be done that way," he said wearily. "I thought for a moment—?"

"You thought that I would kill wantonly with the weapons of the outlaws," the Deacon interrupted bitterly. "You thought that I would destroy my fellow men for the privilege of gaining life for myself!"

"Samson destroyed ten thousand Philistines with the jaw-bone of an ass," Mormon Tucker quoted sonorously.

"Did David fight Goliath with his bare hands?" and Ma Tucker leaned across the bed to lend force to her question. "Did the hosts of the Lord fight with their bare hands at Jericho?"

Brigham Smith sat up suddenly. "They fought in the cause of Right," he boomed, and his great voice throbbed with the sudden knowledge of discovery. "What a fool I have been!"

"They shall wander from darkness into Light," Mormon Tucker quoted thankfully. "Sometimes it takes the fire that sears the soul to make that light, Brigham!"

His eyes swung around to the door when a sharp rap sounded on the panel. Then the door was opened suddenly, and Utah Young stepped into the room and cleared his throat.

"We need you at once, Mormon," he announced,

and tried to keep his voice quiet. "Will you come with me?" and he glanced meaningly at the wounded man.

Mormon Tucker was on his feet like a cat. "Yes?" he barked sharply. "Speak up, man!"

"One of our men has just come in from the north pasture where we are holding that stock for shipping. He just about got here," and the tall rider stared at the Deacon with resentment showing plainly on his tanned face.

"Who was the rider?" Tucker asked quietly, but his eyes held a new light of determination.

"It was Sam Smith," Utah explained slowly. "He was shot through the shoulder, but he got away to bring us the news."

"Talk up, man," and Brigham Smith glared at Utah Young with little ridges of muscle playing about his lips. "Who shot young Sam?"

"Outlaws," Utah explained briefly. "They made a raid while all this other excitement was taking place. They drove off that forty head of gentled saddle-stock we were holding for the Diamond Bar!"

"And they shot my brother Sam," the big foreman murmured to himself. "Shot him because he would not protect himself."

Utah Young grinned savagely. "Sam protected himself," he corrected grimly. "He killed one of those raiders, and wounded another one after they shot him through the shoulder. Then he came fogging in to warn us back here at the ranch. Sam wasn't too proud to fight!"

"You mean they are coming to attack us here?" and Ma Tucker rose to her feet and gripped the tall buckaroo by the arms. "Right here on the M T?"

Utah Young stared steadily into her brown eyes. "They are coming," he muttered gruffly. "So I told the other boys to get their rifles and shells and man the granary. You better come on out, Boss!"

Brigham Smith tried to rise, but sank back with a groan of pain. "I can't get up," he muttered. "If Roaming Reynolds was here to help us!"

He held up a hand when high heels thudded on the planking out in the hall. Utah Young crossed the room in three strides and threw open the door. He shouted with excitement when he whirled to face the watchers by the bed of Brigham Smith.

"It's them! Roaming Reynolds and Texas Joe, and they brought Betty back with them. You got yore wish, Deacon!"

"Get back to the granary," and the voice of Brigham Smith was stronger. "Tell the boys to kill every outlaw they see. You better go with them, Mormon!"

Mormon Tucker whirled on his heel and ran from the room with Utah Young. He met Roaming Reynolds in the hall, and paused to take his daughter in his powerful arms. Then he

195

gripped the tall cowboy by the hand and stared into the cold blue eyes for a long moment.

"The Deacon wants to see you, Reynolds," he whispered with a smile. "We have another mighty fighting man on the M T now, thanks to you and your steadfast courage!"

"I better not go in, Boss," Reynolds said quietly. "I admire the Deacon, but the man don't live who can take my guns from me when I am facing him. You know that without me telling you, Mormon!"

Mormon Tucker smiled broadly. "Brigham wants to fight the outlaws," he explained, and failed to hide the happiness in his deep voice. "Go in and see him while I help the boys in the granary. Eagle Dupree is leading his pack against the M T!"

As Tucker broke away and followed Utah Young through the back door, Roaming Reynolds turned to the girl and Texas Joe. "Guard the front door just in case of, button," he told the boy. "Me and Betty will stop and see the Deacon. You go in first, Betty."

Betty Tucker gripped his hands tightly and stared up into his face. "Don't fight with Brigham," she pleaded earnestly. "Please, Roaming!"

The cowboy smiled. "Yore father said he has changed," he reminded her. "We'll go in together."

Brigham Smith smiled hungrily when Roaming Reynolds pushed the girl into the room. Held out his hand and pulled the girl to a seat beside him while he searched her pretty face anxiously. Then he sighed contentedly and spoke to Roaming Reynolds.

"You met Hip High Hardy?"

The cowboy nodded. "I met him!"

"He is dead?"

"I always keep my promises!"

Brigham Smith looked puzzled. "I don't understand what you mean, Reynolds. Do you mind making yourself clear?"

"Utah Young told Roaming about that short-cut to the river," the girl interrupted. "He and Texas Joe were waiting there when Hardy and I came along on our way to Rainbow Canyon."

"But this promise," the wounded man prompted.

"Utah made Roaming promise to kill Hardy for what he did to you and me," the girl continued. "Utah is my cousin, and he had to stay here to protect the other women. Hip High Hardy is dead!"

A fleeting frown crossed the Mormon's face when he closed his eyes. Then he opened them as suddenly, and held out his big right hand to Roaming Reynolds. A smile brightened his bearded face and made him look years younger when he spoke.

"You are a man, Reynolds," and his deep voice boomed with sincerity. "I've been a fool, and I'm saying that I'm sorry. Will you shake hands with me and be my friend?"

Roaming Reynolds caught his breath while he stared hard at the smiling Mormon. Then he was across the room gripping the extended hand between his muscular fingers.

"Proud to do it, Deacon," he chuckled. "I knew you was a fighting man all along if something would just wake you up. I could see it way down deep in yore eyes!"

Brigham Smith smiled happily and held the grip while his brown eyes sealed the promise he was making in his heart. "You are right," he agreed. "I fought like the men of old, and I thought that I was a man of peace because I did not resort to weapons."

"Betty said the same thing," Reynolds added. "We were talking about it on the way home from the river."

"Will you leave us for a moment?" and the Mormon looked expectantly at Betty and Ma Tucker. "I want to talk to Roaming in private."

The cowboy frowned when the two women got up to leave the room. Ma Tucker put her arms around Reynolds and kissed him on both cheeks. Held him tightly in her arms with her cheek pressed against his shoulder.

"Thanking you, Roaming," she whispered

198

softly. "I'd be a happy mother if you were my son!"

She smiled wistfully and left the room with Betty, and Brigham Smith caught the cowboy's hand and pulled him to a seat on the bed. Searched his hard face for a long moment, and his voice was soft and friendly when he spoke.

"It's about Betty, Reynolds," he began slowly. "Are you in love with her?"

The cowboy stiffened suddenly. Then he shook his head slowly. "I'm not in love with any girl," he answered, and his voice held a note of bitterness. "It wouldn't be fair to the girl, and besides, I can't stay very long in one place. That's why they call me . . . *Roamin'!*"

"I have seen it all along," the Deacon answered thoughtfully. "You could take Betty away from me if it was your desire to do so!"

The cowboy shook his head vigorously. "It was that tap on the head you got from Hardy," he answered. "You and Betty are the same kind of people, and I'm wishing you happiness. I know she loves you . . . *pard!*"

Brigham Smith stared with amazement, and his voice held a deep note of awe when he spoke. "You are a man, Roaming Reynolds," he whispered. "You have opened my eyes, and from now on I will try to be one also!"

Roaming Reynolds released his hand and stood up. He stared at the bearded young face, and then his two hands went down to his belt and lifted the pistols of Hip High Hardy. Reversing them, he extended them by the muzzles to Brigham Smith.

"I had a hunch when I took these off of Hardy," and his voice was metallic. "I brought them for you, Deacon. Keep them close to yore hands at all times, and use them like they was intended to be used if that gang of owl-hoot buckaroos break through our line!"

Brigham Smith took the guns and hefted the balance. They fitted his big hands perfectly, and his face was almost handsome when he smiled up at Roaming Reynolds. Gone was the sober, serious look from his brown eyes, and the cowboy nodded with satisfaction.

"I'll use them, Roaming," and the Mormon laid down his right-hand gun and shook hands again to bind his promise. "We Mormons fight for our women!"

Roaming Reynolds was the sober one when he glanced at the door and leaned forward. "Eagle Dupree was here in this house to-night," he whispered. "He was holding Betty a prisoner back there in her room!"

Brigham Smith rose to a sitting position before the pain forced him back against the pillows. Then his hand stretched out and pointed to the feather of the king eagle on his pillow.

"Did he?"

"It fell to the floor when I broke into the

room," Reynolds muttered. "Betty was on the floor by the bed where a bullet could not reach her, and Dupree went through the window. I was wondering why he did not shoot, and now we know. I better get on out to the granary, Deacon!"

The big man sighed and closed his eyes. "I can never repay my debt to you, fighting man," he muttered. "But I will try by being the man you think I am."

"The man I *know* you are, pard," Reynolds corrected. "Now I am going to blow out the candles and take over my work. Like Mormon Tucker said, I'm Ramrod when powder begins to burn on the M T!"

Brigham Smith nodded his head. "Send Betty in if she is still waiting, Reynolds," he requested wistfully. "Betty has always admired fighting men, and mebbe so—?"

CHAPTER XIV

Roaming Reynolds thought he heard retreating footsteps when he left the Deacon's room and walked through the long hall. Betty Tucker was waiting in the office, and she left her chair and came toward him when he stopped in the doorway.

"The Deacon wants to see you," he said absently. "Never saw such a change in a feller in all my life. He's a fighting man now, Betty."

The girl took a deep breath and then smiled with her lips while her brown eyes tried to conceal some hidden emotion. "I knew it all the time," she whispered. "And you, Roaming. Where are you going?"

"Going to do the thing I know most about," he answered gruffly. "I hired my guns to yore father to rid the M T range of rustlers."

"But they are far away by this time," the girl answered, and edged closer to him. "You can't follow them in the dark."

"We followed Hardy in the dark," the cowboy answered bluntly. "That hoss-band must be headed for Rainbow Canyon, and I got me an invite to see the sunrise up there some fine morning."

The girl gasped and clutched at his hand. "You wouldn't go up there?"

"Why not?" he grunted, and rubbed the handle of his gun. "Didn't Eagle Dupree come down here?"

"Roaming," and the girl stared up into his hard fighting face. "We can't lose you now after all you have done for us. I never saw Ma kiss another man except Father. She loves you too, Roaming!"

Roaming Reynolds flushed under his tan and shifted uneasily. Then he shook his square shoulders and glanced suggestively toward the sick-room down the hall.

"I told the Deacon I would send you to him right away," he muttered. "You got to go to him, gal. Me and him is pards, and that big feller has been hurt bad enough right now!"

The girl coloured with embarrassment and nodded her dark head slowly. "You are right, Roaming," she whispered. "But promise me that you will take care of yourself no matter what happens."

"I always have up to now," he answered more gently. "A gun-fighter has to take care of himself if he wants to keep on working at his trade."

His lips tightened when the girl recoiled with a look of fear sweeping her face, and he hitched up the broad belt at his hips and jerked his head toward the Deacon's room. The girl nodded and shuddered as though a chill wind had struck her, and the tall cowboy smiled with eyes that glistened like glare ice on a frozen stream.

"Gun-fighter," she whispered as though to echo his words. "Must you always be a gun-fighter, Roaming Reynolds?"

He nodded stiffly. "There's always a fast gun-slick waiting to measure yore time," he growled. "He always thinks he is the fastest, and he won't take no rest until he finds out different. It's always the same wherever I go, and now you know why I keep on roaming."

"But if there is only one, you could settle down after you have met him," the girl suggested hopefully. "It is only when you strike out for a new place that you meet these . . . killers!"

He stared at her with a faraway look in his blue eyes, and shook his head. "A gent with a rep will come a long ways looking for show-down," he muttered. "It's something in the blood that makes 'em come!"

"In the blood," the girl repeated. "You mean it is in your blood also?"

Roaming Reynolds jerked up his head while a question widened his eyes. Then he nodded as though he had just made a startling discovery.

"In my blood too," he admitted, and his deep voice sounded sad and older than his years. "I don't know what it is, but it keeps driving me over the hills to see what's on the other side."

Rifles roared suddenly from the big granary before the girl could frame an answer. The cowboy changed instantly and ran to a window. He hunkered down on his heels and lifted his head slightly above the edge of the sill while the girl watched him with fear-widened eyes. Sixguns were flaming in the darkness behind the blockhouse, and Roaming Reynolds loosed his gun automatically when he sidled toward the door.

"Looks like we got us an army of fighting men here on the M T," he grunted. "Them owl-hooters done brought it to us, and some of them won't be riding back to see the sunrise."

"Roaming," and the girl clutched at his arm. "You can't go out there now!"

He shook her away roughly. "I'm gun-boss on the M T when powder begins to burn," he growled. "You stay here in the house with the Deacon, and right now he's trying to sit up to try out that brace of shooting irons I brought him. Hurry in there and side him!"

"You stay here," the girl pleaded. "They will kill you if you go out there now!"

"Texas Joe and me will ride out around and get behind them fellers," Reynolds said grimly, and his smile was as cold as the blue of his fighting eyes. "I told the Deacon you would be right on in!"

He was through the wide doorway before she could argue further. Texas Joe was waiting by the porch with the horses, and the lad swung up and followed Reynolds without asking questions. Wherever the tall cowboy went there was sure to be fighting, and the button smiled happily and rubbed the grip of his old sixgun.

Back in the big house, Betty Tucker stood uncertainly for a long moment as though lost in thought. Then she squared her shoulders and took a deep breath. Moved down the hall and opened the door to the Deacon's room like a person just awaking from a dream.

"Betty," and the wounded man smiled with his brown eyes while he held out his left hand. One of Hip High Hardy's guns was clutched in the big right hand, and the girl ran toward him with a little cry of fear.

"You too, Brigham," she whispered. "You have the killer look in your eyes!"

Brigham Smith sighed happily and patted her rounded shoulder. "None are so blind as they who will not see," he answered, and she lifted her head to stare at his bearded face. Brigham Smith smiled again and showed his strong white teeth. "And I was blind," he added softly.

"They will kill him," the girl whispered, and shivered violently.

The Deacon let his hand slide down to the covers. "You mean Reynolds!" and the joy went out of his deep voice.

The girl nodded and wiped away a tear. "He has done so much for us," she said by way of

206

explanation. "For Mother and me, and for you."

Brigham Smith nodded slowly. "That is right," he admitted. "Look at me, Betty."

The girl turned her head and met his gaze. For a long moment the big man studied her features, and then he sighed softly and turned his head away.

"You love him," he muttered, but there was no bitterness in the accusation. "I don't want to see you hurt yourself, Betty. Roaming Reynolds is a fighting man who lives by his guns, and he will never be any different."

"But you are different," the girl answered musingly. "I never saw such a change in all my life."

"That is right," the Deacon admitted, and a brief frown crossed his face. "You think perhaps the rule might reverse itself?"

The girl flushed and bit her lip. "I don't know what to say," she answered miserably. "It frightens me when I see that terrible expression in the eyes of men. They want to kill . . . kill!"

"There were those deer out there in the snow," the Deacon said thoughtfully. "Fighting for their young ones, and for their mates. And if I remember rightly, the does did most of the killing."

Betty Tucker straightened up and stared at the wounded man. "I remember," she whispered. "When Hardy threatened me, even Mother had the same look in her eyes. She would have killed him if she could have reached my gun!"

"It is something in the blood," the Deacon said soberly.

"Brigham! Roaming Reynolds used those very same words!"

"And Reynolds has taught us all several things," the Deacon answered slowly. "Blow out the candle, Betty. We should not have a light with those raiders attacking the M T."

Betty Tucker ran lightly across the room and snuffed the thick wick with her moistened fingers. Then she came slowly back to the bed and seated herself near the Deacon. He reached out and caught her hand, and the girl jerked slightly when he pressed a subtle warning.

"Someone comes," he whispered just above his breath. "Be very quiet."

The roar of rifles drowned the rustling sound while the silent watchers peered at the window. The girl gasped when an object crept up over the sill. Brigham Smith sucked in his breath and moved slightly, and the girl knew that he was raising his right arm to cover the sill with the gun in his big hand.

She held her breath and waited. The top of a high-crowned Stetson shoved slowly into view and tried to pierce the darkness within. A metallic click told of a gun-hammer being eared back, and Betty Tucker screamed softly when red muzzle-bloom lighted the darkened room. The explosion blasted against the ceiling and echoed deafeningly, and she felt the twitch of the Deacon's big arm when the bucking sixgun recoiled in the wounded man's hand.

A red haze blinded the girl, due to the sudden burst of light after the intense darkness. Black powder extinguished the light almost instantly, and Betty Tucker moaned softly when the leering face seemed to dissolve under the impact of the heavy forty-five slug. Brigham Smith grunted softly and sank back against the pillows with a wavering sigh that told of weakness.

"Brigham!"

Betty called the big man's name sharply while she stared at the empty window. Brigham Smith moaned softly, and the girl knew that the strain had been too much for his sapped vitality. She held tightly to his left hand and waited for consciousness to return, and she smiled grimly with stiffened lips when rifles crashed from the granary.

"Wolves," she whispered fiercely. "Killing lobos that skulk in the night!"

"They got Bull," she heard a hoarse voice murmur. "Somebody in there with the Deacon, but there won't be long!"

The girl cringed when two stabbing bursts of flame gouted out from the heavy shrubbery beyond the window. Brigham Smith was breathing deeply, and occasionally he moaned as though in pain. The girl threw herself across his broad chest and gripped the handle of her gun, and her brown eyes glowed in the darkness while she watched the window.

Again she crouched down when a steady stream of bullets hissed through the window and thudded into the far wall. Waited until the round of shots had whistled harmlessly over her head, and then her right arm came up slowly and levelled down to cover the broad sill.

A tall hat showed suddenly above the sill, but some intuition warned the girl to hold her fire. For a few seconds the hat bobbed up and down, and Betty Tucker sneered with her lips when she saw the gun-barrel below the hat. Silence for a moment. Then a tousled head slipped slowly into view.

Betty Tucker clenched her teeth and pressed the hair-balanced trigger with a gentle squeeze. She caught the bucking gun on the recoil and jabbed angrily as though she could feel the punching shock behind the heavy slug of lead. Moaned softly when the head jerked back like an apple on a string, and she gasped softly when it appeared again in the window.

Her thumb caught the heavy hammer and held it so against the pull of the trigger. No man could stand up against the shock of a half-ounce slug, but Betty Tucker could see the head rising swiftly. Realization came to her when she heard a hammer being cocked. There had been *two* men shooting into the room, and she slipped the heavy hammer under her thumb when her sight centred on the target.

A hoarse scream stopped as suddenly as it had started when the head disappeared from the sill. Came the thud of a thrashing body in the shrubbery, and the girl jerked violently when a groping hand caught her by the shoulder.

"I'll kill you," a deep voice growled savagely. "We Mormons fight for our women."

Betty Tucker twisted like a cat and tried to escape from that powerful grip. Then she ceased struggling when she saw that the hand belonged to Brigham Smith. He was drawing her down toward him, but his weakness was stronger than the strength of the girl, and she renewed her struggles when she saw the shadow of his right arm raise with the sixgun gripped in the big hand.

"Brigham!" she screamed with all the power of her lungs. "Don't shoot, Deacon!"

She turned sideways and came up on her left elbow while her eyes stared at the rising gun sky-lighted against the window. Her eyes widened with unbelief when she saw the Deacon's thumb slipping on the hammer. Moaning softly she brought the barrel of her gun down smartly against the side of the wounded man's head, and

Brigham Smith groaned and slumped back on the pillows.

The gun dropped from his fingers and clattered on the floor. Betty Tucker crawled out from under the heavy left arm that pinned her down, and then she was on her feet crouching across the bed while her eyes stared at the window for another attacker. A soft moan drew her glance back to the bed, and the girl stepped back and jerked the spent shells from her gun while her teeth nearly met through her lower lip.

Her breath came in wheezy gasps while she plucked fresh shells from her gunbelt and thumbed them through the loading gate. Then she holstered the gun and dropped to her knees beside the bed, and her fingers reached out to stroke the swelling lump on the left side of the Mormon's head.

"I had to do it, Brigham," and her voice was a whispered sob of anguish. "You were going to kill me!"

Brigham Smith moaned softly. The girl levered to her high heels and ran across the room in a crouch. Dipped a cloth in cold water standing in the stone basin, and the wounded man gasped when she pressed the cloth to his forehead. Betty placed her left hand on his head and continued her ministrations. Somewhere she had been told that a waking person rouses normally when a hand is placed on the forehead.

A movement made her hold her breath. Brigham Smith was stirring slowly, and she heard the deep respiration that told of returning consciousness.

"Brigham," she whispered softly, with lips close to his ear. "Please wake up, Brigham!"

"Betty," and his answer was a gusty sigh. "Are you hurt, my darling?"

"Oh, Brigham," and the girl sobbed with reaction. "I am so sorry I had to hit you!"

Silence while the wounded man paused to gather his strength. "You hit me?" he whispered, and his deep voice expressed his unbelief.

"You went out of your head," the girl sobbed. "You held me with one arm while you tried to cock that gun with the other hand. You thought I was an outlaw, and you were going to shoot me!"

"I did that terrible thing?" and his voice was filled with horror. "I—I can't think clearly right now."

"You must think, Brigham," the girl pleaded, and became calm when she recognized his need. "You must not slip back again," she said more strongly.

She held tightly to his two hands as though to give him some of her own strength. Brigham Smith had suffered too many shocks, and she knew that his mind might slip if he lapsed again into unconsciousness. Fiercely she gripped his limp hands while her voice whispered into his ear.

"It's Betty, Brigham. Staying right here to side you all the way down the river. You saved my life, Brigham. Please talk to me!"

The wounded man seemed to stiffen as though to listen. Then his grip tightened a trifle to tell of his concentration, and the girl smiled in the darkness.

"I saved your life?"

"Yes, yes. The outlaw was just getting ready to shoot when you pressed trigger. Now do you remember?"

Brigham Smith sucked in his breath tremulously. "I remember," and his voice was stronger. "I killed one of my fellow-men to-night!"

"He would have killed me," the girl whispered. "Even in your delirium, you said that a Mormon always fought for his women-folks!"

Silence for a long moment while the Deacon digested the news. "I'd kill a thousand times for you, Betty," he whispered finally. "I'm thanking God that you did what you had to do!"

The girl shuddered suddenly and began to sob. Brigham Smith loosened one of his hands and gently patted her shoulder. His deep voice was like a softly booming bell when he comforted her.

"You were guided, my child. I would rather die a thousand times than hurt you."

Betty Tucker raised her head and listened. "It wasn't that," she whispered, and quieted herself.

"Two other men shot through the window after you fainted."

"Two other men?"

The girl nodded. "They came to kill us," she whispered tensely. "It was all like a horrible dream!"

"Will you tell me?" he asked softly, and stroked her hair with his free hand.

"They came like that first one," and the girl shuddered. "I shot one time, and I could hear the bullet thud against bone. The man dropped, and then it seemed like his head came right up again. Not until he cocked his gun did I realize that it was another man, and I pressed the trigger just in time."

"You killed two men?"

"I killed two wolves," the girl answered savagely. "You were lying there unconscious after saving my life!"

She stopped suddenly when the sound of her own voice grated against her ears. Her hands began to tremble violently, and the Deacon caught them and pressed them against his heart.

"It is a sign," he said solemnly. "You saved my life, Betty. More than that, you saved my soul. I would have been eternally damned if I had killed you!"

"You didn't know," the girl defended quickly. "You have suffered so much the past few days!"

Brigham Smith sighed contentedly. "And I

215

have learned so much," he answered softly. "I am stronger now than I have been in all my life."

Betty Tucker held his hands and smiled when she felt the steady pulsing under her fingers. A prayer was in her heart when she realized that the mental crisis had been met, and had been passed successfully. No danger now that the big man would lose his mind, and she closed her fingers tightly and gripped him like a man.

"I am glad," she said simply. "You are stronger than you have ever been in your life. Your mind is clear, and you see things as they are, instead of as you want to see them."

"Yes," and Brigham Smith returned her grip strongly. "Roaming Reynolds taught us these things, and the scales of ignorance fell away from my eyes so that I might learn."

The girl jerked suddenly at the mention of the cowboy's name. "Roaming," she whispered. "He is out there somewhere in the darkness fighting for us. If he should be killed . . . ?"

Brigham Smith sighed and dropped his hands. "We would lose the best friend we ever had," he said slowly, but once more his voice was weak with weariness. "We can only wait, Betty. But we can pray for him while we are waiting for the dawn!"

CHAPTER XV

Texas Joe breasted up to Roaming Reynolds and asked a question with his narrowed grey eyes. The tall cowboy turned and swept him with a glance that caught the question, and he jerked one arm toward the holding pens.

"Keep to the corrals and work over in back of Dupree's raiders," he rasped. "When we get in position, cut loose with all you've got to make 'em think we're an army. Let's go!"

A dozen guns were blazing at the granary. Bullets thudded into the heavy logs or whined off into space like angry hornets. Rifles answered steadily from inside the big building, and Roaming Reynolds smiled when he thought of the couple back in the ranch house. No need to worry longer about Brigham Smith. The Deacon had come into his own; from now on he would be a fighting man of the first water.

The smile faded into a frown when he thought of the girl. Deep breasted and long of limb like the girl he had always pictured in his camp-fire dreams. Strong enough to pard a man, with all the feminine softness he admired in a girl. A girl who could laugh and cry; one who would love a man into forgetfulness, or fight like hell's own fury if danger threatened the man of her heart.

He shook his shoulders angrily and tightened his lips while his calloused palm rubbed the handle of his gun. Texas Joe was watching him with a knowing look on his thin face, but the boy turned his head when Reynolds growled deep in his throat.

"Yo're wrong, button," he barked harshly. "Get going like I told you!"

Keeping in the deeper shadows, the two riders walked their horses until they had passed the spitting fireflies behind the granary. Satisfied at last, Roaming Reynolds turned his horse and reached for the Winchester under his left leg. Growled a low order to Texas Joe, who followed every movement.

"Pump yore magazine empty and reach for yore sixgun just as we ride our spurs toward them. Chances are they will break and run, and that will give our boys something to shoot at!"

"The boys might shoot at us," Texas Joe objected. "You thought of that, pard?"

Reynolds smiled in the darkness. "Good head, Joe," he praised. "After we flush that bunch out into the open then we cut around back the way we come. Line out for the house, but keep in the shadows."

They stood their horses among the trees and sighted at the gun-flashes behind the granary. Both guns began to roar savagely, and lead started to pour into the attackers until both magazines were empty. The cowboy neck-reined his horse when the outlaws began to answer with whining lead. Sliding the hot rifle down in the saddle-boot, he reached for his sixguns and spurred his horse forward on the run.

Texas Joe had noticed that extra sixgun in the shoulder holster, and he grinned crookedly while his hand reached to the harness he had made for himself. He scratched with both feet and yipped the Texas yell, and his calloused thumbs began slipping the heavy hammers while he fanned out and followed Reynolds in a mad charge of thundering hooves and snarling sixguns.

Rifles and pistols blazed back at the riders to pluck at their clothing with avid, searching fingers of hot lead. They could hear the howl of surprise that greeted their sudden charge, and the trained horses weaved right and left as though they were following a cow-critter when culling out a shipping herd.

A faint light began to break through the darkness when the moon came up over the high pinnacles of Zion Park. Texas Joe pulled his horse up short and holstered his sixguns like an old-timer. Then he pulled his rifle from the scabbard and reloaded with sweating, smoke-grimed fingers. Dropping from the high saddle, he bellied down on the ground and sighted carefully at a group of saddled horses.

A single guard was holding the horses while

his companions attacked the granary. Texas Joe pressed trigger and snarled with vicious satisfaction when the horse-guard threw up his arms and sagged to the ground. The button began to drop bullets in front of the lunging horses, and they stampeded into the night with snorts of terror.

"Flat-footed, dang yuh," Joe muttered, and rubbed the hot barrel of his saddle-gun.

Roaming Reynolds was spurring towards the corrals, but the boy paid no heed. He reached to his pocket and reloaded his gun; levered a fresh shell into the breach and sighted carefully down the long barrel. Men were milling about in the shadows shouting hoarsely to each other. Three of them made a break for the horses, and Texas Joe smiled grimly when rifles barked sharply from the blockhouse. Two men fell in their tracks, and he sighted along the barrel of his Winchester and pressed the trigger with a gentle squeeze to drop the third fugitive.

Here and there a man showed himself, only to be met by deadly lead from the granary. Guns blazed furiously and then stopped with a suddenness that made the stillness beat down with an oppressive quietness. Texas Joe worked his way back to his horse and leaped to the saddle. Roaming Reynolds was nowhere in sight, but the button kept to the shadows and worked his way back to the corrals.

Two figures crouched back in the shadow of the tack-shed, but the button spotted the jutting shadows that lanced out across the open space. He studied these carefully with his head cocked bird-like to one side, and then he pursed his lips and whistled softly. The shadows jerked back abruptly, and a hoarse whisper keened through the gloom.

"That you, Joe?"

"In the flesh," the button answered in his deepest voice. "Hold yore fire while I come among you and Sam!"

He grinned when he swung toward the tack-shed and slipped around the corner. Utah Young and Sam Smith faced him with guns ready to flame, and they lowered the weapons when Texas Joe started to talk.

"You get them quail me and Roamin' flushed from cover?"

"So it was you?" Utah muttered. "Me and Sam saw them break and run, and I know of three long-riders that won't twirl a wide loop no more."

He whirled suddenly when thudding hooves rattled across the yard. Texas Joe sprang forward and knocked down his arm just before the young Mormon pressed trigger.

"That's the gun-boss," the boy snarled hoarsely. "You want to look before you start throwin' lead!"

Roaming Reynolds came in and swung down

with a grunt. "Saw you two," he muttered. "Nice work you done on that remuda, Joe. Them jiggers is all afoot and we might as well get on with our snake-killin'!"

"We got to stay down out of sight, Roamin'," Utah remarked. "Them boys back in the granary has got oncommon good sight. Out here we look all the same rustler to them."

"Right," the tall cowboy agreed. "But we can work up in back of the house and cut in on the river road. I heard shooting back there not long since, and sounded like some of it came from the house."

"I see flashes," Sam Smith cut in. "And the Deacon down with his head under him."

"Not him," Reynolds contradicted. "The Deacon has a hog-leg in each fist, and right now he's ready to fight for the M T while his cartridges holds out."

"Betty is with him," Texas Joe remarked carelessly. "And that gal can call her shots every time. What we waitin' for?"

Roaming Reynolds nodded and mounted his horse. The four riders circled the corrals and rode into the shadows of the big house. Texas Joe stared for a long moment; pointed to the Deacon's window with the barrel of his gun.

"Three dead men yonder," he chuckled. "Reckon there was some shooting from the Deacon's room, Roamin'!"

Roaming Reynolds stared and shook his head. "The Deacon won't ever walk into a man with his bare fists again," he muttered. "Let's get down the trail!"

They skirted the timbered lane and came to the river crossing where Canuck Avery had met Brigham Smith. A gust of pistol fire spouted from the gravelled shelf, and the four riders reached for their rifles and levered shells.

"Let 'em have it," Reynolds growled. "The bushwhackin' sons!"

Four riders roared like one to send the group by the ford scurrying for cover. Roaming Reynolds spurred his horse and hit a high lope down the trail while his hands holstered the long gun under his left leg. A smooth pair of passes filled his hands with smoking steel, and Texas Joe skinned back his thinned lips and thumbed the hammer of his Colt between jumps of his deep-chested horse.

Utah Young and Sam Smith fanned out to the sides to cut off the fleeing outlaws, and when the smoke cleared away, a single man was standing near the flowing water with both hands raised high above his head. Roaming Reynolds rode up to him and swung down to the ground.

"Yore handle, hombre?" he growled. "You better talk sudden!"

"Pete Jordan," the outlaw muttered sullenly,

but his slitted eyes showed the fear in his heart when he stared at the ring of weapons. "I was only doing what I had to do."

"That goes for the M T too," Reynolds answered bluntly, and pointed at the bodies scattered along the trail. "Mebbe yo're hankering to join yore pards?"

The outlaw shuddered and licked his lips. "You can shoot, Mister," he muttered. "I'd get it nohow if I unbridled my jaw."

"Eagle Dupree?" Reynolds asked quietly.

Pete Jordan nodded slowly. Not much taller than Texas Joe, who was watching him with no attempt to conceal the hatred in his grey eyes. Two long-barrelled forty-fives were belted around the outlaw's hips, and the cartridge loops of his belt were empty. A battered grey Stetson was pulled low over the sloping forehead, and Jordan shifted his rusty boots and shrugged his thin shoulders.

"I was hitting out for Rainbow Canyon," he muttered. "You ain't never seen the place of a sunrise, Reynolds."

The tall cowboy straightened with a jerk. "I got me an invite to drop around there and take a look," he answered slowly. "I might do it before long."

"I'll sell out cheap," the outlaw suggested softly, and tipped his head back to watch Reynolds from under the drooping brim of his hat. "And it won't cost you no dinero," he added softly.

Utah Young stared at the vicious face and turned to Reynolds. "Better take him back to the M T," he suggested coldly. "The other boys might have some ideas now that the Deacon has woke up."

Sam Smith crowded his horse forward. "What you mean by that, Utah?" he asked slowly. "About Brigham waking up?"

"The Deacon is packing two guns now," Texas Joe interrupted, and his grey eyes watched the effect of his words on the prisoner. "I'd like to be there when the Deacon takes it to Eagle Dupree for what he done to Betty."

Pete Jordan leered slyly. "Not the Deacon," he contradicted, and grinned impudently at Roaming Reynolds. "Right now Eagle has the gal back in Rainbow. That's for why I been shooting off my mouth!"

"Guess agin, Mister," Texas Joe sneered. "Yore boss high-tailed through a window when Roamin' come up on him in Betty's room. He didn't pack the sand to stay for show-down!"

Jordan stiffened suddenly and stared at the button. "Tain't so," he denied slowly. "Eagle never showed up, and the raid was a blind for him to get the gal. Right now he's holdin' her back in Rainbow Canyon!"

"You was with that bunch what shot me," Sam

225

Smith drawled slowly, but his hand tightened on the grip of his gun. "Yo're a knowed killer and a rustler, and there's plenty of bent limbs hereabouts. What you say, Boss?" and he turned toward Roaming Reynolds.

The tall cowboy was studying the rising dawn at the top of the Vermilion Cliffs. His face was thoughtful while he pieced out the events of the night, and Texas Joe gigged his horse forward as though he had read his companion's thoughts.

"You reckon there's anything in what he said, Roamin'?"

"We can't take any chances," the tall cowboy muttered. "It's been quite a spell since we saw Betty and the Deacon, and there was gun-fire from the house. On top of that, this jigger says that Eagle Dupree never showed up during the fight at the granary."

Sam Smith set his jaw and reached for the long rope on his saddle. His left shoulder and arm were stiff from the wound he had received, but now his face was like granite while he shook out his coils and built a finicky loop.

"Yo're going to hang and rattle, Jordan," he said softly. "And I aim to kick yore hoss out from under you!"

Utah Young nodded his head in silent agreement. Roaming Reynolds frowned and held up his left hand, and even Texas Joe scowled at the interruption.

"Not so fast," Reynolds grunted. "You men of peace got no proof that Dupree got Betty. We got to be sure before we do something we can't mend afterward."

Young Sam Smith turned angrily and crouched over his sixgun. "If Dupree got Betty, it means the Deacon is dead," he snarled. "We Mormons fight for our women-folks!"

"Yeah," Reynolds drawled thoughtfully. "And I got me an invite to Rainbow Canyon. Looky, Utah," and he turned to the tall young Mormon.

Utah Young scowled and stared at the fighting face of the gun-boss. "I'm lookin'," he growled, and stared at the face of Pete Jordan. "Say yore say, Reynolds!"

"Fan that hoss of yores down the hind legs and get back to the M T," Reynolds answered quietly. "Find out if Betty and the Deacon are all right, and then get back here on the run."

"And miss out when you jiggers have a necktie party?" Utah barked. "Send the button!"

"Texas Joe stays here with me," Reynolds answered stiffly. "I have a plan, Utah, but I got to know for shore. One way or another I aim to see that sunrise up in Rainbow Canyon, but we got to know if the gal is safe before we barge in there setting off the fireworks."

"You'll wait?" and the tall Mormon wheeled his horse.

Reynolds nodded slowly. "We won't know until

you get back," he pointed out. "Now you hit yore hoss with the hooks and make tracks!"

Utah Young turned to glower at the prisoner. "If anything has happened to Betty Tucker, you won't live long enough to say yore prayers," he muttered, and scratched with both feet to rocket his big bay up the trail.

Texas Joe slid from his saddle and cut a latigo-string from the cantle. Sam Smith read his intention and barked sharply at Pete Jordan. The gun in his right hand lent weight to his command.

"Hands behind yore back, rustler. You'll get a chance if Utah gets back with good news. If he don't . . . ?" and the Deacon's brother pointed to the rope on his saddle-horn.

The outlaw paled slightly and turned with his hands behind him. Texas Joe made a loop and snared the thin wrists; made his ties and spun the prisoner roughly to face Roaming Reynolds. The young gun-boss nodded approval and raised his head to stare at the rimrock high above.

"You mentioned Rainbow Canyon, hombre," he said softly. "Talked like you knew a way in there."

"There's only one way in, and one way out," Jordan muttered. "But you couldn't find it on yore lonesome. I'll lead you in, and the rest is up to you."

"We could get in without him," Texas Joe suggested. "They rustled forty head of hosses last

228

night, and that bunch is bound to leave sign."

"That hoss-band is on the way to Red Hoss," the prisoner sneered. "Eagle has a sale for them and no questions asked!"

Roaming Reynolds hooked his right leg over the horn of his saddle and reached for the makin's. He rolled a brown paper quirly slowly and licked the edge with his tongue. Flicked a match to flame with his thumb-nail while his blue eyes held steady on the increasing light high above on the Vermilion Cliffs.

"Dupree won't ship them M T hosses," he said softly. "The train don't make the pick-up till late afternoon, and she still lacks a half-hour till sunrise."

"I want a chance," Jordan croaked hoarsely. "You and the boss has been edging at each other ever since you rode into the Strip. You and him is headed straight for a draw-and-shoot, and right now Eagle is priming his cutter to smoke you down!"

"Like as not," Reynolds murmured. "What's that got to do with this chance you was talking about?"

"I'm leading you to him," Jordan muttered. "If I cut her straight, you can turn me loose to get me a fresh start. I'll go straight, so help me!"

"Straight tuh hell," Texas Joe sneered. "And you can have yore choice of a bullet or a rope!"

"Bridle yore jaw, button," Reynolds said

sternly, and turned to study the pleading eyes of the prisoner. "You mean you won't lead us into a trap?"

"I'd get killed if I did, wouldn't I?" Jordan muttered sullenly.

Sam Smith reached out a hand and played with the hondo on his long rope. Roaming Reynolds shook his head and took a deep breath. The young Mormon straightened slowly and waited.

"You'll get that chance if yo're telling the truth, Jordan," Reynolds promised quietly. "Yonder comes Utah fanning the breeze, and he carries news from the way he's sitting his saddle!"

All eyes turned to the trail and watched the tall Mormon racing toward them, riding forward in the saddle like all mountain men do. He slid the deep-chested horse on its haunches and grinned at Roaming Reynolds while he caught his breath after the jolting run.

"They're safe," he almost shouted. "Three dead outlaws under the Deacon's window back yonder to count that shooting you heard. Every one of them owl-hooters shot through the head, so that makes Jordan out a liar!"

The prisoner leaned forward with the fear of death in his little eyes. "The gal safe?" he whispered. "You mean Eagle didn't get her?"

"Eagle didn't have the sand to make another try," Utah sneered. "He must have high-tailed when he saw his pack was losing out. What you say now, Boss?" and he turned to watch the face of Roaming Reynolds.

"I hired out to do a job of work," the tall cowboy answered sternly. "I'm going to do it or go down trying. I just now made a deal with Pete Jordan."

Utah Young stared with his jaw dropping. Sam Smith scowled and shook his head. Texas Joe slid his horse beside Reynolds with his hand on the grip of his gun.

"This outlaw is going to lead us into Rainbow," Smith muttered. "What you think, Utah?"

"He ain't," the tall Mormon barked. "He's going to stretch rope before we start cutting for sign!"

"Better change yore mind, feller," Texas Joe warned softly. "Roamin' is boss here, and he usually knows what he's doing. Get 'em told, pard," and Joe slid his sixgun out and carelessly covered the two scowling Mormons.

"We ain't killers," the tall cowboy said sternly. "We got nothing again this jigger except that he runs with bad company. We couldn't find our way into Rainbow Canyon by our lonesome, and I'm giving him a chance to make a clean start providing he don't try to cut a rusty. There's some good in most fellers if you just keep down yore mad and uses yore head."

"They nearly killed the Deacon," Sam Smith growled. "And they meant to kill me to boot."

"They didn't kill neither one of you," Reynolds pointed out softly. "Tain't like a Mormon to kill his fellers just to work off his mad!"

Sam Smith twisted uneasily and turned to look at Utah Young. "Looks like we forgot ourselves, Utah," he murmured slowly. "When a heathen like Reynolds can point out what we ought to have seen all along!"

"Unsay them words, Mister!"

Texas Joe was leaning forward in the saddle with a frown of anger on his thin face. "You called my pard a heathen!"

Sam Smith smiled under his silky black beard. "Meaning that Reynolds ain't a Mormon like me and Utah," he corrected with a grin. "And me and Utah is thanking him for the lesson."

"That suit you, Roamin'?" and Texas Joe turned to stare at the tall cowboy.

"Fair enough," Reynolds murmured with a smile. "Now you holster yore hardware and catch up that hoss yonder for Jordan. I aim to see the sunrise back there in Rainbow Canyon!"

CHAPTER XVI

Pete Jordan shuddered while he led the way through twisting rocky passages that cut back into Rainbow Canyon. Roaming Reynolds and Texas Joe rode side by side just behind him with Utah Young and Sam Smith bringing up the drag. The tall cowboy glanced at the prisoner and followed the staring eyes to a soft spot on the trail.

The marks of a single horse were indented in the red loam; the marks of a long-legged horse travelling fast. Reynolds edged up to Pete Jordan and pointed with his thumb.

"You know them tracks?" he asked softly.

Jordan nodded his head and shuddered again. "I'd know 'em anywhere," he whispered. "The boss has been through here recent. He never misses with rifle or hand-gun, and with me up here in the lead . . . ?"

"Mebbe you'd rather have a rope," Utah Young growled savagely. "You took yore choice back by the river!"

"Man of peace," Jordan sneered. "When you Mormons get up yore mad yo're worse than Injuns!"

"Like you said," Sam Smith answered coldly. "I figger right now that yore boss is shy a lot of his wide-looping hands."

"Getting back to me," Jordan changed the subject hastily. "It ain't much farther to the valley, and I was promised a chance."

"He's right," Roaming Reynolds agreed quietly. "We can find the way in from here," and he turned to study the scowling face of Texas Joe.

"Naw yuh don't, Roamin'," the boy answered quickly. "You can pick one of them Mormons to do what yo're thinking about!"

"Yo're taking orders, Joe," the tall cowboy said sternly. "Right now I'm picking you for my right-hand man. To do the things I can't do myself, and I can't trust the job I got in mind to Utah or Sam."

The two Mormons turned swiftly with frowns of anger on their bearded faces. Young faces that had never known the touch of a razor. Utah Young thrust out his jaw and snapped a question while he hunched his powerful shoulders into a crouch.

"Hard words, Reynolds," he barked. "Better you explain what you mean!"

Roaming Reynolds faced the pair with the smoky blue barely showing between narrowed lids. "I back up any talk I make," he answered softly, but his voice was edged with a subtle threat. "You fellers has been men of peace all yore borned days. I come in here to this damn Strip and show you the error of yore ways, and you ain't got used to the change yet. You salty

234

jiggers has had a taste of blood, and you like it too much to suit me!"

"Meaning him!" and Utah Young jerked a thumb at the silent prisoner.

"Meaning him," Reynolds answered coldly. "I might be a gun-fighter, but my kind of people either lives or dies by the code. I passed my spoken word, and I ain't never broke it up to now. Is that plain enough?"

"Reckon it is, Roaming," Utah muttered, and came out of his crouch while he shook his flat-topped hat slowly from side to side. "You was sayin' when I horned in?"

"I was saying that I promised Pete Jordan a chance," the gun-boss continued in the same drawling tones. "A chance to go straight and make a man out of himself. Riding up here on point the way he's doing, he stops first bullet if Dupree or some of his owl-hoot hands spots us coming. Like shooting a sitting duck on a pond!"

"Thanks, Reynolds," the prisoner murmured. "I might have gone straight long ago if some gent with savvy had snubbed me up in time. I won't be forgetting."

"You was looking at me," Texas Joe interrupted in his deepest voice. "Spell it out, pard."

"Ride back with Jordan to the mouth of the Canyon," Reynolds continued thoughtfully. "Tie him loose when you hit the river, and don't you get no ideas about whittling."

Texas Joe flushed with anger and slipped his hand down toward the smoke-grimed gun on his thin leg. "Call them words back, Reynolds," he barked viciously. "Or else you and me quits pardin' right here and now!"

Roaming Reynolds moved his right hand like a flash and caught the leaping gun that jumped into view. Texas Joe was caught flat-footed with his gun in leather, but his face twisted into a scowl of deadly determination.

"Shoot, or unsay it, feller," he croaked, and his changing voice screeched on a high note. "I'm coming out to match my draw again yore drop!"

Roaming Reynolds stared for a moment and flipped his wrist. The spiking gun disappeared as quickly as it had leaped to view, and the tall cowboy's voice was soft with regret while a slow flush of shame coloured his tanned face.

"Unsayin' it, pard," he muttered huskily. "Had no call to mis-doubt you any way you look at it. Sorry I spoke like I did, and here's my hand to prove it."

He did not raise his deep voice while he stared at Texas Joe with a light of admiration in his blue eyes. The half-grown boy gulped noisily and stuck out a hand that trembled like a leaf in the wind.

"I couldn't match you, Roamin'," he muttered, and turned his face to hide the scalding tears. "But I'd have gone down kickin' before I'd have turned yeller so's you or those Mormons could have seen it."

He gripped the tall cowboy hard and kept his face turned until he had gained control of himself. Then he turned toward Utah Young and snarled like a cornered wolf.

"You started this ruckus? You want to make something out of it?"

The tall Mormon recoiled and then a slow grin spread over his bearded face. "Not me, Tex," he answered slowly. "Yo're a better man than I am, or the boss wouldn't have picked you for this job. The same goes for Sam Smith yonder."

"Dag-nab you jiggers nohow," Texas Joe gulped. "I feel worse than if you had hoorawed me for a yearlin' with the velvet still on my hawns!"

"The sun is comin' up yonder," a dry voice interrupted harshly, and all eyes turned to stare at Pete Jordan. The little man was watching the serrated rimrock high above, and Roaming Reynolds drew a deep breath and nodded his head.

"Don't lack much to sunrise," he agreed. "Get goin' you two. I'm counting on you to line out straight when you get away from the Strip, Jordan!"

"Yo're a man, Reynolds," Jordan muttered huskily. "I owe you something for giving me a chance. Better call off meeting Eagle!"

The gun-boss stared coldly. "Keep on talking," he grunted.

"He's that fast," Jordan continued earnestly. "I saw Hip High Hardy call the boss one day. Had both hands hooked in his belts with his fingers touching the gun-handles. Eagle made his pass and caught Hardy flat-footed before he could flip his cutters!"

Roaming Reynolds shrugged carelessly. "I ain't never met a gun-hawk that fast," he admitted quietly, but the joyous light of anticipation leaped into his blue eyes to make them glow hotly. "Better get started, Joe."

"The valley is around the next bend," Jordan said simply. "Eagle has the stone house at the far end. So long, Roaming."

Texas Joe came up and caught the lead reins with his left hand. "I'll tie him loose like you said, Roaming," he growled. "After which I'll come foggin' back to give you the lend of my guns!"

The tall cowboy smiled when Texas Joe spurred his horse and started down the back trail with the prisoner in tow. Utah Young took a deep breath and straightened in the saddle.

"Any orders?" he asked quietly.

Roaming Reynolds jerked his head toward the bend in the trail. "We go single file from here on," he said quietly. "You gents stay out of the play if we find Dupree alone!"

"Except that I'm taking second if he downs you," Utah Young growled deep in his throat.

"I'm taking third," Sam Smith echoed swiftly. "For what that killer done to Brigham!"

Roaming Reynolds gigged his horse forward without answering. They turned the bend in the trail and stopped to stare across a long grassy valley knee-high with blue-stem. A band of brood mares was grazing at the far end, and Sam Smith jerked violently in the saddle when a rifle crashed from the fringing brush on the left side.

Roaming Reynolds slapped down for his gun and kicked with his spurs at the same time. Then he was charging across the bottle-neck with flame roaring from his hand. His horse hit the brush and crashed through without slackening speed, and the tall gun-boss balanced forward on the muscled withers when the big animal leaped a windfall as high as his shoulders.

The timber-trained horse slid to a stop on the far side, and Roaming Reynolds stepped down with his shoulder-gun in his fist. He grunted softly when he saw the body of a man in the brush, and he was turning the outlaw over when Utah Young cleared the windfall and hit the ground a-running.

"You get him, Roaming?"

Reynolds shrugged and pointed to the man on the ground. "Centre," he said quietly. "I was hoping he would live long enough to talk."

Utah Young glared savagely. "Sam," he gulped.

"He fell forward on his face. That tell you anything?"

Roaming Reynolds straightened up and nodded his head. "Dead," he murmured. "I hate to face the Deacon."

The faint echo of gun-fire sounded from far down the trail. "You reckon the button had trouble?" Utah asked anxiously.

Roaming Reynolds closed his eyes for a moment. "If he did, it's too late now for us to help," he whispered, and raised his eyes to the glowing walls of Rainbow Canyon. "It's sunrise," he muttered.

"I'm taking back that promise, Roaming," Utah said jerkily. "If Eagle Dupree is waiting yonderly, I'm cutting him down on sight!"

Roaming Reynolds leaped forward and gripped the Mormon by both arms. A terrible rage made his hard face stiff and craggy, and his steely fingers bit to the bone to send Utah Young to his knees with a moan of pain. The tall cowboy's voice was a muffled roar when he spoke.

"Mebbe you made a mistake, Utah!"

He straightened his arms and lifted the tall Mormon to his feet like a child. Utah Young gasped and tried to speak above the pain that made him helpless in that relentless grip.

"Yeah," he panted. "I made a mistake!"

Reynolds opened his fingers and stepped back. Utah Young stumbled and caught his balance with difficulty, and his arms hung down at his sides like shreds of cloth. The cowboy shook himself and sucked in his breath like a horse that has made a hard run.

"Sorry to man-handle you that away, Utah," and once more his deep voice was under control. "I'd kill the man who made me break my word!"

"Gawd!" the Mormon murmured. "You could break my arms with your fingers. I went out of my head there, Roaming. I'm asking you not to hold no grudge!"

Roaming Reynolds was breathing easily while he slowly nodded his head. "I lost my head like you did," he admitted. "And a gent can't do that in my business and keep on living."

"No wonder you handled the Deacon," the Mormon whispered, and followed the cowboy's gaze to the tops of the cliffs. "It's sunrise!"

Roaming Reynolds walked to his horse and mounted to the high saddle. He turned to glance at the dead outlaw; sent his horse at the windfall and leaped over without speaking. Utah Young followed across the narrow bottle-neck, and sat his saddle when the cowboy swung down and made a swift examination of Sam Smith.

"Through the heart," Reynolds said softly. "And he had the makings of a fighting man!"

Utah Young did not answer. He was staring at a group of squatty buildings up ahead when Roaming Reynolds covered the face of Sam

Smith with the black flat-topped beaver. The Mormon pointed to a stone house sitting off to one side.

"That's where Eagle Dupree lives," he muttered softly. "He'll dry-gulch us when we ride up to speak to him fair!"

The gun-boss shook his head positively. "Not Dupree," he contradicted. "He would cut off his gun-hand before he would shoot a man in the back!"

Utah Young jerked around and stared incredulously. "Dupree is an outlaw," he grated harshly. "He robs and kills without conscience!"

Reynolds nodded his head. "But he lives by the code when it comes to burning powder," he answered quietly. "Eagle Dupree is a master with his tools, and he works according to rules of the game. He calls his shots and puts his lead where he calls 'em, and he thinks more of his reputation than he does of all the money in the world."

The voice of Roaming Reynolds was quiet and confident while he talked of the thing that meant more than life to him. Utah Young stared at the craggy face and stroked his bearded chin. Then he shook his head slowly.

"Like you said," he answered in a far away voice. "We Mormons have been men of peace for so long that we cannot understand. Is it pride that makes a gun-fighter toe up to scratch with empty hands, when he knows the man facing him is going to kill him if he can?"

"Something like that," Reynolds agreed. "You get a feeling that you don't want to live if the other feller is the best. Down in yore heart you know he ain't, and dogging it would put a gun-boss in hell for all his living days. And even after he shuffled off," he added thoughtfully.

"Young Sam," Utah muttered gruffly. "Lying there stiff as a tarp while you and me sit our saddles wind-jamming. What we waiting for?"

Roaming Reynolds brought himself back to realities with a jerk. He neck-reined his horse toward the group of buildings without speaking. Pointed toward the stone house and sent the horse loping through the blue-stem while his right hand drew his gun and jacked the spent shells from the cylinder. His thumb and finger plucked fresh cartridges from his wide belt and worked them through the loading gate automatically, and then he spun the cylinder and holstered the weapon with a smooth flirt of his supple wrist.

"I'll call him to come out," he said simply. "You fan out ten paces and sit yore hoss. I don't blame Dupree for living back here in Rainbow Canyon. Looky yonder!"

Utah Young followed the pointing arm with his eyes and caught his breath. The early sun was painting the sides of the steep towering cliffs with all the vivid colours of the Rainbow. Off to the side a mountain stream gurgled noisily over lava rocks, and tall bracken lined the banks with varying changes of living green.

"Hoss heaven," the Mormon murmured. "Wait until the Deacon sees this."

Roaming Reynolds was sitting straight in the saddle with his blue eyes fastened on the stone house. No sign of life among the cluster of buildings off to the right, and the pole corrals were empty of stock. The tall cowboy loped right up to the low porch and swung down to anchor his horse with trailing reins. Utah Young fanned out ten paces away and waited with his hand close to the gun on his leg.

"Dupree!"

The cowboy's voice echoed hollowly when he shouted the name of the famous outlaw. He waited a moment and repeated the call with a brassy twang in his drawling voice. Then the tall gun-fighter drooped his shoulders and mounted the three stone steps.

Utah Young drew his gun and fastened his eyes on the big oak door. Roaming Reynolds turned the handle and pushed through without hesitation. Then he turned and jerked his head at the Mormon.

"Light down and come on in," he growled. "We might as well find us some proof while we got the chance."

Utah Young swung down and pouched his

pistol with a sigh of relief. Mounted the steps and stared at the litter of sacks the cowboy was pulling from behind a curtain. Bank wrappers and Wells Fargo canvas, filled with clinking gold and rustling greenbacks.

"He could live like a king," the Mormon gasped. "And he stayed here when he knew he was whipped."

"He don't know it yet," Reynolds grunted. "No gun-fighter ever does until he meets a better man."

"Can't figger out why the place is deserted," Utah muttered. "Dupree must have had all of twenty-thirty men in his gang."

"And he lost quite a few," Reynolds reminded dryly. "The feller that got young Sam was left here to guard the place. Give me a hand with this stuff!"

"You going to take it?"

"Why not?" Reynolds grunted. "Dupree can't be no madder than he is right now. We can hide it until this ruckus is over, and after that the law can mebbe straighten things out. The Law," he grunted contemptuously.

Utah Young nodded and helped stuff the loot into the heavy canvas sacks. Roaming Reynolds dragged these out on the front porch and threw them to the ground. Then he climbed down and pushed them under the house where they could not be seen. Levered erect and walked over to grab the trailing whangs with his left hand.

"They will stay there until we want them," he muttered, and swung up to the saddle. "Now we better get back and blind young Sam's hoss."

Utah Young shuddered. "You mean to pack the body back?"

"That boy gets put away proper," Reynolds growled. "With the Deacon waiting back there on the M T to read the services!"

Utah Young did not answer until they reached the body of young Sam Smith. He caught up the grazing horse and made a blindfold with his bandanna while Reynolds busied himself with ropes. Then he led the snorting animal close, and held the bit while the tall cowboy lifted the body and laid it face-down across the saddle.

"Never thought Sam would get it," Young muttered.

"None of us know when we are going to get it," Reynolds growled, and made his ties on ankles and wrists. "You lead that hoss," he added, and handed up the bridle reins to Utah Young.

"Them shots we heard back on the trail," the Mormon said suddenly. "Like as not we will be leading two hosses back to the M T."

Roaming Reynolds stiffened. "Meaning what?" he asked jerkily.

"Yore pard," the Mormon muttered. "He's only a button, and he was back there with Pete Jordan!"

"Take a hitch in yore jaw," Reynolds growled savagely, but his craggy face showed the worry that was in his mind. "Joe might be a button, but you seen for yoreself that he was all man. They didn't get him, I tell yuh!"

His deep voice was so savage that Utah Young dropped his eyes and glanced hastily away. Roaming Reynolds jumped his saddle without touching the oxbows. Sent the tall bay roaring across the long valley with the hooks biting at every jump.

"I hope yo're right, Boss," Utah Young muttered under his breath, and followed slowly with his burden, "but it's my guess that the Deacon will read two services. Men of peace," he grunted with heavy irony.

CHAPTER XVII

Texas Joe sat turned in the saddle while he led the horse of Pete Jordan back through the twisting mazes. The little outlaw was a different man from the cringing Pete Jordan who had led Roaming Reynolds into Rainbow with the fear of certain death in his heart. He carried himself with a jaunty air of hopefulness, but Texas Joe scowled and maintained his watchfulness.

"I'd bc proud to side a boss like Roaming Reynolds," Jordan remarked. "Like yo're doin', Joe," he added when the boy stared at him with open suspicion.

"You was sidin' quite a man yore own self," Joe growled. "I don't cotton none to a gent what sells out!"

"He's a cold killer," the little outlaw answered defensively. "He ain't never yet took a chance even when he faced them hombres he put in Boot Hill."

"You mean he didn't give 'em a chance?"

Pete Jordan shuddered. "Would you or me have a chance with Eagle Dupree?" he asked slowly. "Take you, for instance. You never got yore cutter out of leather back there behind the M T ranch house."

The button frowned angrily. "You call that a

chance?" he snarled. "And him with his iron in his hand?"

"Him having it in his hand saved you a killing," Jordan muttered. "When Eagle Dupree makes a draw he always shoots, and he shoots mighty straight!"

"A gent can't die but one time," Joe grunted. "I'd have took a chance to keep him from getting Miss Betty."

"Shore you would," Jordan agreed. "And right now you'd be waiting for the shovel-crew to dig you a three-by-seven. Eagle Dupree has killed more than a dozen men, and he ain't got a bullet-burn on him!"

"Yah," Joe sneered. "But now there's a new gun-boss up here in the Strip, and I'll be siding him when he catches up to Eagle Dupree to give him show-down. How much farther to the river?"

"Mebbe two miles," Jordan answered, and scanned the fringing brush nervously. "You feel anything funny?" he asked in a whisper.

Texas Joe stared coldly. "I ain't bothered none with imagination nor a guilty conscience," he growled. "What for kind of a feelin' you talking about?"

"Like eyes watching us," Jordan murmured. "I'd be as good as dead right now if Eagle knew I led you and Reynolds back through here!"

Texas Joe was half-turned in the saddle to watch his prisoner. He jerked around when Pete

Jordan caught his breath with a look of terror in his eyes. A snaky loop hissed through the air to pin the cowboy's arms down when he started to slap for his gun, and Texas Joe was dragged sideways from the saddle. The breath was jolted from his body when he landed on his back, and a pair of running half-hitches flipped down the rope to snare his rusty boots.

"Lie still, yearlin'," a soft voice purred, and Eagle Dupree stepped out from the brush and stooped swiftly to finish his ties with a hard knot.

Pete Jordan stared and kicked with both spurred boots. His horse lunged ahead and was brought up short as the end of his bridle-reins fastened to the nubbin of Texas Joe's saddle. Eagle Dupree leaped forward and jerked the little outlaw from the saddle just as Texas Joe rolled over mouthing curses in a shrill boyish voice.

"Tie me loose, yuh sneakin' killer. Yuh don't dare to face a man!"

The tall outlaw threw Pete Jordan to the ground and turned with a smile on his dark face. "You ain't a man, Joe," he said quietly. "Or I'd have shot you from the saddle when you come back-trackin' like a Pilgrim!"

"Man enough to smoke down a few of yore owl-hoot hands," the boy shrilled. "I was man enough to stay and fight when you run away!"

Eagle Dupree changed swiftly. His face froze into a mask of cruelty to make him look like an Apache brave. His right hand snapped to his holster. Hung there when he regained control of his temper, and then he dropped his hand and smiled at the angry youth.

"So you think I ran away, eh?" he almost whispered.

"Yuh dogged it," Texas Joe barked viciously. "When you knew Roamin' was comin' through the door!"

Eagle Dupree straightened slowly and stared down into the blazing grey eyes. Then he shook his head slowly. "You don't know much about the code, button," he murmured, and the contempt in his soft voice cut the boy's pride worse than a whip could have done. "I don't shoot from the dark like you might have heard."

"You was afraid of Roamin'," Joe sneered, and grinned when the tall outlaw gripped his slender hands to control his anger. "You knew he had you beat with yore own tools!"

Eagle Dupree threw a glance at Pete Jordan and turned again to Texas Joe. "Stop and think a minute, Kid," he suggested quietly. "I was outside where nobody could see me. Yore pard was in the room with a light behind him. Spell that out and tell me the answer."

Texas Joe gulped and nodded his tousled head. "Reckon yo're right, Mister," he admitted. "But nohow, you didn't get the gal!"

The outlaw shrugged. "Time enough," he

muttered. "She can't go anywhere, and I have other business to attend first."

"Yeah," Joe growled. "Like meeting a better man than yoreself."

The outlaw controlled his anger with difficulty. He took a quick step forward with his hand raised, and then he stopped when he saw the sneering grin on the boy's grimy face.

"Yo're just a yearlin'," he said disdainfully, and shrugged his muscular shoulders. "Now you save yore wind while I make medicine with my friend Pete Jordan."

Texas Joe had sense enough to stop his badgering. Pete Jordan shuddered and levered up to squat on his boot-heels. His hands tugged against the thong that held them behind his back, and the tall outlaw leaned over swiftly. A knife flashed in his left hand to cut the saddle-string, and Pete Jordan crouched down and rubbed his swollen wrists.

"So you led the enemy to my camp?" Dupree said softly.

"They'd have found it nohow, Boss," the little outlaw shouted. "You gave Reynolds an invite yore own self!"

"So I did," Dupree agreed softly. "And I was not home to receive him."

"He give me a chance, he did," Jordan moaned piteously. "He give me a chance to light out and start goin' straight!"

"Straight," the tall outlaw sneered. "You ever hear of a gent going straight once he took the wrong fork of the trail?"

Pete Jordan dropped his eyes and continued to rub his wrists. Texas Joe watched the little scene with his lips curling. No pity in his grey eyes when Jordan turned his head and stared as though asking for help.

"There always has to be the first time," the button heard himself saying. "The way it looked to me, Pete was going to give the straight and narrow a whirl!"

"You ain't lived long enough to know," Dupree barked. "So I'm telling both you and him. It ain't been done up to now!"

Pete Jordan licked his lips and stared at his small hands. "Reynolds give me a chance," he croaked huskily. "He could have killed me back there by the river, but he held his shot and let me live!"

"Big-hearted," Dupree sneered softly. "Never let it be said that my rival was more generous than me. I aim to give you a chance myself!"

Pete Jordan straightened slowly and stared at the dark cruel face. "You mean it, Eagle?" he whispered incredulously. "Yo're goin' to give me one more chance?"

Eagle Dupree nodded his black head slowly. "That's what I said," he murmured, and stepped across to lean over Texas Joe.

The button sucked in his breath and tightened his tough muscles. He jerked when Dupree reached out his left hand and lifted the old forty-five from the worn holster, and then his snarling voice ripped savagely against his clenched teeth.

"Drop my cutter, you killin' lobo! The man don't live what could lift my hardware if my hands were free!"

Eagle Dupree shrugged carelessly and stepped back to Pete Jordan. The little outlaw watched him like a cornered mouse watches a cat, and Dupree smiled coldly and stared for a long moment until Jordan dropped his eyes. Then his left hand twitched out suddenly to holster the borrowed gun deep in the holster on the little outlaw's right leg.

"There's yore chance," he grunted softly. "And it's more than you deserve!"

Pete Jordan raised both hands with a squeal of terror. "Yuh can't do it, Eagle," he shouted hoarsely. "It's no less than cold murder!"

"It's a chance," the tall outlaw murmured coldly. "Take it or leave it."

"Just a minute, yuh ringy owl-hooter," Texas Joe drawled slowly. "You ain't got the guts of a squirrel. You know you got him beat before he starts, and I can give a name to that kind of a chance!"

Eagle Dupree ignored the taunt and continued to stare at Pete Jordan. The little outlaw whim-

254

pered and clasped his hands together across his narrow chest.

"Hip High Hardy pistol-whipped me one time," he moaned. "You saw the time I went up again that flip-draw of hissen. Then you slipped yore cutter before Hardy could clear leather, and I tell you it's dirty murder!"

Eagle Dupree continued to stare with his steady dark eyes.

"Leading Reynolds and his Mormons back here in Rainbow Canyon," he said quietly. "To kill me without giving me a chance. What would you call that, Pete Jordan?"

"He was bringin' you show-down," Jordan rasped hoarsely. "You told him to come in sometime and see the sunrise!"

Dupree shook his head slowly. "No dice," he murmured. "And I'm givin' you a chance."

"You ain't," Texas Joe snarled viciously. "You know he's boogered so he can't hit the handle of his cutter. Tie me loose from this rope and holster that iron back on my leg. I'll take that chance, yuh ringy lobo!"

Eagle Dupree smiled with his eyes while his lips held in a stern straight line. "I don't doubt yore courage, button," he answered quietly. "But right now I'm talking to a man who has eaten my salt, and who swore loyalty to me. Stiffen up yore nerve, Pete."

Pete Jordan glanced at the sun-painted cliffs of

255

Rainbow Canyon. Back again to the lush grass where a small stream flowed noisily over the lava rocks. Then he sucked in a great draught of air and squared his thin shoulders.

"Shoot," he muttered. "And I'll haunt you to yore grave!"

Eagle Dupree stepped forward like a cat and slapped with his open left hand. The blow rocked Jordan back on his run-over heels; left a row of livid welts on his pallid cheeks. Gradually the terror left his slitted grey eyes and he straightened his stooped shoulders slowly while his hands unclenched and dropped down to his sides.

"That done it, Eagle," he said quietly. "I ain't been much of a man in my time, but like the button said, a gent can't die but one time. It's cold murder, but I'll take the chance."

"That's better," Dupree murmured. "Now you brace yoreself and stop shaking. When you get ready, just make yore pass. Yore last one," he added softly.

Pete Jordan clenched his fists and closed his eyes tightly. His face showed the fight he was making to steady himself, and gradually the tremble left his fingers. Then he opened his eyes and smiled wanly.

"I'm ready, killer," he said softly. "You didn't look for it, but I can die like a man!"

His right hand rapped down like a striking snake with fingers spread wide to fit the handle of the old gun. Eagle Dupree waited until the long barrel hissed against the worn leather and poised on the lip of the scabbard. Then he twitched his right shoulder in a blinding flash of speed, and a rocking explosion seemed to belch from his hand before the movement had been completed.

Pete Jordan jerked back under the shock that also jerked his arm to complete his draw. His thumb slipped on the hammer to throw a shot off to one side even while he was falling forward to measure his length. Eagle Dupree watched critically, and when Texas Joe jerked his eyes around, the ivory-handled gun was once more snugged in leather. A curl of acrid smoke floated up to make a gun-fighter's halo above the tall outlaw's head.

Pete Jordan fell to the ground and bounced a time or two. Then the toes of his rusty boots rattled briefly to trample the grass. An oppressive quiet caught an echoing explosion from up on the cliffs, and Texas Joe threw himself against the tight-twist rope that held him captive.

"Murder," he snarled shrilly. "You don't pack the sand to tie me loose and put that same cutter on my leg!"

Eagle Dupree turned with a shrug. "It *would* be murder," he said quietly. "Pete Jordan was way faster than you with a sixgun, and you saw what happened."

"I saw," Joe shouted. "And he died like a man

the way he said. Even a thief like you can't take that away from him!"

"I wouldn't do it," the outlaw answered softly. "I might take a gent's money like that old poet said, but I wouldn't try to rob him of his good name. Pete Jordan died like a man, but he got what was coming to him."

Texas Joe stared up into the hard black eyes and gritted his teeth. "You'll get it, rustler," he grated bitterly. "There's a better man lookin' for you right now. You know it the same as me, and I can see it down in them snaky eyes of yores!"

The calmness fell away from Eagle Dupree like a discarded coat. His lips twisted while the fires of hell leaped high in his dark eyes, and his hands were gripped tightly while he stared at the button and fought for self control. Texas Joe shivered involuntarily, and the move restored the outlaw to reason.

"I nearly sent you after Pete Jordan," he said quietly, but his voice was chilled with the ice of a terrible anger. "Like I told you before, I never kill children. You was talking about Roaming Reynolds being fast!"

Texas Joe sucked in his breath. He had seen the flashing draw that waited until Pete Jordan had almost cleared leather. He could not be sure that he had seen the outlaw's hand move, and his grey eyes darted down to the holster thonged low on Dupree's right leg.

"Swivel holster," he sneered. "Yuh killed him on a sneak!"

Eagle Dupree stiffened again and relaxed immediately. His right hand moved slowly to his holster and lifted the long-barrelled sixgun. Held it in his left hand while his right tugged at the hand-moulded holster while Texas Joe stared his unbelief.

"Takin' it back, outlaw," the boy muttered softly. "I might have knowed it wasn't a swivel-scabbard when I see the tie-backs. But you knew you had him beat before you started," and once more his rasping voice was bitter with denunciation.

Eagle Dupree smiled and nodded his head. "Part of that is true," he agreed honestly. "I knew I had him beat, just as I always have known it when I faced a gun-hawk who thought he was fast. I am the gun-boss of the Strip and I always will be!"

"You won't," Texas Joe contradicted flatly. "Roamin' is the boss, and there's one gun-hawk who don't booger worth a hoot. I see him make several passes, and he's got you faded!"

"Fast, eh?" and the outlaw's voice was a whisper of joy. "You ain't hoorawing me, Kid?"

Texas Joe sneered. "Hoorawing a gent what has been around as long as you have?" he grunted. "What I'm telling you is Gospel!"

"The money means nothing to me," Dupree

whispered, and his dark eyes glowed with a strange fire. "I wouldn't want to live if I thought . . . ?"

"If yuh thought some other fast gun-passer had yuh beat with yore tools," the boy finished for him. "So it looks like yo're about through up here in the Strip!"

Eagle Dupree stared thoughtfully for a long moment, and then his eyes switched to the body of Pete Jordan. He straightened suddenly and shrugged his shoulders back, and when he turned to Texas Joe again the old mask of coldness covered his dark face.

"Roaming Reynolds cut into my play last night," he stated quietly. "He kept me from taking something I wanted, but I expect her soon nohow!"

Texas Joe laughed raucously. "Then you didn't hear?" he taunted.

Eagle Dupree frowned. "Didn't hear what?"

"About the Deacon and Betty Tucker smokin' yore owl-hooters down," Joe continued.

"Not the Deacon," Dupree contradicted. "He won't be bothering any one for quite a while, and the gal wouldn't kill a fly."

"That's what you figger," Joe chuckled. "But there were three long-ridin' sons all sprawled out under the Deacon's window when we rode past there. They tried to bushwhack a sick man, and every dang one of them rustlers is shot plumb through the head. Looks like yo're wasting yore time waiting for them to bring Miss Betty back to you!"

Eagle Dupree stared and twisted the ends of his little moustache. Satisfied that Joe was telling the truth, he rubbed his square chin and shook his head slowly.

"Can the leopard change his spots?" he murmured softly. "You mean to tell me that Brigham Smith used a gun?"

"I'd tell uh man," Texas Joe answered heartily. "Roamin' took them fancy cutters offen Hip High Hardy after he had rubbed him out. Made the Deacon a present of them same cutters, and looks like the Deacon learned almighty fast. Looks like no dice again, Mister!"

Eagle Dupree jerked his head toward the far end of the canyon. "You say Reynolds went up to look for me?"

Texas Joe nodded. "Him and Utah Young, along with Sam Smith," he answered without hesitation. "They ought to be back this way when they find you missing."

"Three to one," Dupree muttered, and tugged at his moustaches. "But two of them are Mormons, and they don't count for much when it comes to gun-talk!"

"You might be surprised," Texas Joe warned. "You got something on yore mind?"

Eagle Dupree reached into his pocket and

pulled out a feather. The feather of the great king eagle, and he broke it between his fingers while Joe watched every move intently. Then the outlaw leaned over and stuck the broken feather in the collar band of the dead man's shirt.

"I'll do the same for yore pard," he said quietly, and stared hard at Texas Joe. "You can tell him I said so."

"Tell him yoreself," Joe barked. "He ought to be back here soon after hearing them shots when you murdered Pete Jordan yonder."

"You was a man, I'd give you the same chance Pete Jordan got," the outlaw muttered.

"I'm gun-size," Joe snarled. "Throw off these ties and let me get up on my hind legs. Put my old cutter on my leg and call the time yoreself!"

"That would be murder," Dupree said gruffly. "You ain't lived no where's near long enough to have the feel of a gun. This is the third time I let you live because you was a yearlin' with the velvet on yore horns."

"I'm coming eighteen and full growed," Texas Joe shouted angrily, and bit his lips when his voice broke and ended in a shrill scream. "You mangy, hoss-rustlin' son of a tarantuler!"

Eagle Dupree smiled and then began to chuckle. "You got spirit, button," he praised quietly. "But like I told you, you don't pack around enough years to face me for a shoot-and-draw. You tell yore salty pard what I said. And you might tell

Miss Betty that I meant every word I said about that feather!"

"Doggin' it, eh?" Joe taunted, when the outlaw disappeared back in the brush screen. "You don't pack the sand to stay and face Roamin' for a show-down!"

Eagle Dupree swung up to his saddle and came back to the clearing. "I got business this morning," he said without emotion. "And right now yore pard has too much help. I reckon he will keep until the time is right. So long, button."

"*Hasta la vista*," Texas Joe shouted. "Till we meet again, yuh murderin' son of a wolf!"

CHAPTER XVIII

Betty Tucker stretched her tired muscles and glanced down at the bearded face of Brigham Smith. The big man was sleeping soundly, and the girl's face clouded momentarily when she saw the long-barrelled gun clutched in her right hand. She shivered when she turned her eyes toward the window where the first light of dawn was giving notice of a new day.

The girl arose slowly from her seat on the bed and tiptoed toward the door. Making her way back to her own room, she bathed her face in the stone basin and tidied her hair with quick little pats. Pans were rattling back in the big kitchen, and Ma Tucker looked up with an unspoken question in her brown eyes when Betty entered the room.

"He's asleep," the girl said softly. "Where is Father?"

"Reading the services behind the granary," Ma Tucker answered simply. "The boys buried eight men when the light came up in the sky."

Full red lips quivered for a moment, and then Betty Tucker was in her mother's arms. "I hated to do it," she sobbed. "Those two men I killed last night."

Mrs. Tucker patted her heaving shoulders. "It

264

was kill or be killed," she answered firmly. "The survival of the fittest, daughter."

"And Brigham," the girl sobbed. "He is a killer like . . . like . . ."

"Like Roaming Reynolds," Ma Tucker answered with quiet satisfaction. "Sometimes there is such a thing as carrying peace too far. Your father said the same thing just before he took his prayer-book and went out there to read the services."

"Roaming?" the girl asked suddenly, and held her mother at arm's length. "Where is he?"

"Gone," the older woman answered quietly. "He and Texas Joe rode away with Utah and Sam. They started for Rainbow Canyon."

"They will be killed," the girl gasped. "That is the hide-out for Eagle Dupree and all his gang!"

Ma Tucker sniffed. "I don't think there is much of that gang left after last night," she said quietly. "And we owe it all to Roaming Reynolds."

The girl nodded and started for the hall. "I am going to meet Father," she explained. "Roaming might need help."

"You get your breakfast first," Ma Tucker answered practically. "Roaming Reynolds won't be needing any help."

Betty Tucker walked through the long hall and out on the porch. Mormon Tucker was just coming across the yard, and the girl waited for him with a finger to her lips. She pointed to the side room and spoke in a whisper.

"Brigham is asleep, Father. I am worried about Roaming and the boys!"

"They started for Rainbow Canyon," the big Mormon muttered. "Nothing was seen of Dupree after the fighting began."

"I'll have horses saddled while we eat our breakfasts," the girl answered. "He might need our help, Dad. Somehow I have a feeling that something is wrong."

Mormon Tucker nodded and stroked his long black beard with his left hand while his right unconsciously rubbed the handle of his gun. He followed Betty back to the kitchen; took his place at the table and ate in silence after offering a short prayer. Ma Tucker stared at him when he arose from the table and hitched up the gunbelt on his big hips.

"Where are you going, husband?"

"Betty and I are riding to Rainbow Canyon, wife," the big man answered slowly. "Betty has a feeling."

Ma Tucker nodded her head emphatically. "I have a feeling too," she admitted seriously. "Perhaps you better hurry!"

The two walked swiftly across the yard where a pair of deep-chested mountain horses were rein-tied at the corral. Mounted up and rode down the tree-bordered lane in silence, and Mormon

Tucker stopped his horse abruptly when they rounded the bend by the ford.

"We buried eight men," he whispered solemnly. "Look yonder, daughter!"

"Six more," the girl gasped. "They were the ones we heard running away. Now we know why those saddle horses were scattered all over the north pasture."

"Someone must have killed the guard and turned the horses loose to prevent the outlaws from making an escape," Tucker murmured, and shrugged his big shoulders. "They won't ever be any deader than they are right now, and our duty is toward the living!"

He sent his horse into the shallow water and crossed the ford with the girl rubbing stirrups at his side. Betty Tucker pointed to a high ridge where a solitary horseman was silhouetted against the sky.

"I wonder who that can be?" she murmured.

Mormon Tucker clutched her arm. "It looks like Eagle Dupree, but he must be a mile away," he whispered.

"And he comes from Rainbow Canyon," the girl added. "We must hurry, Father!"

She hit her horse with the hooks and sent him rocketing across the river bottom and through the pass that led into Rainbow Canyon. Twisting and dodging the brilliantly coloured shoulders of rock that jutted out from every side, and Mormon

Tucker was the first to see the bodies on the ground when they came to the narrow bottle-neck.

"Two men down," he muttered, and sent his sweating horse up the sloping grade.

He slid his horse to a stop; was bending over Texas Joe when Betty Tucker clattered up behind him and stepped off to slide on braking boot-heels.

"Howdy, Boss," the button said calmly. "Take yore knife and cut me loose from this lass-rope."

Mormon Tucker fished for his frogging knife and severed the wrapped coils with swift strokes. Texas Joe sat up and rubbed his wrists; smiled at Betty Tucker until he saw her staring at the body of Pete Jordan. Then he crawled across the ground and retrieved his old sixgun.

"Eagle Dupree done that there," he said gruffly. "His name was Pete Jordan, and he led us back here to Dupree's hide-out. Roamin' promised Pete a chance to quit and go straight, but Eagle was waiting back here in the bresh. Snared me out of my hull with a finicky loop before I could slap for my cutter!"

"Then he tied you up," Tucker growled, and jerked his head toward the body. "After which he murdered Jordan!"

"He called it giving Pete a chance," Joe muttered. "Put my gun in Pete's holster and told

268

him to take a chance. Finally Pete screwed up his nerve, and he died like a man!"

"You mean he shot it out with Dupree?"

Texas Joe smiled grimly. "Dupree waited until Pete was just on the edges of clearing leather," he explained dryly. "Then Eagle made his pass, and I never even saw his hand move. Then Pete was lyin' there on his face with his boots rattling a fare-thee-well."

"We saw Dupree riding away," the girl answered softly. "It's a wonder he didn't kill you, Joe."

The boy flushed and swallowed a lump in his throat. "He wouldn't give me the same chance he give Pete," he snarled. "Said I was a kid button what hadn't lived long enough to get the feel of a gun. Likewise, he said he wanted me to live to deliver some messages," and the boy turned his head and stared at the girl.

Betty Tucker jerked and caught her breath sharply. "A message for me?" she asked in a whisper.

Texas Joe nodded his sandy head. "Said to tell you he was saving a feather for you. Sounds like Roaming Reynolds coming down the draw."

Roaming Reynolds and Utah Young came pounding through the narrow pass at a headlong pace. Both threw their running horses to sliding haunches when they saw Texas Joe on his feet talking to the Tuckers; Roaming Reynolds slid to the ground and came forward to grab the boy by the shoulders.

"Thought you was done for, pard," he said jerkily, and then he saw the body of the little outlaw. "You do that?" he asked slowly.

Texas Joe shook his head. "Eagle Dupree done it," he explained, and told the same story he had recited to the Tuckers. "He called it giving the little feller a chance!"

"Pore jigger," the tall cowboy murmured. "I believed him when he said he was going to cut 'er straight from here on out!" Then he turned swiftly to Mormon Tucker. "How come you and Betty to be down here?"

"Betty and her mother had a feeling that something was wrong," the big Mormon explained. "We saw Eagle Dupree way up on top of the rim, and we hurried here to see if we could help. Joe was all tied up in that rope, and you see the rest."

"Eagle said to tell you he would settle with you after he had finished some other business," Joe interrupted softly. "He's fast as ball-lightnin', Roamin'!"

The tall gun-boss turned slowly. "I've heard he is," he answered in a slow drawl, but his blue eyes were glowing hotly. "He say where at he'd be waiting?"

"He never said," Joe shrugged. "What become of Sam Smith?"

Roaming Reynolds drew a deep breath and

glanced at Utah Young. "You tell them," he muttered.

"I left his hoss back behind that bend," the tall Mormon muttered. "Sam was in the saddle."

Mormon Tucker stepped forward and gripped him by the arm. "He wounded?"

"He's dead," and Utah Young turned his face away. "Only one outlaw left back there in the Canyon, but he shot from cover and got young Sam right through the heart. Reckon you will have to tell the Deacon, Mormon!"

Mormon Tucker stared in absolute silence. Then he glanced down at the body and turned to study the face of his daughter. She caught the pleading look in his dark eyes and lowered her head.

"I can't tell him," she whispered through stiff lips. "Don't you think he has had enough already?"

"He would want to read the service," Utah said softly. "Me and Roaming figgered to take the body under the Deacon's window. We could hold the service there."

Mormon Tucker drew himself up and sighed. "I will tell Brigham," he stated soberly. "Brigham is a man, and he has tasted the salt of flowing blood. Shall we go?"

"I'll get the other horse," Utah answered, and neck-reined his mount; glad for a chance to escape.

"Him," Texas Joe said softly, and pointed to the body of Pete Jordan. "He earned a decent burial, Boss. I'm asking you to plant him proper, and read the service over him for what he done."

"Spoke like a Christian, son," the big Mormon agreed heartily. "Blind his horse while Betty starts on ahead. Lend me a hand, Roaming."

"I got the proof on Dupree now, Boss," the tall cowboy muttered when Joe went after the outlaw's horse. "Must be close to a hundred thousand in gold and currency back there in the Canyon!"

Mormon Tucker stared hard. "You leave it there?"

"Left it for the law if same ever gets up this far," Reynolds grunted. "Eagle won't need it no more nohow."

"This war is nearly over, Roaming," the Mormon said slowly. "We can't afford to take any chances now. Ma and Betty and myself have come to think a heap of you, cowboy!"

Roaming Reynolds turned his face away and shrugged. "Eagle is the fastest gun-boss I ever cut sign on," he muttered. "I got to take it to him."

"You mean to face him in a gun duel?"

Reynolds nodded shortly. "According to the code," he muttered. "He thinks he is the fastest up here in the Arizona Strip, and I *know* I am."

"But you have broken his power," Tucker argued. "Let the law finish up the rest!"

272

"You know there ain't no law up here in the Strips," Reynolds clipped bluntly. "It might take him quite a while, but Dupree would start all over again. Besides that, you got to think of the gal."

"Betty!" Tucker gasped. "I had forgotten about that, Reynolds. He left word with Joe that he was keeping a feather for her!"

"You better ride on ahead with her," the cowboy murmured.

"I'll stay with the bodies," Tucker answered. "You ride ahead and cheer her up. She feels badly about those two men she shot last night."

Roaming Reynolds stared for a moment and then mounted his horse. Rode through the pass and overtook the girl at the next bend, and she smiled wanly and drew up to wait. The cowboy studied her pretty face and reached out his right hand.

"Shake, pard," he said sincerely. "You had to do what you did, and don't let it fret you none."

The girl gripped hard and held on to his hand. "It was terrible, Roaming," she whispered. "I felt the same blood-lust in my heart that I told you was a mortal sin. Those brutal faces at the window, and Brigham lying there unconscious," and the girl shuddered violently.

"They shoot the Deacon again?"

The girl shook her head. "Brigham shot the first one," she whispered tearfully. "When the gun

273

bucked in his hand, he must have fainted. Then those other two . . ."

The cowboy patted her shoulder gently. "I know," he murmured soothingly. "We saw them when we rode past in the moonlight. You needn't fear for the Deacon after last night. He's all man from hocks to horns!"

The girl came closer and sobbed on his shoulder. "You won't leave us, Roaming?" she whispered. "You will stay on the M T with Ma and Dad . . . and me?"

The cowboy stiffened and set his lips firmly. "I don't ever stay long in one place," he muttered. "I'm a gun-fighter, Miss Betty, and I reckon it's too deep in my blood."

"Brigham is a gun-fighter, too," the girl whispered. "Don't you like us just a little, Roaming Reynolds?"

"More than a little," the cowboy answered heartily. "I feel like I've been here half of my life. Never was treated better!"

"Then you will stay?"

Reynolds waited until she raised her head and studied his face. "I reckon not, Betty," he answered stubbornly. "The Deacon will soon be well again, and a better man never lived. He thinks a heap of you, little gal."

Betty Tucker caught her lip between even white teeth. "I guess he does," she answered wearily. "I guess maybe he needs me. Shall we ride on?"

She released his hand and sent her horse toward the river ford, and Reynolds glanced back over his shoulder. Utah Young and Mormon Tucker were each leading a horse, and Texas Joe came spurring up with fire blazing in his grey eyes.

"What did you do to Miss Betty?" he demanded hotly.

Roaming Reynolds regarded him coldly. "Might be best for you to mind yore own business," he growled. "Barging in like a Pilgrim every time you lose yore fool head."

"Might be I do," the boy snarled. "But you got no call to make that gal cry like you went and done. Eagle Dupree wouldn't do that!"

Roaming Reynolds became strangely silent. Texas Joe turned in his scarred saddle and scowled at his tall companion. Reynolds was watching the girl crossing the river ford with a strange stricken expression on his hard face. Only now the hard blue eyes were soft with a light that Joe had never seen in them before.

"Roamin'," he whispered contritely. "I didn't mean all them things I said. Don't look like that, pard!"

Roaming Reynolds turned his head away. "Reckon you wouldn't savvy, Joe. Don't know if I do myself. It's this away, feller. I'm a gunfighter with something down inside of me that I can't resist. Just can't help myself when some fast gun-boss cuts my sign and gives me the high-sign. It ain't something that you can see nor put a finger upon, but it's there just the same. He knows it, and he knows that I know it, and I'd go to hell with my boots on before I'd let him cut his rusty!"

The boy stared with awe in his grey eyes. "Yuh really feel that away, pard?"

The tall cowboy nodded silently. "The other gent feels the same way," Joe announced solemnly. "I could see it in the eyes of Eagle Dupree when he was tallying off yore points in his mind." Then he scowled. "What's that got to do with that pretty filly up yonder?" he demanded roughly.

Roaming Reynolds relaxed with a grave smile. "Everything," he answered softly. "Things mean for ever and ever with her. Brigham Smith is her kind of folks, and he won't ever give back a step in anything he starts. He's been loving Betty for a long time."

"Well cut my cinches," Joe whispered. "Slap me to sleep for a knot-head if I didn't booger like a Pilgrim and cloud up the sign. Sayin' I'm sorry I run off at the mouth that away, Roamin'!"

"The Deacon," Reynolds said slowly. "Right now he's hurt bad and fighting a battle with himself because he killed a man that meant to kill him. On top of that we're bringing in young Sam; the only brother he ever had. We got to think about that big feller, pard."

"And yo're steppin' aside because of the

Deacon," Joe said slowly, and shook his head. "Figgerin' he needs the gal more than you do."

Roaming Reynolds turned and stared with his cold blue eyes. "I'm telling you for the last time, button," he warned softly. "You link me up again with Miss Betty, what Eagle Dupree did to you won't be a patch on what you got coming!"

Texas Joe looked away and slowly bobbed his head. "Like you said, Roamin'," and there was genuine fear in his grey eyes at what he read in the tall cowboy's face. "Let's drop back and give them two a hand."

"You drop back," Reynolds grunted. "I'm foggin' ahead to tell Betty to break the news easy. No good getting the Deacon all worked up right now. Might be best to let Ma tell him."

He spurred ahead and crossed the river in a shower of spray. Betty Tucker was just dismounting at the big porch when the cowboy slid his horse to a stop and stepped off to catch her hand.

"Betty; hold up a spell."

The girl waited with head lowered, and he saw a tear on the long lashes. "Yes, Roaming."

"Better get Ma to tell him," Reynolds said softly. "I'll go with you while you let her know. Chin up, pard."

The girl nodded and started up the steps. Through the long hall with Reynolds at her side, and they tiptoed past the Deacon's door and on into the big kitchen. Ma Tucker left the big wood range and caught the cowboy in her arms to hold him close.

"You are safe, son," she murmured close to his ear. "We were worried about you."

"Sho now, Ma'am," Reynolds muttered. "Me and Tex was all right. But Betty and I want to tell you something."

Ma Tucker drew her breath in sharply and glanced at her daughter. A puzzled expression crept into her eyes when she saw the sad look in the brown eyes. A sadness that was reflected in the blue eyes of the tall young cowboy in her plump arms.

"Something to tell me?" she repeated.

"Young Sam Smith," Reynolds muttered. "We're bringing him home. He's gone west, Ma!"

"Young Sam! Not dead?" she whispered tensely.

Roaming Reynolds nodded. "Utah Young is bringing him home, and we thought mebbe you better break it to the Deacon. Sam was shot back there in Rainbow Canyon, but the feller that did it won't never bushwhack anybody else!"

Ma Tucker began to sob and then checked herself abruptly. "No time for tears now," she said in a choked voice, and squared her broad shoulders. "We will go in together. Brigham would never forgive us if we didn't tell him at once, and thank God the Deacon is a fighting man!"

CHAPTER XIX

"I'm afraid, Roaming," and Betty Tucker came close to the tall cowboy and gripped his arm hard. "I'm afraid the shock will be too much for Brigham!"

Roaming Reynolds took a deep breath and squared his shoulders. "We got it to do, little pard," he muttered, but for once his hard face showed that he was worried. "I'd rather face a salty *buscadero* with his gun a-smokin' than break the news to the Deacon."

He began to move down the hall with the girl by his side. He hesitated at the Deacon's door until a deep booming voice called impatiently from within.

"Come in, Roaming. I've been waiting for you!"

Roaming Reynolds gulped and turned the knob. Pushed into the room and stopped for a moment to study the big man in the high bed. Brigham Smith smiled gently and extended his right hand. The handles of his twin guns peeped out from under his pillows, and the tall cowboy high-heeled across the floor and gripped the Mormon hard.

"Glad you made the big pull, Deacon," he murmured softly. "Was afraid there for a spell I'd have to throw you a rope to help you out of the bog."

"Roaming, I prayed for you," the Deacon said softly. "I knew you had gone into Rainbow Canyon. Seems like I've known you a long time, pard!"

His eyes wandered to the side and saw Betty Tucker in the door behind Reynolds. Brown eyes that opened wide when he extended his left hand to the girl.

"I heard you ride out, Betty," he said softly. "Are the boys all right?"

The girl nodded and turned her face away. The big man frowned when Ma Tucker came into the room with a sad sweet smile on her comely face. Brigham Smith glanced up at Reynolds, and then settled back as though to brace himself.

"Sam?" he breathed softly. "It's about Sam!"

Roaming Reynolds jerked a trifle and turned his head. "It's about Sam, Brigham," Ma Tucker answered gently. "He rode out to Rainbow Canyon with Roaming and Utah. Mormon is bringing Sam home."

"Bringing him?" and the wounded man leaned forward. Then he relaxed with a nod of his head. "When a man is close to the Border, he sees and senses things that pass him by when he is well and strong," he murmured softly. "I knew it when you came into the room, Roaming. My brother Sam . . . has gone . . . *West!*"

Roaming Reynolds nodded his head slowly without meeting the pleading brown eyes. "He was shot from ambush," he muttered gruffly. "He didn't suffer none, Brigham!"

The bearded young Mormon sighed deeply. "It was Destiny," he murmured, and closed his eyes while his lips moved silently. Roaming Reynolds slowly took off his high-crowned Stetson and bowed his head. Ma Tucker and Betty prayed silently until Brigham Smith murmured and opened his eyes.

"The man who killed Sam?" he asked, and now his deep voice was harsh.

"Dead," Reynolds muttered fiercely. "He didn't live more than a minute after he dry-gulched young Sam. I got the varmint personal," he added softly, but the blue in his eyes glittered feverishly.

"Mormon would know that I would want to read the service," Brigham Smith whispered, and glanced toward the window.

He sat up with a jerk when he saw the flat-topped beaver of Mormon Tucker just above the sill. Utah Young was standing just opposite, and the two big men raised a litter and stood in silence with uncovered heads. Brigham Smith looked long at the peaceful quiet face of his younger brother until Ma Tucker crossed the room and handed him a small open book.

Betty Tucker began to sob softly, and Roaming Reynolds nudged her savagely with his elbow.

281

The girl gasped and bit her lips, and all the room was silent when Brigham Smith began to read in a soft booming voice that somehow held the mellowed tones of an old bell.

Texas Joe stood outside and stared down at the scuffed toes of his rusty boots. His young face was twisted with savagery affected to hide the panic in his youthful heart. Afraid to look up lest he should disclose the scalding tears in his squinted grey eyes when his grimy right hand rubbed the grip of his gun.

"And thus we consign this clay to earth again whence it came," the Deacon intoned gently, and waved his big left hand while he closed his eyes.

Mormon Tucker and Utah Young picked up their burden and moved silently away. Texas Joe disappeared and came into the room a moment later to take his stand beside Roaming Reynolds. Brigham Smith turned his head and held out his hand.

"Glad you came back safe, Joe," he said heartily. "And now we must think about the living!"

"Yeah," the boy muttered. "There's them what has lived too long!"

"Right," the big Mormon agreed promptly, and turned his head to study the face of Roaming Reynolds.

Roaming Reynolds nodded shortly. "I'll be

hitting out," he grunted. "As soon as I have cleaned my guns!"

Betty Tucker shivered at the icy tones of his vibrant voice. "Must you?" she whispered.

"He must," Brigham Smith answered firmly. "And after that, my roaming friend?"

"After that I'll be roamin' along," the tall cowboy murmured quietly. "There's lots of places over the hills I ain't never seen yet."

Betty Tucker moved back and leaned against her mother. Her brown eyes held steady on the strong column of the cowboy's neck, and Ma Tucker circled her waist and squeezed with silent understanding. Utah Young came suddenly into the room before Brigham Smith could frame an answer.

"Look!" and his harsh voice swung every pair of eyes toward him. "We just found this on the door of the granary!"

He held a feather in his right hand. An eagle feather with a bit of white paper wrapped around the thick quill. The eyes of Roaming Reynolds narrowed down to pin-points of glistening blue, and his voice was barely audible when he spoke to Utah Young.

"A message; like as not it was meant for me!"

He stepped forward and took the feather from the tall Mormon's hand. Tore off the paper and smoothed it on his knee while the others watched him in silence. Then he read the paper and smiled with the corners of his hard mouth, and held up his left hand.

"Roaming Reynolds,
This is your last chance, or mine. I am willing to fight for the things I want. I will be waiting at the LAST CHANCE in Red Horse if you come alone. I alone am the gun-boss of the Arizona Strip. A fair show-down at ten paces if you pack the sand. According to the code.
Eagle Dupree."

The tall cowboy read the note quietly but in a clear steady voice. Then he tucked the paper in an upper pocket of his vest and stared thoughtfully through the window where the brilliant peaks of the Vermilion Cliffs shimmered with changing colours in the sunlight.

"You better not go, Roaming," Brigham Smith murmured softly. "We need you here on the M T!"

Tenderness in that deep voice, and a shy note of suppressed affection. The affection that one strong man holds for another who has proven his worth. The cowboy nodded his head and continued to stare through the open window.

"I'll go," he contradicted flatly. "I wouldn't miss meeting the Eagle for anything I could name!"

"Nothing, Reynolds?" the Deacon asked softly, and his brown eyes wandered across the room to study the sad face of Betty Tucker. "Is there nothing that would cause you to change your mind?"

"Nothing," and the cowboy's tone was final. "Empty hands at ten paces against the fastest gun-boss in the Strip!"

He turned when scuffling boots sounded in the hall. Mormon Tucker was framed in the doorway, and the owner of the M T stared at the feather in the cowboy's hand.

"Has Eagle Dupree been here again?" he asked in a whisper.

Brigham Smith answered clearly. "He sent this by one of his men. Dupree wants to meet Reynolds for a show-down!"

"You won't go," and Mormon Tucker's voice was emphatic. "I won't allow it!"

Roaming Reynolds straightened and hitched up his sagging gunbelt. "I go where I please," he stated harshly. "No man tells me what I can do!"

Mormon Tucker flushed. "I mean that we need you here at the M T," he corrected quickly. "After what you have done for all of us!"

"You won't need me at all if I am faster than Eagle Dupree," Reynolds grunted. "If I don't face him now, I could never hold up my head again!"

"But he has no gang to speak of now," Utah Young broke in. "Mormon read services over eight men out behind the granary. Someone shot the horse-guard, and if any of them owl-hooters got away, he made it on foot. I think Pete Jordan was the only one left."

Reynolds turned and stared at Texas Joe. "Shooting that hoss-guard was a Texas trick," he said thoughtfully. "That was some of yore work, button!"

"I admits it," Texas Joe answered proudly, and stuck out his chest. "When we goin' in to meet Eagle Dupree?"

"*We* ain't," Reynolds corrected harshly. "The bid said to come in alone. That makes it a sixgun solo, pard!"

"Shore," the button agreed. "Like Hip High Hardy. I just stand by in case he's backed up by one of them curly wolves what ran in his owl-hoot pack."

"Wrong again, feller," and the cowboy glared at the lanky kid. "Yo're making a hand here on the M T, and me, I'm rolling my soogans. There's places over in the canyon of the Colorado I never have seen."

Mormon Tucker glanced from the hard face to the man on the bed. Betty Tucker had come close, and now she was staring down at the gun on her right leg as if afraid to raise her dark eyes.

"We might have trouble back in Rainbow Canyon, Roaming," Tucker suggested. "Eagle

286

Dupree is holding at least two hundred head of our stock back there."

The cowboy shrugged. "Dupree won't be back there," he said confidently. "He won't be troubling you or yores any more, Mormon!"

Mormon Tucker shrugged with resignation. "I'll see you in the office," and left the room abruptly.

Roaming Reynolds walked over to the bed and held out his hand. Brigham Smith gripped him hard and smiled wistfully. The cowboy's lips moved slowly.

"Good luck, pard," he muttered.

Betty Tucker raised her head and shook hands like a man. "I'll give you back your gun now, Roaming," she said hesitantly. "I won't be needing a gun anymore," and she glanced at the Deacon.

"Congratulations," and the cowboy's smile was sincere. "Be good to my little pard, Deacon!"

Brigham Smith smiled and patted the two guns near his hands. "I'll wear them from now on, Roaming," he promised. "A Mormon always fights for his women. I'm thanking you personal for showing me the light!"

Roaming Reynolds matched the smile and backed to the door. "Be seeing you around," he muttered, and stepped into the hall. Shook hands with Utah Young and growled at Texas Joe who followed him to the office.

"Better line out for work, button. You ain't going with me!"

Texas Joe scowled and walked out of the room. Mormon Tucker tendered a tight roll of bills which the cowboy took and shoved deep in the pocket of his scarred chaps. Held out his hand and gripped the Mormon while he growled in his throat.

"Thanks for the job, Boss. You won't be bothered no more with them owl-hoot buckaroos. I'll be gearin' my tops and lining out for town!"

"About Betty," Tucker said slowly. "You've done things to that gal-chip of mine, Roaming. Even Ma can see it, not to mention the Deacon. Can't you think this matter over and mebbe so change your mind?"

A pair of soft plump arms folded around the tall cowboy and held him tight. Roaming Reynolds stopped with a jerk and then smiled when Ma Tucker turned him and held him close.

"It's Ma I'm in love with," he said with a twinkle in his blue eyes, and then he stooped to kiss her cheek. "I wish you were my mother, Ma Tucker!"

"I'd be a real mother to you, son," and Ma Tucker watched his craggy face hopefully. "It would be like falling in love all over again to have you for always, and Mormon thinks the same as I do."

Roaming Reynolds flushed to the roots of his

brown hair and shifted his feet uneasily. "I better go," he muttered. "I better go before I loses my nerve," and he kissed Ma Tucker and ran from the room with spurs jingling.

Ma Tucker looked at her husband without speaking when Betty came slowly down the hall. Then she jerked her head toward the kitchen, and Mormon Tucker followed her with a slow smile on his florid face. The girl walked to the porch and stared across the yard until Roaming Reynolds roped his own horse from the remuda and fastened his heavy saddle snugly.

Thirty-five foot tight-twist rope on the left side of the saddle, with Winchester snugged under the saddle-fender. Light bed-roll behind the cantle, and a pair of worn saddle-bags on the broad flanks. Leather-covered ox-bows, with California chains on the bridle. Three-quarter rig with a single cinch. Tie-fast loop on the maguey, and the girl ran across the hard-packed yard.

"Don't you dally, Roaming?" she asked, and pointed to his tie-fast rope.

The cowboy held up both hands and counted his fingers. "I'm a tie-fast man, Betty," he grinned. "You see I still got all my fingers."

"But your rope is so short," the girl continued. "Our men all use fifty-foot ropes."

"Know they do, but I wouldn't know what to do with all that twine," Reynolds grinned. "If I can't stop a critter with what I got, the chances are he'd hang me with all that extra rope."

"Funny," the girl murmured. "You are a tie-fast man, and yet you never stay long in one place."

The cowboy glanced at her quickly. Gone was the smile from her pretty face, and now he twisted uneasily at the soberness in her throaty voice.

"I likewise said I never dally," he reminded gruffly. "Reckon I better be riding along."

"Roaming," and the girl reached out and held his left hand. "I'm asking you to stay, cowboy. We all need you here on the M T. It won't be the same if you ride away for keeps!"

She came closer to him and threw her arms around his neck. Kissed him full on the lips and clung to him while little sobs shook her shoulders. Roaming Reynolds frowned and patted her awkwardly.

"I ain't been here long, little pard," he said softly. "You have Mormon and Ma, and Brigham Smith. The Deacon is the squarest pard I ever run across in all my travels."

"I know," the girl answered from the hollow of his broad shoulder. "But even the Deacon asked you a question. He asked you if there was nothing here that would make you stay!"

The cowboy shifted his feet and continued to pat her shoulders. "And I answered the Deacon honest," he muttered. "Something churned all up inside when I got that note from the Eagle. Something bigger than anything else that ever come my way!"

"Bigger than love?" the girl whispered.

Roaming Reynolds nodded. "Bigger than love," he answered huskily, and tightened his big hands. "It would always be that way, little gal. I'm just trying to be honest with myself, and honest with all the rest of you folks who think I'm a square-shooter!"

"Will you kiss me, Roaming?" and the girl raised her head and waited for him to speak.

"No'm," the cowboy muttered, and turned his eyes away.

The girl stared at him and drew back. Her arms still held him, but now the look in his eyes had changed to something she had never seen before. Smoky flame burned deep behind the blue, and little ridges of corded muscle jutted out around his jaws to make his lips straight and ruthless.

"You are thinking about Eagle Dupree," she whispered.

"Yeah," and his voice was harsh. "With yore arms around me, and him waiting to put a broken feather in yore pretty hair. He won't ever do it, Betty!"

"You are fighting for me?"

Roaming Reynolds drew a deep breath. "He'd get you shore if I didn't get him," he said slowly.

"But I'd meet him nohow, because I just couldn't help it."

The eager light of hope faded from the brown eyes of the girl when he admitted the truth. She stepped back and held out her hand; gripped him hard while she said her good-bye.

"We're praying for you, Roaming. Some day you will find the place you want to call your home, and we all want you to be happy."

Roaming Reynolds nodded and jumped his saddle without touching the stirrups. "So long," he growled, and hit the tall sorrel with his hooks.

Betty Tucker watched him ride down the lane, and there were tears in her brown eyes when she turned at a touch on her arm. Texas Joe was standing behind her, and he pointed to the bunkhouse where a saddled horse was tied to an upright.

"Don't you go to frettin', Miss Betty," he growled deep in his throat. "That tall jigger done took me for his pard, and he can't shake me that away. I'm sidin' him all the way down the river if I have to give him draw-and-shoot to do it!"

"Joe! Are you leaving us, too?"

"Got the itching heel, Ma'am," the boy answered soberly. "There's lots of places over the hills I ain't never seen yet!"

"Don't go, button," the girl pleaded. "You will only get killed."

"That there's another thing," the lanky boy

flared angrily. "I'm tired of bein' called a button. I'm man-growed and gun-size and I've killed my man like the rest of this gun-totin' crew!"

The girl's eyes clouded with remembrance. "So you have," she admitted quietly. "And you have the same look in your eyes, Joe. I know we can't hold you here, but please try to do what you know is right."

"Like Roamin'," the boy grinned. "I've learned lots of things from that salty jigger."

"I know you have," the girl sighed. "And so has Brigham."

"Miss Betty," and Joe fiddled with his hat. "I saw you kiss my pard. Did he say he was comin' back here to stay?"

The girl shook her head slowly. "He won't be back, Joe. We all wanted him, because we love him for what he is. I wanted him most, but . . ."

"I know, Miss Betty," the boy muttered. "All us gun-fighters is the same way. Down inside there's a hell burning that makes us want to match guns with some other salty hombre when he goes on the prod and cuts loose his wolf. Reckon we won't never be no different."

"You too, Joe?"

The boy nodded vigorously. "I'd kill the jigger what bested my pard or run in a sneak," he muttered viciously. "That's why I'm tailin' after Roamin' to give him the lend of my gun in case Dupree has outside help."

Betty Tucker smiled and shook hands soberly. "I'm glad of that, Joe," she said softly. "Stay right with Roaming wherever he goes. And if he wants to come back, the M T will always be his home."

"Yes'm," the boy growled. "When you and the Deacon going to get spliced?"

"Joe!"

The girl stared at him and then turned away. Texas Joe scowled with shame and stumbled toward his horse. Then he was in the saddle roaring down the lane with his slicker-pack tied behind the saddle. Up ahead, Roaming Reynolds was riding slowly, unmindful of the shadow dogging the tracks of his horse. Eagle Dupree was waiting in Red Horse.

CHAPTER XX

An old day was dying, and a new one was being born when Roaming Reynolds rolled his blankets and kicked out the embers of his breakfast fire. Geared his horse and left the brakes in the river bottom of Antelope Valley with Stetson pulled low over his watchful blue eyes.

The twisting canyons and lower cliffs were still hidden deep in hazy darkness where the false dawn had failed to penetrate. That weird half-light that precedes the rise of the sun by a full half-hour, and lowers a mantle of darkness slowly in an effort to retard the filtering fingers of light.

Farther south the lofty peaks of Grand Canyon reared darkly against the sky-line with the morning stars twinkling coldly. Between was the Arizona Strip bordered by Utah, Nevada and Arizona to make a triangle. Paradise for blood-lusty men wanted by the laws of all three states.

Men who had made gun-history in Dodge City and Tombstone; outlaws from Montana, Wyoming and Nevada. Sheriff-killers from Texas and the Indian Territory with federal rewards on their heads. All were here with death in the scabbards on their legs for the man who tried to collect bounty.

Jesse James had been sold for cash by one of his trusted friends, but here in the Strip, such treachery was unknown. There were no bounty hunters, because each man carried the brand of the hunted. They might kill each other in personal combat, but they were banded together against a common enemy. The Law was unknown in the Strip.

Roaming Reynolds thought of these things while he allowed his horse to blow on the crest of a high ridge. Rainbow Canyon was miles behind him. Red Horse was a short hour ahead. Mormon Tucker and his riders could gather up their horses without danger; could dot the hidden range with the unmarked graves of raiders who had died with their boots on.

The cowboy took a deep breath and pointed his horse toward the distant town. The sunrise was not gradual. It burst above the distant peaks like a red raider destroying an enemy. Complete darkness one moment; blinding light the very next. The new day was born full-grown.

Roaming Reynolds was like a tired man who has slept well. New strength flowed into his saddle-toughened body with the rising sun. He shook his bridle reins and squared his shoulders like a man who has work to do. An expression of contentment made his tanned craggy face almost peaceful while he loped along the rocky trail and drank in the fresh beauty of the morning.

New scenes like this one were the very essence of living. New adventures waited in those forbidden places he had never seen. Distant pastures were always the greenest, and one never knew what waited just over the next hill.

The tall cowboy stiffened when the thought struck him. He knew what waited over that next long hill, and when he reached the crest he drew his gun and checked the loads. Five fulls with the balanced hammer riding on an empty. He slipped the long-barrelled gun a time or two in the moulded leather to make sure that it worked smoothly and without a hang. Then he gigged his sorrel forward and rode down the long slope where Red Horse sprawled ungracefully on the valley floor.

The look of peace had left his face now, and his blue eyes were alert and watchful when he walked his horse across the planking of Wolf Creek. The twisting street was deserted except for a freighter who was harnessing his jerk-line teams in a blackjack corral. And wasteland teamsters are not curious.

A huge boulder jutted out at one side of the street. Roaming Reynolds reined his horse to a walk and rode around it warily. Frame houses started at the bend, and halfway down on the opposite side a red stallion was rail-tied in front of the saloon. Above the board awning swung a sagging sign that bore a message and a name.

"THE LAST CHANCE."

The cowboy twisted the corners of his mouth and headed straight for the tie-rail. He knew that blooded stallion; knew the calibre of the man who waited to stake his life on the one last chance that remained to him. A gambler plays his cards until the last one has been dealt off the deck, and even then he will call for a show-down.

Roaming Reynolds swung down easily and made a slip-knot in his hair *mecate*. The light in his blue eyes softened the craggy outlines of his hard young face when he rubbed against the blooded stallion. An eager light of anticipated happiness; the joy of meeting a master for the highest stakes possible. His right hand unconsciously slipped the gun that hung low-thonged on his batwing chaps. Then he shouldered through the swinging doors and stopped just inside until his narrowed eyes had shed the bright sunlight.

A fat bartender leaned sleepily against the back-bar with his eyes half-closed. He opened them wide and stared at the tall cowboy, but Roaming Reynolds gave him only that first swift glance. The long room was empty except for a tall slender man who stood midway of the bar playing with the glass in his left hand. Long slender fingers that spun the glass out and caught it again to cuddle it deep within the circle of his palm.

He smiled when he noticed the light of eagerness that transformed the cowboy's face. Nodded approvingly when he saw the easy balance of the hand-made boots spread wide apart. Frowned for an instant when his dark eyes swept up and rested on the symbol of his own supremacy. The feather of the king eagle tucked under the sweat-stained hat-band.

"You got my message," he said softly, and nodded his well-shaped head again. "I knew you would come if you got over Hip High Hardy."

"He was fast but uncertain," the cowboy answered softly, as though stating an indisputable fact.

"We found him," the outlaw admitted casually. "We read the sign where he stopped with the girl to drink the horses."

"He died like a man," Reynolds admitted, and Eagle Dupree knew he was paying a tribute to the courage of the dead. "Which is more than I can say for Canuck Avery."

Dupree shrugged. "Not that it matters now, but Canuck was a rat," he muttered carelessly. "And he died like one!"

Roaming Reynolds nodded slowly. "There was a fighting man born on the M T that night," he changed the subject. "I carried the guns of Hardy back to the Deacon. He used them on the men you sent to do a job of work. From now on, Brigham Smith is the gun-boss on the M T hoss spread. Thought you might like to know."

Eagle Dupree smiled and waved his hand; his left hand. "He won't be boss very long," he remarked confidently. "After I have left a broken feather in his hand, I will take the girl with me to Mexico."

Roaming Reynolds dropped his head forward a trifle; studied the thin handsome face with expressive eyes that told of his admiration. Eagle Dupree was straight and tall in the tailored broadcloth suit that fitted him with faultless perfection. His calf-skin boots were polished and glove-fitting, and every part of his muscled body was poised with supreme confidence in himself.

"But you are not going to Mexico," Reynolds answered softly. "You are going to stay right here in the Arizona Strip!"

Eagle Dupree stared for a long moment. Then he raised the glass in his left hand and drank slowly without taking his eyes from the face of his enemy. Replaced the glass on the bar with a flirt of supple fingers, and smiled again when he pushed away from the polished bar.

"One of us is wrong," he said softly. "Until you came, I did real well in the horse trade. My saddle-bags are heavy with gold that will buy me a respectable Rancho across the southern border."

Roaming Reynolds straightened up suddenly and stared. "You found the gold?" he asked with doubt in his deep voice.

"I can read sign with the best," the outlaw answered with a smile. "I saw where you and Utah Young had entered my house; traced the tracks to where you had hidden the loot under the porch."

The cowboy shook his head slowly. "You got oncommon good eyes, Dupree," he praised reluctantly, and then his tall frame straightened. "About Pete Jordan?"

Eagle Dupree shrugged. "You gave him a chance," he answered lightly. "So I gave him another one."

Reynolds shook his head. "You didn't," he contradicted. "You knew you had him faded before you made yore pass!"

"Right and wrong," Dupree growled softly. "I gave him a chance he didn't deserve, but I knew I had him beat. I always know that last!"

His voice twanged on the last word while his dark eyes stared unwinkingly at Roaming Reynolds. The cowboy shrugged his shoulders and curled the corners of his mouth.

"You coppered a shore-thing bet," he sneered.

"Hard words, Mister," the outlaw snapped, and then relaxed with a smile. "But I didn't grant yore young pard the wish he requested. He likewise wanted a chance."

Roaming Reynolds tightened with unspoken threat in every line of his sinewy frame. "If you had done Joe a hurt, I'd shot you through

301

the middle and watched you tick out slow," he growled like a bear. "Like you know, they live longer that away."

"Yeah," Dupree answered softly, and smothered a yawn behind his left hand. "Pete Jordan came through at the last moment," he added in a tone of respect. "He made his pass like a man, and he went away like one. I was going to give him the coward's slug through the middle, but he earned a brave man's bullet through the heart!"

"We found him," Reynolds admitted gruffly. "Mormon Tucker cut Texas Joe loose from yore lass-rope not long after you dogged it out of Rainbow Canyon."

Eagle Dupree straightened and tightened his lips. "Did you say I dogged it?" he purred silkily.

Reynolds shrugged. "You knew I was up at yore house," he answered bluntly. "You knew I was coming down through the mazes with the hooves of my hoss smoking. You didn't wait!"

"And there was a lady present," Dupree pointed out quietly. "A lady, three men with itching fingers, and guns on their legs!"

The cowboy stared thoughtfully and finally nodded agreement. "That's right. So we took young Sam Smith back to the ranch, and likewise Pete Jordan. Pete got buried decent, and Mormon Tucker read the service."

"Sam Smith killed?"

"You knew it," Reynolds rasped hoarsely. "You said you was good at reading sign. You must have found yore guard back there stiff as a tarp when you snuck back there to get the dinero!"

Eagle Dupree leaned forward and pointed with the fingers of his left hand. "You said I sneaked back there," he growled softly. "Better watch yore words, cowboy. It might make the difference as to where I put my shot!"

Roaming Reynolds grinned and then became deadly serious. "Sorry," he murmured. "Yo're a lot of things, Dupree, but you ain't neither a sneak or a coward."

"I can say the same for you, Reynolds," the outlaw echoed softly "And you got my message."

Reynolds nodded. "It said to come alone, and I slept out in the brakes last night. Loped in early so we wouldn't be bothered none."

"I heard you coming across Wolf Creek," Dupree answered with a smile. "Knew you was alone from the rattle of hocks."

"According to the code," Reynolds added. "But that money outside won't do you any good."

"Money will do a lot of things," Dupree answered with quiet assurance. "It will even make a woman change her mind. I want the girl," and he shrugged expressively. "Like you know, I take what I want!"

"Most of the gold was taken from the herds of Mormon Tucker," the cowboy said musingly, and he nodded while his lips puckered in thought. "Brigham Smith and Betty Tucker will be married next week, and I will send that gold to them for a wedding present."

Eagle Dupree chuckled with enjoyment. Anger clouds a man's brain and slows up his gun hand, and the outlaw had never shot second in his long career. Most gun-men blustered and bellowed . . . and died. Not so Eagle Dupree, and he read Roaming Reynolds accurately.

He sensed that the tall cowboy was dangerous competition, and the knowledge only added to his enjoyment. The blood tingled through his healthy body like warm wine, and his dark eyes were almost affectionate when he locked glances with Reynolds.

"I thought we might be friends that day I met you at the depot," he remarked quietly, and then paused while he shook his head slowly. "But we are too much alike in some respects. One of us would have to be the boss."

"I'm no bounty hunter," the cowboy answered as evenly. "But I've always hated a hoss thief, and you were the Ramrod of those owl-hoot buckaroos. I set out to bust them up, and we finished the job yesterday like you know. Then I got yore message after the Deacon had read the service over young Sam, and I came in to meet you . . . alone!"

"The sun is an hour high," the outlaw answered

in the same soft voice. "I do not like to ride far in the heat of the day."

His indolence fell away from him like a cloak to leave him poised and deadly. Gone was the sleepy look from his dark eyes that now glittered expectantly. His right hand was even with the bottom pocket of his embroidered vest; taloned above the worn ivory grip of his long-barrelled Colt. His weight was balanced lightly on the thin soles of his boots, but in the greatest moment of his life, he wanted no advantages.

"Draw," he whispered softly. "I'll follow like yore own shadow!"

Roaming Reynolds shook his head slowly one time. "A shadow is an eye-wink too late," he reminded grimly. "We'll go at . . . when. You say the word for both of us!"

Grudging admiration flickered across the slitted dark eyes for a brief instant. Then it was gone when the outlaw frowned, like the remnants of night had wiped out the false dawn back in Antelope Valley. Eagle Dupree crouched forward like a stalking wolf and slowly shook his head.

"Not me," he whispered, and his voice vibrated like the blade of a knife that had been thrown point-first into hard wood. "Fat ain't got nothing particular to do right now. Let him say the word!"

The cringing bar-dog jerked erect and wet his

lips. Roaming Reynolds deliberately turned his head and smiled. He was leaning forward with his right hand shadowing his gun; fingers fanned out loosely to fit the worn walnut handle.

"Fair enough with me," he murmured, and his deep voice purred like the water of a brook rippling over worn rocks. "Yo're elected trail-boss, Fat. Give the Go-ahead whenever yo're so minded!"

The bartender wiped his mouth and straightened up with new importance. A life hung in the balance; would be snuffed out like a candle on the very next word that fell from his flaccid lips. He sensed this big moment in his drab life; lived it to the full while two strong men waited and watched each other.

Hoof-beats whispered faintly across the planking of the bridge spanning Wolf Creek. Both gun-fighters heard it and tilted heads to listen without dropping their eyes. The bar-dog also heard it and sucked in his breath with a sound like the wind in the trees. Then he leaned forward and pursed his trembling lips.

"When!"

The two gun-bosses moved like a single man. Shoulder muscles rippled forward like pistons to plunge striking hands down with fingers taloned to fit familiar gun handles. Roaming Reynolds jerked his body to the left without moving his feet, and did not know what prompted him to do it. Made his draw with smooth steel hissing against oiled leather while his thumb slipped the hammer when the leaping muzzle tilted up across the lip of his hand-moulded scabbard.

Eagle Dupree slipped his thumb to drop hammer in that split second of time necessary to make all the movements in a gun-master's symphony. The two reports blended in a roar that rocked the flame in the swinging coal-oil lamps. Dupree's bullet tore a hole in the flapping vest of the shifting cowboy when Roaming Reynolds made that quick body-twist; the side-slip that saved his gun-threatened life.

Eagle Dupree staggered and shifted his feet to catch his balance. Roaming Reynolds caught the bucking Colt in his hand and eared back the hammer against the rocking recoil. His blue eyes blazed like leaping flames, but his hard face was devoid of all expression.

The outlaw was trying to bring his arm up, and the heavy smoking gun sagged in weak nerveless fingers from which vibrant strength was fugitive. His head jerked down with the effort he was making to win his fight, or make it a draw, but his arm refused to move. As though the old man with the scythe were referee, and had already decided the winner.

The ivory-handled sixgun dropped at his feet just before he teetered forward a trifle too far and crashed to the sawdust-covered planking worn smooth by the milling boots of wanted men. Eagle Dupree was dead even before his reflexes sounded his requiem!

Roaming Reynolds straightened slowly and glanced at the fat bartender. That sallow-faced worthy was shaking with fright, and the cowboy stooped slowly and unfastened Eagle Dupree's gunbelt when the polished boots had finished their vibrating tattoo. He picked up the ivory-handled sixgun and snugged it deep in holster leather. Hung the belt over his left arm and walked slowly toward the swinging slatted doors.

"Yo're the only witness, Fat," he said slowly. "Was it a square shake for what a man might call a shoot-and-draw?"

"You gave him a bit the best of it, Roamin'," the bar-dog shouted shrilly. "Like the damn fool I've always heard that you was!"

A fleeting expression of satisfaction flitted across the hard face of the victor. "Be seein' yuh, Fat," he grunted, and stopped again. "Eagle has money in his clothes," he stated calmly. "See that he gets a decent burial and a choice grave . . . in Boot Hill!"

He shouldered through the swinging doors and smiled slowly when he saw a third horse tied at the whittled rail. Texas Joe was leaning against the rail chewing on a barley straw, and he tried to appear unconcerned when the cowboy spoke.

"Howdy, Texas, I saw you tailin' me when I left Antelope Valley early this morning. You can do me a big favour, pard!"

"Yuh never saw me," the lanky boy snarled. "I kept to the shadders and hid on the turns. You wouldn't hooraw a feller, Roamin'?"

"Me and Eagle and Fat all heard you when you rattled across Wolf Creek," the cowboy grunted. "It was rightly what you might call the pay-off."

"Ruint my blanket and cut strips to muffle that jug-head's hooves," Joe barked. "You never heard him!"

The tall cowboy smiled grimly and waved his hand. "Ask the bar-dog in the Last Chance," he grunted. "About the favour we was talking about."

"Give it a name, pard," and Texas Joe scowled when his changing voice broke on a high note. "I saw you down that Ramrod of the owl-hoot buckaroos. That makes you gun-boss of the whole damn Strip!"

"There ain't no more owl-hoot buckaroos," the cowboy corrected quietly. "Eagle Dupree robbed the M T and sold off the stock. The money is in those saddle-bags on that big red stallion yonder. The stud belongs to Mormon Tucker, so you take it back to him. You see those saddle-bags behind his cantle?"

Texas Joe nodded his head. "Done patted 'em and hear the clink," he growled, and took no chances on his changing voice. "What about it?"

Roaming Reynolds turned his face to hide the smile. "Give the gold to Betty and the Deacon for a wedding present from you and me!"

"Yo're really givin' up the gal?"

Roaming Reynolds scowled fiercely. "You forgettin' what I said one time, button?"

"But I done rolled my soogans, pard," the thin-faced boy objected. "You said we was pards, and I figgered on goin' over the hill with you!"

The hardness left the face of Roaming Reynolds. "I was waiting and a-honing to hear you say that, Joe," and his deep voice was gentle. "You take the gold and the stallion back to the M T because I don't dare to go back now. I never had no truck with women-folks, cause they booger me into a stampede every time!"

The boy frowned and then brightened up. "I'll do it, pard," and Texas Joe tightened his belt. "On top of that I'll kiss Ma Tucker and Betty for you. Where will I meet you?"

"Back there in the valley where you was trying to hide when I saw you tailing me," the tall cowboy chuckled. "And there might come a day when I ride back here to kiss the bride my own self."

Texas Joe pursed his lips and made a derisive sound. "Not you," he sneered, and then his face became serious. "Any message?"

"Fly at yore chore now and get it done,"

Roaming Reynolds growled. "There's a heap of things over the hill you and me ain't never seen, and we got something down in our blood. Get goin', button. That next range of hills yonder. I'll be waiting right there, pard."

Center Point Large Print
600 Brooks Road / PO Box 1
Thorndike, ME 04986-0001 USA

(207) 568-3717

US & Canada:
1 800 929-9108
www.centerpointlargeprint.com